Please do not remove
cover from book

to the
Winds

Published by LONGSTREET PRESS, INC.,
A subsidiary of Cox Newspapers,
A subsidiary of Cox Enterprises, Inc.
2140 Newmarket Parkway
Suite 118
Marietta, GA 30067

Printed in the United States of America

1st printing 1996

Library of Congress Catalog Number 95-82230

ISBN: 1-56352-278-0

This book was printed by Maple-Vale Printing

Cover/jacket design by Laura McDonald
Book design by Neil Hollingworth

Digital film prep and imaging by Advertising Technologies Inc., Atlanta, GA

to the
Winds

a novel

Madison Jones

LONGSTREET PRESS
Atlanta, Georgia

Other novels by Madison Jones

Last Things
Season of the Strangler
Passage through Gehenna
A Cry of Absence
An Exile
A Buried Land
Forest of the Night
The Innocent

For Oxford, Budge, and Ward: aging friends

Contents

to the
Winds

One

A man thirty years old has got no business to be thinking all the time about his boyhood. I'm not married but I have this good, responsible job at Cummings Feed and Seed Store down by the river in Nashville and I've got my own, fairly busy life to lead. Still I keep thinking and thinking back, just as if what-all happened to me and my family was a kind of a sickness I just can't quite shake off. Maybe I got so deep in the habit of our tribulations that I never will be able to put them clear out of mind. My best medicine, I've found out, is telling my story to somebody. So this time I'm telling it to you.

I grew up near Riverton thirty miles north of here. Riverton is a big prosperous town now but the real boom only got started when I was a middle-sized boy in the 1950s. Then, though it had been growing ever since the war, the town still had a population of just about 2,500. Our little farm was only three miles away by road, though from the look of the countryside up there it might have been twenty miles instead of three. You went west out of Riverton a block from the square on a banked-up state highway, across half a mile of floodland to the big bridge over the river. On the other side you turned sharp north and ran under bluffs and almost straight-up wooded hillsides till you started climbing in a circle that finally took you up to the top of the ridge. There were just four houses along the road, little ones stuffed into hollows. And one tiny grocery store right where the slope began. Our house wasn't on the main road, and neither was the edge of our property. You turned off down a dirt track that was always muddy in wintertime and passed through a short stretch of woods that my daddy had sold off to the timber people before I was born. Then you passed a downsloping field, ours, on the left and came to our house with three big oaks and a locust and a white, white sycamore tree around it.

The house faced woods across the road, and a hollow you couldn't see at all in summer because of the foliage. By the time I was born the house was a house, all right, though not many years before it had been still the same log cabin my great-grandfather built. When our family got too big — or, rather, long after the family got too big — my daddy added two rooms on the back. But instead of logs he used second-grade lumber and scraps that he probably got free, or maybe in part stole, from Mr. Cutchin's sawmill. Then he covered the siding with old roof shingles, so that part of the house looked like something he'd found deserted somewhere and managed to drag up and tack on to the back of the old building. No bathroom, though. We still had the outdoor privy, a little off-square, when we finally moved away. We didn't have running water, either, just a hand-dug well out back. In the 1950s, even in the '40s maybe, we could have had electricity if Daddy had been willing to pay the fee to get it.

Later I'm going to have a whole lot to say about my daddy — Link Moss was his name — but for now I'll just give a kind of a preview. People saw him as just plain not much account, along with weak in the head and unlucky besides. There were things they didn't see but there was a lot more truth in that description than I was willing to admit back then. Once upon a time, long before I was born, our farm had around 250 acres, with more than half of it cleared land good enough to grow a decent crop of corn. By the time I was ten we had ninety acres left and a big part of that grown up in thicket that Daddy said (though I finally knew he never had really meant it) he was waiting on to make trees for selling. Even I could see that would take forever but Daddy always swore it made sense. He said that then he would pay off all his debts and wouldn't have to worry about such as taxes and meeting mortgage payments and repairing things that ought to be thrown away. There were plenty of debts. I think there was at least one financial emergency every month of my life at home, and it's a wonder how we managed to hold on to the place as long as we did.

Daddy was able enough. He was a little stooped but he was strong, and up till he lost three fingers working at Mr. Cutchins sawmill he was mighty skillful with his hands: he could make anything when he wanted to. He didn't lose the fingers all at once. There were three different times, times like a whole lot of others when his mind wandered. These three times cost him one finger off his left hand and two off his right. He took it well and he could still harness a mule as fast as the next man and do any kind of ordinary work. When he wanted to and his mind didn't wander. If he could have controlled his mind he would have done better with a lot of those debts. He would have tried saving something against them.

I never, or hardly ever, blamed him for all those emergencies I had learned to worry about by the time I was ten. All his faults, even when he wandered off and got drunk and failed to make it home that night, didn't keep me from liking him. And he liked me. Except maybe for my little sister Eve, the youngest of us all, I was his favorite. He would find time to sit down and talk to me, no matter what was waiting on him. It might be the mules standing out there harnessed to the plow in the tobacco patch next to the house, or it might be Mama yelling at him at the top of her voice to come do something. He paid them no mind. He was a man with all the time in the world and he might sit there squatted on his heels a solid hour beside where I was playing in the dust under my favorite oak tree, telling me stuff.

He was full of old tales and information about hunting and animals. "Now you take a coon," he would say. "Chester, a coon is got more natural sense than aire dog or cat or a heap of folks has got. A coon could go to the first grade and do better'n Dud and Stack put together done." (Dud and Stack, along with Stack's twin Bucky, were my oldest brothers.) "Once hunting I come up on my dogs baying their brains out on a hickory tree. I looked up and seen the dangest big buck coon in Clayton County. That coon done something I won't never forget. He lifted up his paw same as a man would, and if he didn't thumb his nose at them dogs I ain't your daddy sitting here. Same as a man, them four fingers just open and close, open and close. I went right straight on off and left that coon alone."

He would get excited when he told me such stuff, just like it was all happening right there in front of, or in this case above, his eyes. He had small eyes, a kind of runny blue, but they got big and bright at those times. Excitement would stretch his wide mouth still wider, and usually he would snatch off his hat, exposing the bald and almost pointed crown of his head. When a tale was especially exciting he was likely to throw his hat clear away, up on the porch or something, waking up a dog or two. I believed that about the coon, and all the other lies he told me, on up till I was high-school age.

As I said, I was around ten when I started to be a worrier. I worried about debts and I worried about Daddy and I also worried about my brothers and sisters. There were eight of us, five boys and three girls. I was next to youngest, the youngest boy, and the oldest one of us all was Dud who was nineteen when I was ten. It wouldn't be true at all to say that the bunch of us came off short when the Lord dished out the brains. If I do say so myself, I came off all right. So did my little sister Eve. And Coop, the youngest boy but me, did best of all by a long shot. We were the ones that took after Mama, I guess, who was a mighty sensible woman . . . even when she was mad about something, which she was a lot of the time. But the rest of us either took after Daddy or else after some ancestor who wasn't any heavyweight either. Whoever, none of them were big winners in the brains department.

Except for Stack's twin Bucky, who I'll save to talk about last, we all went to school, of course. But Eve and Coop and I were the only ones that made it all the way through to graduate. Dud and Stack spent two years in almost every-other grade, at least, and then got passed on just because their teachers were sick of them. Both of them quit as soon as the law allowed, when they were sixteen. At that time Dud was in the seventh grade, I think, and Stack maybe the sixth, both of them looking like giants in the class room. My sisters Dorcas and Mabel, especially Dorcas, didn't do any better as students, but most of the time they got passed along for being nice. Because they were girls, though, and had an eye out, they stayed on till the classes they'd started with finally graduated. Except that Dorcas (who called herself Caress though nobody else in the family did) was so pretty I doubt she ever would have got passed along even for being nice.

But the biggest loser by far in the brains department was Bucky. I never liked to hear him called a moron but that's what he was — or else an idiot, born that way. He looked it, too, with his mouth that was always hanging open and eyes that kept rolling back in his head. If there wasn't anything to make him excited he could talk some, and if you tried you could get sense out of him. I could get more out of him than anybody and I think I knew a lot more than anybody else what went on in his head. It wasn't like people thought. He could surprise you with things he knew. I was the only one not surprised that summer when we found out he had a steady job and didn't mean to live off the family anymore. At least it was a kind of a job, it was work, even if it wasn't a kind most people would be proud to do.

More and more it came to be that Bucky would go off somewhere by himself and stay a long time. Pretty soon he was staying away overnight too, now and again, and finally he got to the point that he only showed up at home a couple of times a week. At first Mama worried about him. He wouldn't, acted like he couldn't, tell her where he went. I soon discovered and told her, and once she found out he knew how to swim she quit worrying. He had built him a sorry little hut down on the river bank. You couldn't see it from the road or even from the bridge and I only found out about it by following him down there through the woods.

Bucky was upset when he saw I'd found him out. He puffed up his lip at me and said, "Go, go," pointing back towards home. I got him over it by praising his hut, even if it was a sorry thing. It was made out of old planks and slabs and sheets of rusty tin he had found somewhere. Inside, it was just big enough for a man to stretch himself out from wall to wall. There was a little space for a window in the back wall and a door on leather hinges. By the time I had gone inside and shut the door and come out again my praise had got to be heartfelt. It was a neat place, here on the bank with willows and scaley-bark trees and the tall yellow bluff behind it and the whole big smooth-faced river lying out there bright in the sun. He saw how much I liked it and after that I was welcome, though nobody else was.

Taking the short cut through the woods it was just a mile or so down there and all that summer I visited him three or four times a week. Pretty soon he was working on an old piece of a boat he had found along the bank. I helped him some, even snitching a few tools from home for him to use. He never got it to where it wouldn't leak but he didn't mind. When the leak got to be too much he would just go to bailing. In fact, having some water in the boat was handy because the fish he caught could flop around in it and stay alive till he got back to his hut. Then he would put them in a chicken-wire cage he kept in the water at the foot of the bank. I've seen the time when he would have a couple of dozen old mud cats swimming around in there. At first I didn't know what the dickens he wanted with them, he wouldn't say. Pretty soon he told me, though. "T-t-tu sell," he said. He was selling them to Markham's grocery store in Riverton for ten cents a pound.

If you didn't look right into Bucky's face or try to make him talk, you'd forget he was a moron. He was a little clumsy, his fingers were always bruised up or cut from hitting them with his hammer or sticking fish hooks in them. But he could do what he needed to. How he learned that quick all he knew about fishing I'll never be able to figure out. He mostly used chicken guts to catch catfish, and worms and minnows for bass and bream he caught around the mouth of Stump Creek where it emptied into the river. He seemed to know just exactly where to find the fish. He'd be paddling along maybe ten or fifteen feet from the bank, then all of a sudden grab up his anchor, which was an old piece of limestone with a hole through the middle, and quiet as a cat sink it in the water. Once he got his line out he wouldn't move or make any kind of a sound no matter what. I had to do the same or he would get mad and make horrible faces at me, screwing up his lips, showing me his crooked teeth, glaring from under the brim of that straw hat that looked like somebody had trampled and then thrown away. I watched and watched him, wondering sometimes if he was still breathing. When he started to get a bite he would move, but that was just a matter of going stiff all over. He might have been about to spring. "Gu-gu-gu," he would say when the fish got on. "Gu-got him." And all the time he was hauling it in he would keep making little noises in his throat that didn't even sound like words.

What I finally found out, though, was that selling fish was just one of Bucky's jobs. I found out about the other one when I was in town one day with Mama and Eve. While Mama, and Eve with her, went to the grocery or someplace, I would always go down beyond the courthouse to Mr. Blount's mercantile store, because it had a lot of things I liked to look at and wish for — shotguns and fancy fishing reels and shiney leather boots. (What I would have given for a pair of those boots!) It was a big store that went way back, with lots of counters and shelves for me to explore and find things I hadn't noticed the last time. The big ceiling fans swashing over my head made it cool in there, too.

The one clerk, Mr. Casey, stayed up front around the cash register, but Mr. Blount himself spent a good part of his time in his little office in a back corner of the store. That day, I was following along the last row of counters fingering pocket knives and fishing tackle when I happened to look up straight at Mr. Blount's office door. I dropped the pocket knife I had in my hand; I couldn't believe what I saw. The figure standing just inside Mr. Blount's open door, beat-up straw hat and filthy shirt and all, was Bucky. From behind his desk inside, Mr. Blount's uplifted, round red face was looking straight at him, saying something. I moved a few steps closer, out of Mr. Blount's line of sight, and listened. Mr. Blount was saying, "Come on, Bucky. That's the dried-upest looking mouse I ever seen. How long he been dead?"

That was what Bucky had in his uplifted hand, a dead mouse.

"Nu-nu-not —," Bucky said and fell silent. I knew good and well his eyes were rolling back in his head.

"I bet you didn't even catch him in my store. How many nickels you got for him so far?"

Bucky's head was jerking around but this time no sound came out.

"I ain't paying you no nickel a mouse for ones you catch at the grocery or someplace. Got to come out of my store. Come to think of it, I bet that's the same one I paid you for a couple days ago. Th'ow that thing away."

"I-I-I —."

"Get on out of here, Bucky," Mr. Blount said, not in a mean way, though. I hurried to get out of there myself before either one of them saw me.

I didn't tell Mama or anybody else, I was ashamed to. I started to talk to Bucky about it but I saw right off he wouldn't understand, much less stop. Of course, because he was doing it at stores all over town, it was bound to get back to our family pretty soon. And, in fact, I didn't have to wait and worry about it much more than a week.

It came one evening when we were all in the kitchen at the supper table. I think when Daddy built that table it was probably big enough for the whole family, but now even with Bucky gone it was too little. Of course, with the big woodstove and the safe and all, there wasn't much space left over. Anyhow, the only ones of us with enough room at the table were Daddy and Dud who sat at the ends. Mama used to sit where Dud did now but he was so big and caused so much trouble in the crush that Mama finally swapped places with him. When it came to eating, he was just like Daddy and needed plenty of room for his elbows and for leaning this way and that when he felt like it. He went at it like Daddy in another way too. Both of them were powerful, noisy eaters and it was a good thing when they got put as far away from each other as possible. Before that, when it was all sort of gathered together, they made such a racket chewing and clattering with their knives and forks you could bare-ly hear what anybody said.

Most of the time there was plenty that got said at our table, the biggest part of it in arguments or else the kind of ribbing likely to end with either Dorcas or Mabel or both of them getting up burning mad and stalking out of the kitchen. Of course, little Eve never did, never got ribbed at all. She was everybody's pet. She sat, with the other two girls and Mama, across the table from us boys and right across from me. That made it so I could reach and put chicken livers and other stuff she liked on her plate.

Coop was the one who brought it up about Bucky that evening. Coop liked to stir things up sometimes and he waited for a minute when there wasn't any noise but what Daddy and Dud made eating. Just from look-ing at his face — it had a kind of a greedy, waiting expression — I knew what was coming and bent my head down.

"Anybody here know what Bucky's up to?"

Mama looked at him. She was kind of a short woman, running to flesh just a little, with gray-streaked hair and a jutting chin and gray eyes that could get quick all of a sudden and fasten hard on a person. "The fish business," she said, with a hint of something like suspicion in her look. "I'm right proud of him. At least I got one makes a living."

"The only one," Dorcas said in a spiteful way. She and Coop hadn't long been through exchanging shots at each other.

"Well, you can be twice as proud now, Mama," Coop said, ignoring Dorcas. "He's got him another business besides."

Mama just looked at him. You could see how much Coop enjoyed having everybody waiting. His mouth, tight at the corners like Mama's, was just barely not grinning. Daddy and Dud both stopped eating.

"Well," Mama finally said. "What?"

"I look for him to get rich and pay off the mortgage," Coop said.

"What business?" Mama said, her voice meaning it.

"The mouse business."

A few seconds of stillness came.

"The which?" Daddy said.

"Mouse business. He gets a nickel for every mouse he catches at the stores in town." Coop waited for this to settle. "Sometimes he sells the same mouse at three or four different ones." He paused again. "Bucky's a businessman. Going to amount to something. Not like us."

Those last words were for Dorcas, whose full, painted lips were hanging open. She was already pale, and getting paler. A few seconds more and, in a voice amounting to a whimper, she said, "Everybody at school'll know it." A pair of exactly matched tears came welling out of her eyes, and after that a sniffle broke the quiet. The second sniffle came from Mabel, who was suffering through the same thoughts just a little bit behind Dorcas. But Mabel wasn't pretty like Dorcas and crying just made her fat, pimpled face swell up and turn even redder than it naturally was.

"They'll laugh at us," Dorcas whimpered. "They'll say we're trash."

"They think it already," Mabel said in a voice like gargling.

"Shush your big mouth, gal," Daddy said with some heat. "We ain't no trash. Tell them 'bout your granddaddy. Tell them keep their faces shut."

"You got to stop him, Link." This was Mama. Her mouth got stiff for just a second. "Shaming us like that."

"He don't know no better. Everybody knows Bucky. Ain't no shame to it."

"It's shame to us. Look at these gals. You got to stop him."

"I can't stop him. He's a growed boy, done left home. Poor fellow's got a right to make a living." Daddy looked down as if just now remembering he hadn't finished the cabbage and cornbread on his plate. "I don't see nothing wrong in it nohow." He began to eat again.

In that little voice of hers Eve said, "It's a good way to get nickels."

Nobody else said anything and after a minute Dorcas and Mabel, still sniffling, got up and left the kitchen. Mama's mouth had set in that stiff way and her eyes were bright but I could tell she'd decided not to make a fight of it at the supper table. It wouldn't have done any good, and it didn't do any good later when she tried again. Daddy wasn't what you would call a strong man but when he got his mind set on something, he could be just like a big rock. Anyway, as I found out pretty soon, he had another reason.

One evening down in the barn when Daddy was starting to feed the mules I saw him take money out of the feed bucket. It looked like it might have been as much as five dollars. Daddy turned and saw me seeing him and told me, meaning it, to keep my mouth shut. But I kept watching secretly and got to the bottom of it. Every week or two, without anybody but me ever seeing him do it, Bucky would sneak up and put money in that bucket — fish and mouse money. It was hard to picture, but all Daddy's moaning about needing money for debts and such had someway got to Bucky, too, moron or not. Being secret about it was Daddy's idea, I know. But Daddy needn't have warned me to keep it quiet. I wouldn't have said anything anyhow.

Two

You can see already that my growing up was not all just tribulation and nothing else. I worried plenty more than my share, all right, even when I was little, and there was good reason for it. I would start dreading mortgage and tax times a whole month before the last day actually came around, and keep asking Daddy and Mama both if they had the money . . . which they usually didn't till it was almost too late. All we made on the place came from the three acres of tobacco our allotment allowed and a small corn crop and a few hogs and a cow and a calf or two along, and it never was enough. Daddy would get jobs and after a little while either get fired or, for some cooked-up reason, like backache, quit. It was the same way with Dud and Stack. Coop was a lot more dependable but he never had good-paying jobs except for one he had down in Nashville the summer when he was sixteen. But he quit that one after two months and came back home. It was like the only place even Coop could put up with in a steady way (for several more years, anyhow) was right there with the family where there wasn't any work except by spells. They say an idler's mind is the devil's workshop, and Dud especially, with Stack to back him, was always coming up with cockeyed schemes that led to trouble. Once in while it even got to be serious trouble, like with the law. So you can see my reasons for worrying even before the worst of our troubles started.

But I didn't worry all the time. I have a world of good memories of things that were fun, hunting and fishing and swimming in Stump Creek and playing with Eve, keeping her happy. And a lot of funny things, too, with me part of them sometimes. One I remember best happened when I was seven or eight.

It came from going to the picture show that had started up in town not long before. Dud and Stack took me. I'd never seen a picture show and Dud and Stack hadn't seen but a few. All of us got carried away by it. It was a western, about cowboys on a ranch and cattle rustlers that slipped up and drove off the cows and got them down and put new brands on them with a red-hot iron. Of course, the cowboys finally caught up with them and killed all the rustlers and got the cows back. Then the top cowboy married the rancher's daughter and they went off to start a new ranch on the prettiest piece of green land you ever laid your eyes on. We talked about it all the way home and then sat down on the edge of the porch and talked about it some more. Dud said he wished he could live out there where there were cattle ranches and rustlers and all. Stack said he did, too, and that he sure wished he could marry a woman like that rancher's daughter.

The talk finally got around to branding cattle. Dud explained that the cows out there all looked about alike and that you burned your mark on them so you could tell your cows from other people's. This put Stack to thinking. He said there were plenty of cows around here that looked about the same, too. Mr. Simpson, for instance, had one you couldn't have told from our cow. And plenty more just like them, he had seen them all over the place. This brought a silence, with Dud and Stack just sitting looking at each other. It wasn't but a minute before I saw what was up.

"What if our cow wandered off?" Stack said, with his round, blue eyes wide open.

"She might get stole, " Dud said. "Let's do it."

It was too late that day, because it took a long time to get the fire poker bent to suit them. *M* for *Moss* was too hard, so they decided to make the letter *U*. They finally got the poker bent to shape, but then they decided an *S* would look better. They used the *U* to make half of the *S* and they hammered and hammered away at it for an hour on that old anvil in the barn. They finally got it looking kind of like an *S* but they had used the whole stem of the poker doing it, all but the handle. Then they found out they couldn't make any way at all bending the handle to a right angle from the *S*. "It don't matter," Stack said. "We can just lay the whole thing on sideways." It looked to me like it was going to make an awful big brand on that cow

We were dying to do it first thing in the morning but Daddy messed us up. He was getting ready to plow out the tobacco and he spent the best part of an hour in the barn fixing and cussing the mule harness that the rats had gnawed in two or three places. He was still at it when Dud got through milking. We couldn't do it with him around, so, to make everything look like always, we had to turn the cow out in the lot.

When Daddy was finally out in the field plowing, we set about driving the cow back into the barn. It took a while and a lot of running and heading her off, because going back to the barn in the morning wasn't on her schedule. By the time we managed it she was in the worst kind of humor. She was a big cow with bad horns Daddy had never gotten around to cutting off, and she had enough Jersey in her to give her plenty of meanness. Back in the barn she took a kick at Dud. It didn't hit him square but it tore his britches leg. "Old bitch!" he said. "Th'ow that rope around her horns."

The cow was standing with her rump in the corner by the shut front door looking white-eyed and down-headed . . . to me, looking like she might have some notions about charging. "You better look out for her," I said.

"Ain't scared of no milk cow," Stack said. He had moved up within about five feet of her, holding his lasso ready.

"Th'ow it," Dud said. "Else give it to me."

Stack threw it but the loop caught on just one horn and she shook it right off. Anyway, she didn't charge. Stack gathered his lasso and threw it again. It went right this time, around both horns, and he yanked the rope up tight. "Got you, old fool," he said. He had her roped, all right, but I couldn't see how he had her. Neither could Stack or Dud, from the looks of them. Both of them just stood there for a minute or two like they were waiting for the cow to give them instructions. There wasn't a sound but her breath heaving like an old leaky bellows.

"She ain't going to stand for us this-a-way," Stack said.

"I know what," Dud said. "Get outside with the rope and then push the door shut on it, all but a crack. Then pull her head around up against it.

You can hold her from out there. Put your foot up on the door."

Stack did it and tightened up on the rope through the crack. He got her head bent around but that was the best he could do. In a straining voice he said, "Y'all push on her. Get side of her and push."

We did, and after Dud added in a couple of good hard licks with his knee in her side, she came around with her head against the door, groaning. But I got careless. I stepped back without thinking and took a kick in the belly that knock me for a backward somersault and left me sitting there on my butt seeing two of Dud's face looking down at me. "You ain't hurt," Dud said. "Run get the branding iron."

I got up and after a few weaving steps I was all right. We already had the branding iron lying in a pile of red hot coals down the slope behind a tree. The handle was sticking out and I grabbed it and dang near burnt my hand off. I had to run get a towsack to hold it with, waving my burnt hand in the air all the way. But I finally got back to the barn with it, where Dud and Stack both were already at cussing me for a slowpoke.

Except for her heaving, the cow was standing quiet when I first came in the barn. But it looked like the smell of that red hot iron upset her all over again. She started fighting the rope and groaning and then came out with a great loud bellow.

"Lay it on her," Stack yelled through the crack. "I can't hold her all day."

Dud reached and grabbed the branding iron out of my hand. "Goddamn!" he screamed and dropped it. But he went down quick and got the sack fixed on the handle and picked it up. "That other sack there." He meant the one lying in the feed trough beside me. "Put it over her head. Quick!" I wasn't comfortable close around that cow anymore but I did what I was told to pretty fast. Even if I did take a hurting lick on my shoulder from one of them, I got the sack hooked over both her head and horns so she couldn't see. That was just about two seconds before Dud came down on her rump with that hot iron.

The bellow that came out of that cow a minute before was just a cat squall compared to this one. It was so loud it ended up in a crashing noise different from anything that ever had come out of a cow's mouth till now. Really, what I heard was what I was seeing at the same time, that barn door, or part of it, exploding open and the cow right in the middle of it with pieces of lumber floating in the air all around her. There was another noise, though it seemed like I didn't hear it till a little bit later. It was Stack yelling. Then I could see why. The cow, with that sack still over her head, was running and wheeling and bucking and bellowing all at the same time, and Stack was dragging along the ground just barely not under her hoofs. The fool had wrapped that rope around his arm.

This was about the only clear thought I had for the next few minutes. It seemed like everything that could happen did happen. Right off, the dogs got into it, five of them, running and yelling around and under that cow and all over Stack who kept trying to get on his feet and, halfway up, got yanked flat again. Next it was the chickens, because the cow ran up against the chicken house where the hens were setting and flushed them out shrieking and screaming and flapping all over the place like lightning had struck them. In no time the whole show was right up behind our house where Mama was hanging out clothes, and when the cow finally threw the sack off her head, she ran in under a bedsheet that covered her all over clear back to her rump. By then the girls were out there screaming too and running around like crazy. I saw Mama sitting flat on the ground with her feet stretched out, and Stack, from one of those blind whirl-arounds the cow kept making, come right over the top of her head like a yo-yo on a string. The next thing I saw, the cow was on the fence beyond the house, and then through it, and Stack was lying there on his back in the gap half wrapped-up in fence wire. Maybe the worst piece of luck was that Daddy was plowing just about the third or fourth tobacco row out from the fence and had stopped his mule right in front of where that big bed-sheeted whatever-it-was came crashing through. Of course the mule bolted, dragging the plow sideways on the ground, uprooting tobacco plants every-which-way clear across to the other side of the field. The last really loud noise I heard was Daddy screaming cuss words in a voice fit to blast his throat open.

When I got there everybody was crowded around Stack, leaning over him. He was sitting up but he didn't look like he knew where he was. He looked kind of like he had fallen into a threshing machine and come out lacking odd pieces and patches of his clothes and skin both. They finally got him unwrapped and on his feet. For a wonder, he wasn't really much hurt, except his arm which he couldn't use for a week. Mama led him off to the house. The only thing he could say, kind of half under his breath, was, "Goddam, goddamn cow."

The cow wasn't much hurt either. The only damage to her was the big burnt mark on her rump that when it healed didn't look any more like an S than it looked like anything else. The only one in danger of permanent damage was Dud. Daddy went for him, but Dud was quicker. He lit out down the hill and outran Daddy and didn't come out of the woods till late that night when everybody was asleep. I took a flailing for him, but it wasn't too bad. I was just a substitute and Daddy's heart wasn't really in it.

One other funny thing, though this one finally had a kind of a sad ending to it, happened when I was ten or so. That summer a new man named Burger came to Riverton and bought Mr. Vinson's old ten-cent store and opened up an amusement center with electric games and ping-pong and pool tables. I always think of that, and of that whole summer in fact, as the time when Riverton began to change in a way that in not too many years made it into a new kind of place. Which is not really true. It's only that that was the time in my life when I started noticing and thinking about such things. Really, by then, as Daddy used to say, Riverton was already a different town from what it had been before the war.

Anyway, it wasn't long till a lot of boys and young men were hanging out at the new amusement center. Dud and Stack were sometime customers, but this day Dud was there by himself. He came home mad as a snake, swearing he would get back at them. "Them" was a group of four boys he barely even knew by sight, lounging around one of the pinball machines. He could hear them talking about girls and getting them some pussy and, this being a dry county, about how hard it was to get hold of whiskey. Thinking maybe to make some new friends — he didn't have any to speak of — Dud moved in on them. He said he hadn't paid much mind before to their way of talking or to the fact that they had on floppy slippers and T-shirts, one of the shirts with "U of Tennessee" printed on it. At least not till he saw how they were looking down their noses at him.

He said that instead of talking to him, they talked to each other about him, and some of the things they said got him really fighting mad. One thing that stuck with him, that a kind of a pink-faced boy said in a mumbling way over the pinball machine, was, "The Reds are coming." Another one was a crack about chickens, how the hens probably hunkered down whenever they saw him, Dud, open the barnyard gate. It took Dud a couple of minutes to figure out that about Reds coming, but he knew right off what the chicken crack meant. By that time he was not just mad, he was right on the edge of going for the whole bunch of them. Dud was a tall rawboned boy with a lot of tough stringy muscles, and nobody you wanted to be quick to get in a fight with. But there were four of them, two of them pretty good sized, and he finally decided he had better hold off. For the time being. But he was going to get them.

The question was, How? Dud thought about finding out where they lived — he knew one of them was named Burford — and waiting close around and whipping them one at a time when they came out of their houses. He sat around thinking about it for two or three days, on the front porch or the woodpile, talking about it to Stack or Coop or even me sometimes. "I'm going to get them smart-ass bastards. I'm going to. . . . " His lean jaw would clench and you could see his teeth between his lips. I wasn't sure what had happened was really worth all this stewing, but I never said it. Anyway, Dud kept right on until he finally did come up with a plan. Or rather, Coop came up with the plan and Dud jumped right on it.

It took a while because those boys never were at the amusement center when Dud went to find them. But finally they were there, or two of them were, and by that time Dud had his plan all honed and polished. He said the first step came off just like grease. The two boys were brothers, Burfords, and the pink-faced one that had made him the maddest, the one lounging across the pinball machine, had started off just the same way as last time, looking at him like Dud was something straight out of the hog pen. But Dud was calm and they went right for the bait. They even wanted it set for that same night. Dud sweetened the pot by promising them it wasn't 'shine but good store-bought whiskey, and then he added to it by hinting there might be a couple of girls in it.

I had been in on the plan all along, or listening in, and I begged and begged until they finally gave down and let me go with them. I might come in handy. So just after dark all four of us got in Dud's old piece of a Ford, hoping it would start, and drove out to the road and on to a place about half a mile beyond the Stump Creek bridge. Dud turned off onto a dirt track through the woods and parked the car there out of sight. Stack got out with Daddy's old twelve-gauge shotgun and a pocket full of shells. "I'll get on up there," he said. There was a little bit of a moon and for a minute or so we could see him like a shadow moving on up the track between the trees. Then the rest of us went back to the road and walked down almost to the bridge and waited.

Just one car went by before they showed up, about fifteen minutes later. I saw right off there were four of them, which was what Dud was hoping for. The driver, the biggest one and the one that did most of the talking, was Joe Burford . . . which I only found out later, along with the names of the other boys. But they were the right four boys. I was almost shaking for fear Dud would trip up, or something else would happen. But Dud did better than I expected and the only thing that had me going for a minute there at first was when I thought maybe they were sounding suspicious.

"I don't see anything but woods," Joe Burford said. "Where the shit is it?"

I could barely see his face. He had a lot of long light-colored hair and a T-shirt on. Dud's answer came a little slow, like maybe he had to swallow first, but his voice was natural.

"It's up other side them woods. It used to be a kind of a road in there to it, but the old man blocked it off, won't let nobody use it." He hesitated. But Coop's voice, a relief to me, took it up.

"He don't want a lot of people tracking in and out. The law'd notice. He's a sly old man." Then Coop said, "All right to leave your car here, though. People going past'll think you're down there at the creek fishing."

Joe Burford gave an unpleasant grunt. "I can't even see a path through there. Just thicket."

"It is one, though," Dud said.

"We'll find it. It ain't but a little ways," Coop said, turning and starting into the woods. We all followed him, with Dud second and me right behind him. For the first few steps it was pretty open between the tree trunks but then there started to be underbrush, and after a little while, patches of briers. One of the boys behind me said, "Goddamn!" and another one a minute later said, "Shit!" A few more steps and the whole procession stopped, because Coop was having to untangle himself and pick his way around a really big clump of briers. "How much farther?" a voice said. "Fucking briers."

"Just to the top of the slope up yonder," Coop said. "We missed the path."

"Yeah." This was Joe Burford. "Better be whiskey there. Better be good, too. If it's, 'shine, we're not paying you a goddamn penny."

"Don't worry. It's just what you're wanting," Coop said.

A boy behind me said, "What about the gals you mentioned? They going to be there?"

This was for Dud to answer and his need to think about what he would say took a little too long to suit me. But he did all right. "I reckon so. They usually there."

Coop had got his way clear and we followed him on in a winding track that brought us out of the trees to where we could see the shape of a building at the top of the slope. "That's where he keeps his whiskey," Coop said. "In that barn."

"That where he keeps his gals too?" Joe Burford said, in a tone of voice I didn't like.

"Naw," Coop said. "The other side, down the hill. That's his main place. When we get to the barn I'll give him the signal. It's two whistles. To call him up there. Come on."

The clumps of briers had turned into a solid thicket and we had to go in a circle until we came to a thin place. Even then we had to pick our way, so the whole bunch of them behind me were cussing like crazy. When I heard one of them asking if this was the way everybody had to come in, I started worrying. I was scared they were catching on and I tried to think of something. But Coop was quicker. "I got mixed up, missed the path." Then, "Anyhow we're out now."

Another minute or two and we were all out in the clear, at a place maybe a hundred feet from the barn. "Come on," Coop said. "He'll show up soon as I whistle."

Halfway there, with the bunch of them straggling just a little behind me, I could make out the dark hole high up where the barn loft door stood open. Then I thought I saw something, something that moved. It was time. I was holding my breath but I was still walking on, hearing one of them's voice complaining behind me. I saw the flash before I heard it: Boom!

I don't think it was more than a few seconds before the next Boom, but that little space was like time stopped cold, without one sound anywhere in it. The next one wasn't just a Boom. A scream came along with it, a scream to really curdle your blood, and there was Coop stretched out on the ground kicking. Another Boom and it seemed to me everybody was yelling and there was another one, Dud, lying there kicking just the same way. When I looked up I wasn't the only one on my feet but I was the only one anywhere close to the writhing wounded on the ground. People were running in every direction but toward the barn, and two of them had already torn themselves pretty good paths straight through that bank of briers.

It still wasn't enough for Stack, who got carried away. Daddy's shotgun had the plug out and would take five shells, but Stack was a quick loader and he must have fired twelve or fifteen times before things settled down. The last of those boys had reversed his field before he made for the brier patch. I know he took some birdshot, because I heard him let out a bellow before he hit those briers at a dead run. I could still hear him when I couldn't see him anymore and everything else had got quiet. I think he was the one that fell in the creek. It wasn't very far and he was headed toward it. We could hear the splash pretty clear.

It must've been half an hour before all of us could quit laughing. We were still at it strong when we got to the car, and Dud and Stack gave a special howl when we got near to the bridge and saw their car still parked there on the road shoulder. "They still running," Dud moaned. "Har, har, har! Out in the woods . . . still running. God a-mighty!" He pretty near collapsed at the wheel with laughing and he was laughing yet, with Stack cutting in sometimes, when we finally pulled up in front of the house. In fact, after a few more minutes of it Daddy came out in his longjohns and told him to shut up. I was glad when he did. I was more than just tired of it, it was too much. There was something wrong about it, the same way it had seemed to me when he kept on raging around for the best part of a week about how those boys had treated him.

It was all over, though, I thought, except for the satisfied look I kept seeing on Dud's face for the next few days. But then he decided to go to town. Stack, and especially Coop, kept telling him not to, because there hadn't been near enough time yet for the dust to get settled. Dud said he wouldn't, but then he slipped off. He just couldn't stand it. He was dying to see that bunch limping around town with all their brier scratches and bruises.

As it turned out, Coop and Stack were right as rain.

I've already said Dud wasn't long on brains, and this proved it. I don't think he was even careful. I think he went to strut and rub it in on them. It was a mistake. I started worrying long before the afternoon was over, and when he didn't show up for supper I really got worried. So did Coop and Stack. When Mama wanted to know where he was, Coop told her some lie. After supper we borrowed Daddy's old truck that kept stalling all the way and went in to town.

Dud wasn't at the amusement center. The man that ran the place couldn't even remember him. We did find his car parked on the square but no Dud, and driving up and down streets all over town didn't help a bit. We gave up and came home and stayed awake a long time after everybody else was asleep. Finally we went to bed, too, but I couldn't even get my eyes to stay closed. After a while I got up and went out on the porch and sat down on the steps, with all the dogs lying around me on the ground.

It was getting toward full moon and there was plenty of light and crickets and whippoorwills and owls calling. But the sounds just made me more nervous and the light kept me staring off up the road and in every direction. That was why I saw something moving before it even got close, coming toward me out of the woods. Of course I thought right off it was Dud and heaved a sigh of relief. But less than a minute later I was sure it wasn't Dud. I didn't know what it was, and as soon as I could see the thing in a little bit of detail my blood just about froze. First I thought, spook. But after a few more seconds I thought, chicken, a great big chicken, big as a man. I got up on my feet. I never saw such a thing in my life. Just about then was when the dogs spotted it and went streaming out through the gate with racket enough to raise up the dead.

I think I'd stopped being scared even before the dogs got to it and right away hushed up their howling. I'd figured it couldn't be a chicken, it had to be a man fixed up like one, and that man had to be Dud. By that time, with the dogs prancing all around him, he was almost to the gate. He saw me and stopped, then came on, white feathers from head to foot. I mean, he even had them on top of his head, sticking up like a big old crest. At the gate he stopped again and said, in a whisper I could just make out, "Chester. Come help me."

As soon as I could get my legs working I stepped down on the ground and went to him. Even his chin had a few feathers stuck on it. The smell told me they'd used just molasses, though.

"You got to help me. Get some coal oil."

"We ain't got any," I said.

"In the lamps, get it out the lamps. Bring them out here. And don't wake up nobody."

I kept looking at him, up and down. "Why didn't you pull them off?"

"'Cause I'm naked. Them goddamn bastards."

All of a sudden I couldn't help myself. I started laughing and I couldn't stop. I almost went down on the ground laughing.

"Goddamit, shut up! Shut up! And get my coal oil."

But I couldn't help it. I went right on laughing. Till I saw there was somebody on the porch behind me. Then I was sorry and I did stop. But it was too late. Dud had already scuddled back across the road and got behind a gum tree there.

I was even sorrier later on because everybody had waked up and all of them did just what I'd done, broke down laughing. But they were sorry too, afterwards, because Dud was as shamed as I ever saw a man be. And mad. Mad at us for a long time, and killing mad at those four bastards in town. It did something to him, something that lasted on and on that I could see in him once in a while. In fact, I kind of think it was something the whole family finally took from him, in a way. What made it so, I think, was our finding out about those boys, that all of them were sons of new, big folks in town, the ones that were starting to run everything and that people like us couldn't touch, no matter what.

Three

When you're a little kid you forget a world of things that could have told you something. They pass by like the wind and never come back. But sometimes there are things that just get buried in your memory and, for no special reason you can see, pop up years later and tell you something important. It's been that way with me. Now, whenever I get to thinking much about Daddy, I always remember one certain winter night that I had forgot completely till I was almost grown. I'm not saying what happened that night finally told me why Daddy was like he was. But it was a help, like opening a door part ways. I could look through the crack and see some things I never had seen before.

It was raining. Everybody but me, even Mama, had finally gone to sleep, and I was trying to, lying in my bed. But my eyes wouldn't stay shut. I'd squinch them shut but pretty soon they would fly open and I would be looking at that gray rain-streaming window again. It was the third night Daddy had been gone — just gone without a word or sign to anybody, the way he did every once in a while. But never before for so long. We had looked every place we could think of, starting with the jail because we had found him there the last time. He was lying dead drunk on a cot in the cell and we had to leave him till the next day. But he wasn't in jail this time. He wasn't anywhere. He had been to the Hilltop Inn and left there drunk, but that was two days ago. My mind kept circling in the dark and ending up where it started.

But on in the night I heard him. I wasn't sure at first, and after waiting a minute for another noise to come, I got up and stood in the door to the front room where the lamp was burning. I heard a bump, then two more, heavy feet on the porch. He was fumbling at the door, feeling for the knob, taking a while to do it. When the door swung open I stepped back into the dark.

Daddy just stood there like even that dim lamplight had struck him blind. A gust of air blew past him. It made the lamp gutter and almost go out, and for a second I thought he was going to fall down. He held to the door and, after swaying and blundering a little bit, managed to get it shut without even much noise. Then he stood with his back against it, his clothes filthy wet and dripping, red mud all over one side of his face and his bald head. He was looking my way but not quite at me. It was like he was looking straight at somebody else in the room across from him, trying to say something to that person. I saw his mouth make a word I couldn't hear. A little later, barely loud enough, he said, "'pologize."

He wasn't talking to me, I could see that. He wasn't talking to anybody, though I reckoned he thought he was talking to Mama. A minute later, maybe because of the look on his face, I decided I was wrong. That was when he said the words I remember best of all: "It ain't none of my fault."

Who in the world was he talking to? It wasn't Mama, the something accusing in his face made me sure of that.

"It was you." His bald head swayed a little bit and I could see his eyelids starting to droop. "I never been nothing but just like you."

He had to be plain crazy drunk, I guessed, because he wasn't making a bit of sense. I saw him looking again like he might be going to fall on his face and I was at the point of running to help him, when all of a sudden Mama in her big patched cotton gown was in the room. She didn't say a thing. She got hold of his arm, pulling at him, trying to lead him, but he yanked loose and fell back against the door. "Lemme be," he mumbled, never looking at her. "Lemme be."

That was when Mama called Dud. She never said another word, even when Dud finally showed up in his longjohns, blinking, and took hold of Daddy's arm on the other side. For a minute there, it looked like Daddy wasn't going to let them help him and I got the notion he was holding back to say something important. Once they got him moving and almost to his bedroom door he did say something, but it wasn't important. "Raining. Raint the whole time," he said. "Never nothing but rain."

I didn't think, the next day or any day, to ask Mama who it was Daddy thought he was talking to. To me it was all just part of his being mighty drunk and it was years later before it struck me that that person was his own daddy. By then, of course, I knew a lot of things about my grandfather, knew most of them from Daddy's mouth. But they never had really come together for me, not in a way to make me see what I finally saw.

My grandfather had died about ten years before I was born. I knew he owned this land that he passed on to Daddy and that there used to be a whole lot more of it than there was now. But for a long time I thought that when Daddy got his hands on the place it was as big as it ever had been. That wasn't true. I believe the main reason I thought what I did was hearing Daddy say bragging things about his father, like his father had been a mighty important man in the county. I thought he must have been rich and bought and farmed all that land, and I thought it was just Daddy, being the way he was, who had whittled it down to the little place I knew. By and by, because I finally asked her, Mama straightened me out. This land had come in the family not by Daddy's father but by his grandfather, who really was somebody and who had bought it back in the days when the government owned a big part of this county. Daddy's father had already sold off many an acre before it ever came to Daddy's hands.

Looking back, it's clear to me how many of the things Daddy said about his father didn't square with each other. Daddy would tell about working in the log woods with him and it would sound like his father owned the trucks and bossed the men with the saws and axes. But again Daddy would tell about him getting mad and cussing the boss to his face and walking off the job. He was a man that wouldn't take nothing off of nobody, Daddy would say. A proud man. Daddy would talk about his father making whiskey and Daddy helping him. I asked him once if they didn't ever get in trouble with the law, but Daddy said it was all right back then, the law didn't mind, a lot of the finest folks made whiskey. And drank it, too, I reckoned, because he told me a couple of times about his father and him getting drunk together. But other times he told me about the kind of whippings he would get for coming home drunk, because, he said, his father was a man that wouldn't put up with a boy not walking the straight and narrow. That one would get by me, too. There were so many things I never thought to question. Him and his father digging and selling ginseng was another one, though even at that time I thought people who sold ginseng had to be poor as yard dogs.

I don't think Daddy's bragging about his father's importance was all exactly lies. He was like an awful lot of other people. They want so bad to believe something that they do believe it, no matter for the tricks they have to play on themselves. For one thing Daddy was mighty fond of his father. He wasn't much more than a boy when his two older brothers, Clarence and Bill, left for parts unknown, and a year or so later his mother ran off with another man. So it was just Daddy and his daddy.

But that was only part of it, and I think the other part was the biggest thing. Daddy had a couple of snapshots of his father. Growing up I saw them a good many times without really studying them up close. Later on when I did study them I could see what I'd missed before. Cut off the old man's whiskers and he and Daddy were like two peas in a pod. That was what Daddy meant by those words that night when he came home drunk. Except he wasn't talking just about their looks. He meant it all the way, and that there wasn't a thing in the world waiting for him but the same old blundering path his daddy had followed to failure. It was a vision that would come down on him every once in a while, and the only answer he ever could think of was to go and get real drunk. Considering everything, it was a mercy that it didn't come on him oftener than it did.

That might not be right, though, that it was a mercy. Because if you really knew such a thing about yourself, you couldn't ever put it all the way out of your head, much less keep it out. It would always be kind of lurking in the dark, whispering to you. Probably, without your even realizing, it would be giving you hints and notions that might not make a bit of sense. Thinking about it this way, I believe I can understand why Daddy did a lot of the things he did. Like, for example, the business of that sorry tractor he was set on swapping his good team of mules for.

It was an old Allis Chalmers, about as old as they get, I reckon. He saw it sitting on the square in town with a "For Sale" sign on it. I was with him that evening and watched him walk around and around that tractor and finally get up on the seat and start working the clutch pedal and the gearshift lever. When he finished fooling with those, he just sat there on the high seat and finally took off his straw hat. Sitting or walking, Daddy was naturally a little stooped over, but right then for two or three minutes he sat on that tractor just as straight and stiff and tall as a hickory pole. The evening sunshine lit up his white bald head, and his hands gripped on that steering wheel like a man who didn't mean to stand for any backtalk. He made me think of a king I saw in a book once, riding on one of those big dray horses. He made me uneasy, too.

He finally got down from the seat and commenced spinning the starting wheel. The tractor didn't start up but the look on his face stayed the same, kind of victorious-like. "Prob'ly got no fuel," he said. I watched him spend a while in front of the "For Sale" sign, his lips moving, memorizing the owner's name and number. That made me even more uneasy. I said, "It wouldn't start."

"Ain't got no fuel," he said.

"How'd it get here, then?"

"Likely had just barely enough to make it. Smart man'll figure them things."

"Ain't got much paint on it," I said. "Got a lot of dents, too."

But he had stopped paying any attention to me.

He called the man up on the telephone at the grocery. I was standing by and heard him asking questions about the tractor and talking about swapping our team of mules for it. He finally hung up and stood there looking like a man who had just swallowed something so good it was near about too much for him. He kept that same look all the way home in the truck. I kept talking about how good our team of mules was, old Bell and Tom that could pull a house down and never get tired even from plowing new ground all day long. He looked like he couldn't hear me.

Supper was ready when we got home. We hadn't been at it but a couple of minutes before everybody noticed there was something up with Daddy. He wasn't even eating, hardly, just a bite once in while, and he had that same expression he had worn the whole way home. We all got kind of quiet, waiting. When he finally put his knife down on his plate we stopped eating, too. He kind of reared back. I never in my life saw him look so important.

"We're fixing to get a tractor," he said.

Everybody just looked at him. Mama cocked her head sideways.

"I done looked up a mule's behind all I aim to ever. The time's come. It ain't going to be like it was before around here. So you boys might as well to get ready. We going to clear up all that west ground and pull all them stumps and plum bushes and grow more corn and barley and stuff than you ever laid your eyes on. It's time, past time. All a farmer needs is a good tractor and we're fixing to get one."

I never had heard Daddy say so many words all at once so you could understand him. It was like it was all spelled out for him in a vision standing in front of his eyes. I thought that if he had got this worked up in half an hour, there was no telling what he'd be like by bedtime.

"How you going to pay for this tractor?" Mama said. Her face was looking hard, the way it did pretty often these days.

"You needn't to worry your head on that," Daddy said. "It ain't going to cost us a penny."

Mama's face didn't change. "Somebody going to give you a free tractor?"

"He's going to swap the mules for it," I said. Then I was sorry, because Daddy gave me one of his hot beady-eyed looks.

"Them good mules?" Mama said. "The only thing we got on this place any 'count is them two mules. What you know about a tractor? That man's liable to cheat you blind. And us to the poor house."

"They're mighty good mules," Coop said. He liked the mules. So did I.

Daddy just reared back a little farther in his chair and looked haughty. "It ain't too much about a tractor I don't know," he said. "Worked on several. Helped old Cairns overhaul his'n from top to bottom."

Mama's face, with her mouth shut tight, didn't change.

Daddy went on, "This ain't a man to cheat nobody anyhow. Mr. Walt Burns. Got a great big farm out there around Oakton. He's just selling this'n 'cause he's got more tractors than he's got use for."

"Never heard of him," Mama said.

Daddy just drew a long breath and looked up at the ceiling. "A woman don't understand about things. A man can't just stand still, he's got to move on. This here tractor's going be. . . . "

He was off again. When I looked back at Mama I could see she had already got almost to the point of thinking it was another hopeless case. And it didn't help that Dud and Stack both started getting in behind him. When Daddy finally hushed for a minute Stack said, "Good tractor'll work three times fast as a team."

"A man can make money with a tractor," Dud said. The girls looked like they weren't even listening anymore, especially Dorcas who was getting the kind of expression she got when she thought about some boy. Coop was listening but he didn't say anything. He had a way, when his mind was busy on something, of looking kind of up and sideways out of his eyesockets. After a few more seconds, when Daddy started talking again, Mama put her hands on the table and got up and went out the back door.

"There's a woman for you," Daddy said.

The man was supposed to come at seven o'clock in the morning to look at the mules, and Daddy spent the whole evening till bedtime down at the barn currying them and clipping their manes back and their fetlocks and oiling their hoofs with cottonseed oil. When he got through they looked so pretty it made me sicker than ever to think about them getting swapped off, especially for an old tractor that probably wasn't any account. But Daddy just wasn't going to listen, not to me for sure, not even to Mama. He was still riding high when he went to bed and he was up ahead of time the next morning to wait for Mr. Burns. When 7:30 came and still no Mr. Burns, Daddy was looking even sicker than I had been feeling up till the last little while. He stood there kind of hanging on the front-yard fence, looking like all the juice had drained out of him.

About eight o'clock, though, a boy showed up in a truck. Something had happened with Mr. Burns' wife and he couldn't make it at all today. But Daddy could count on him for sure tomorrow morning at seven. In a few minutes Daddy was back on his high seat again. I think he would have busted wide open before the day was over if we hadn't had all that tobacco to set out. I never had seen him work so fast, up and down along those rows like a pump handle, pegging the dirt and putting the plants in. He kept haling us along too, barely giving us time to get a drink of water. Coop, who finally said he had to go talk to somebody in town about a job, just about had to fight his way loose that afternoon.

We were in the house ready for supper when Coop came back. He went in the kitchen and talked quiet to Mama for a few minutes, but all he told us was that he didn't get the job. It was after dark and almost bedtime before I found out what he told Mama. I overheard her telling it to Daddy in their bedroom. Coop had gone out to Oakton and talked to one of Mr. Burns' neighbors who told him that tractor wasn't nothing but a pile of loose nuts and bolts. And Mr. Burns wasn't any big farmer, either. He had an old frame house without any paint on it and a bunch of run-down cows in a pasture half grown up with sedge and buck bushes. I listened hard, waiting for Daddy's voice to come in.

I didn't have to wait long, or listen to more than about five words before I knew Daddy wasn't having any part of it. He said that Coop was just a boy and didn't know nothing, and that Mr. Burns owned bottom land all along Triple Creek. He said it was just some neighbor that didn't like Mr. Burns and wanted to harm him. Besides that, Mr. Burns was going to give a solemn sworn guarantee on the tractor. He said that what Coop needed was a good whupping with a hickory limb. In my head I kissed those mules goodbye.

I slept in the same bed with Coop and we both lay there in the dark for a while without saying anything. Then Coop said, whispering, "He's going to swap them mules for that junk pile, sure." He had been listening, too.

"I know it," I whispered back.

Coop didn't say anything else for a long time. Then, "I got a idea," he said.

"What?"

"Something I heard about, once."

"What was it?"

"You'll see. You got to help me. I'm going to slip out in a minute and go somewhere. You go on to sleep, but I'm going to wake you up a while before daylight. Just don't make no noise when I do."

"What are we going to do?"

"You'll see." He wouldn't tell me. Coop liked secrets. A few minutes later he got up and was out the window as quiet as a snake.

I didn't think I would but I finally fell asleep. After that it didn't seem like but a few minutes before Coop was shaking me, whispering, "Come on, get up." I slipped right in my clothes and followed him out the window and around the back of the house. The dogs tried to come, too, but Coop scared them back.

Half of a late dark moon in the west made light enough to see by, and we spotted the mules in the lot just down beyond the barn. "What we going to do, Coop?" I said, still whispering.

"I'm going to show you. Got to get them in the barn. Quiet-like."

We went through the barn and circled down behind them and got them up as easy as grease. "What we going to do?"

Coop struck a match and lit a lantern sitting in the feed trough. I saw two jugs sitting beside it. "What's in them jugs?"

"Run Bell in the stall, there."

I did, and a few seconds later Coop came in with the lantern and a bridle and a piece of rope. Then he went out and came back with one of the jugs and a funnel and a short span of hose pipe. "You going to dowse her?" I said. "What is that stuff?"

"Wait and see." He threw the rope up over one of the ceiling beams above the feed box. He put the bridle on the mule good and tight and then he tied the end of the rope to the bit at the side of her mouth. "Now," he said. "When I get up in the box and get ready, you pull her head up high with that rope. Keep it held tight. Hang on it, if you got to." He took the hose and the funnel and got up in the feed box. "Now hand me that jug." I did, and he set it on a cross-brace next to his head and screwed the top off. "Pull the rope." I pulled and got her head up but she started to struggle. "That's all right," Coop said. "Pull it a little more and then hold on." I managed it but the mule was struggling harder than ever and groaning now. Then I heard that big hee-haw gathering in her throat. Not much of it came out, though, because Coop grabbed hold hard with both hands and held her mouth shut. A few seconds more and he had the hose pipe in her mouth and part way down her throat. He stuck the funnel in the other end of it and then he had that jug up in his hand, kind of hoisted across his wrist, pouring what I knew from the smell was 'shine.

"That's 'shine," I said, hanging on the rope.

"One thousand proof," Coop said and went on pouring. Poor Bell gagged and heaved and slobbered but there wasn't a thing she could do but keep on swallowing. Coop poured the whole jug, just pausing now and again for her to breathe, and I know he got more than half that gallon down her. After we led her out of the stall she stood there in one place heaving so hard her ears went up and down. Of course, by now I knew what Coop was counting on.

"You reckon she's drunk?" I said.

"She ought to be pretty soon . . . I hope."

There was still the other mule to go and it went off just about like before. Except this time, because it was getting daylight, we were running scared. There was no telling what, if Daddy caught us. Then something that made things worse came in my head. "You can smell the 'shine in here," I said. "Daddy sure ain't one to miss that smell."

We were leading Tom out of the stall when I said that and it made Coop stop in his tracks. He didn't stand there more than a few seconds, though. What Coop came up with showed how smart he was. I think he had just about all the brains that should have gone to Dud and Stack and the girls, except for Eve. "Get that fly spray," he said. "Th'ow it all around. On the mules too. That ought to kill it."

We did it quick. We put everything like it was before, taking the jugs, and opened the door out to the lot and left the mules standing there in the barn heaving. Then we went down to the branch and got a little wet and muddy to make it look like we had gone early to fish.

We came back to the house worrying. We were worried that Daddy might go to catch up the mules too soon and figure it out, and we were worried all that whiskey might have done something worse to the mules than get them drunk. We were lucky both ways, though. It turned out finally that the mules weren't hurt a bit. And Mr. Burns came early, right as we got up from breakfast, before Daddy had time to do anything but put his hat on.

He was outside before Mr. Burns, moving slow, got all the way down from the cab of his truck. Mr. Burns was a fat man with a face red enough to make you think maybe somebody had poured a gallon of whiskey down him. And he had a long, straight mouth without any lips, like a snapping turtle. He said in a loud voice, "Come to see them good mules. They good enough, I'll shore trade with you," nodding his big round head. "Much as I hate to give up that tractor. It's a running fool. But I just got too many tractors."

Daddy had his hat off. "You ain't going to find no better mules than what I got. Pull a oak stump like it was a pine slip. Work all day and get no more'n a sweat up. Quiet, too." He turned around and saw all us boys behind him. "Dud and Stack, go get 'em."

Coop and I followed along, but before we got quite to the barn Coop slowed down and then stopped, and I did too. We stood there waiting, both of us feeling nervous, while Dud and Stack opened the door and went in. We could see the mules standing there just about where we had left them and pretty soon we heard Dud and Stack talking, but not loud. The only thing I heard plain was Stack saying, "You reckon they asleep?" They had the bridles on them now.

"You boys make haste." That was Daddy. He and Mr. Burns had walked most of the way down and were waiting there, with Daddy talking about how easy handled his mules were. I could see Dud pulling hard on Bell's bridle but all he could manage to do was stretch her neck out. "Goddamn!" he said. "What the hell!" He dropped the reins and got around behind her and gave her a powerful kick in the rump. That got her moving, but coming through she bumped hard against the door and then stopped with her front legs spread out wide. I could see her eyes were all the way shut.

"What in the hell!" Dud was back on her bridle pulling and yanking, but the only thing that did was make her all of a sudden open her mouth and start hee-hawing. She must have hee-hawed eight or ten times, and before she got done, Tom, that Stack had finally managed to drag out of the barn, joined right in with her. For a minute there, it sounded like some kind of a mule convention. They made so much noise that the dogs came down to check things out. That wouldn't have mattered except for what Tom did next. Stack had finally turned loose of his bridle and Tom's deciding to go for a walk was his own idea. He took a few trial steps up toward where Daddy, looking like he had been hit with something heavy, was standing with Mr. Burns. Then he staggered like he was going to fall down and took off in a different direction and did the same thing over again. Then he did fall down, right flop on his side, and lay there working his legs like a big old bug trying to get them back under him.

That was too much for the dogs. They came in like something a tornado had set swirling around that mule, baying and yelping and snapping at his legs, till that poor mule in a kind of strangled way started in heehawing again. Then all of a sudden Daddy was right in the middle of them yelling and cussing and kicking dogs in every direction. He even grabbed little Bitsy by the tail and threw her halfway up to the house, where she hit rolling and yelping and then lit out.

After that, things quieted down, and a minute later Daddy was standing there with his hat gone and his arms hanging long at his sides, looking down at the mule. Poor old Tom had finally got back onto his belly. He tried to get up on his legs and couldn't because they went every which way, and so he settled for just staying down there, with his head lolling back and forth and his eyes falling shut. Daddy said, like he wasn't saying it to anybody but himself, "Never have saw any such a goddamn thing in my whole life. What in the hell is the matter with them mules?"

"They got the staggers."

This came from Mr. Burns. From the way Daddy looked at him, you'd have thought he didn't know who Mr. Burns was or how in the devil he had got there. Daddy finally said, "Ain't no staggers. Never have had no staggers."

"It's the staggers. Know them when I see them." Mr. Burns's words sounded like they might have come from somewhere high up, like maybe God had said them, and I don't think it was till right then that it came clear to Daddy how his swap was going down the drain. It made him look kind of shrunk inside his clothes, and his arms hang down longer. But he gave it another try.

"I swear to you, Mr. Burns, I swear to God Almighty them mules ain't never had no staggers. Ain't had nothing. Ain't never even been sick."

But Mr. Burns shook his head in a grand kind of way. I thought how much his mouth, the way he puckered it up sharp in the middle, made it look like a snapping turtle's. In a way I was feeling sorry for Daddy, but it did me good to think old Burns was really the one getting beat.

"It could of been laurel," Stack said, his face getting brighter. "Laurel'll do them like that."

It was something possible and for a little space it perked Daddy up. I couldn't see any change in Mr. Burns's expression but there was this minute when nobody said anything. Then, "It shore can do that to a mule," Daddy said.

"But there ain't no laurel in that lot," Coop said. "Or the woods around here either."

Daddy looked at him, looked hard. I know he didn't really think that that about the laurel was going to be any help, but he felt like Coop, his own son, had come in against him. He was still looking at Coop when Mr. Burns turned around and started back up toward his truck. Daddy went after him and caught up with him but nothing he could say was any use. A couple of minutes later Mr. Burns was in his truck and on the way out.

Daddy never did get suspicious about the trick but he kept on holding those words against Coop. He never quite said so, but I think he finally got to where, by some curious working of his mind, he started thinking of Coop as one the reasons why he never was able to make a success.

Right off, Coop was sorry he'd ever said those words. He hoped that what he found out the next day, and what he found out a few weeks after that and told Daddy about, would help. The first thing was that Mr. Burns had sold the tractor that same day for just fifty dollars, instead of swapping it for two mules worth a hundred anyhow. The other thing was that the man who bought the tractor said it not only wasn't worth fifty dollars, it wasn't worth ten. Coop told Daddy those things but he could see it didn't help.

Four

I always think of Mama as having come from way, way back. I mean, back in time and place both. Of course, it's not really true either way. She never told us exactly how old she was but I think she was born around 1914. That's not really so long ago, though it sure seems like it when I remember the things she told us about the life that used to be. Also, the place where she lived isn't all that far from Riverton and some other towns just as big. But that's now. Back then, she said, Horn County didn't have one place in it that you could rightly call a town, and the thirty miles from Riverton to her old home seemed about like a hundred miles seems now. Dirt road winding through the hills, up and down all the way. Some places along the road you would go two or three miles and never see a house, just woods and maybe a field sometimes. I think her house was the best part of a mile from her next neighbor's. It sounds lonesome but Mama said that, taking it all together, here where we lived was just as lonesome.

Really, talking just about houses and such, her home wasn't very much different from ours in my first years. Our house was made all out of logs too, before Daddy tacked those new rooms on the back of it. We had a water well just like hers, and coal oil lamps, and we lived on a dirt road a good way from anybody else. We had the same kind of stock, if not as much of it, and a garden and a smokehouse and pretty much the same kind of farming tools. In most ways it wasn't much different with us. But there had been other ways. Listening to Mama I would feel like maybe we had missed out on the best part of living.

It was funny about Mama. I was a long time getting it clear in my head that half of what she told us about life back then wasn't that way still when she was a girl. It was like the world she'd heard about from her mama and daddy was just as real to her as the one she remembered herself. She would get them mixed up, I think, and the only way you could tell was to notice how those pictures her words painted never showed her in them. The way she'd kind of stand back and tell it was about the way you'd look for a judge to do. I finally got to noticing that but I never figured why it was, till years later.

Anyway, listening to Mama I would wish our life was more like the one she told about. Hers sounded so much friendlier, for one thing. It didn't seem to matter that people lived so far off from each other and didn't have cars or anything but mules and horses. They were always getting together anyhow, at church and square dances and corn huskings and such. When she talked about the dances, Mama's expression would get a little brighter and kind of faraway, and sometimes one of those old fiddle tunes would come back in her head. "Flies in the buttermilk / Shoo shoo shoo . . ." she would sing in kind of a murmuring voice, like she was looking back through all those years at folks dancing hand-in-hand in a ring. All the dancing I ever saw when I was growing up was at places like the Hilltop Inn, with a juke box groaning out sorrowful love songs and half-drunk boys clutching and heaving their gals around between the tables.

Mama said people were always visiting each other. Saturday evenings and Sundays whole families would show up at each others' houses, bringing maybe blackberries they had picked or fresh butter or jars of pickles or new-baked pies. Apple cider, too, sometimes. Pretty often on weekdays, women, maybe four or five of them, would come with their babies and stay almost till evening sewing or knitting or quilting together. And people would help you out in times of trouble. You didn't have to ask, just let it be known. Give the word and half a dozen men and boys would come and help thresh a crop of ripe wheat that the wind had knocked down. Any worriment or grief in a family, sickness or childbirth or death, would draw in an hour or two more comfort and offers of help than you ever could have use for. Not anymore, not here in Clayton County, Mama would say, surely thinking of the time little Eve had got sick and nearly died and nobody came to help or even comfort. Not even the preacher came, though he might not have known about it because we hardly ever went to church.

Mama knew a lot of old tales that she was always telling us when we were little. Some of them were singing tales with tunes that were real pretty to hear, the way she sang them. I've seen some of them in books since then but she didn't get them out of books, she got them from her mama, I think. She said tales and music were some of the best things she remembered from back then, and she wished there were still fiddlers around like there used to be. We had an old guitar and Dud and Stack both used to pick it some. But Mama said those boys weren't anything at it, besides that the songs they knew weren't even real music. Back then, she said, there were a plenty of folks around that beat all to pieces anything you could hear on a radio nowadays.

Another thing about Mama I remember mighty well was how superstitious she was. I guess the old folks were all that way and she took it from them. We made fun of her, but all that did was make her keep it to herself a little more. She believed in signs and spooks and even bewitchments. Once she made Daddy get rid of a dog she said kept looking at her in a funny way. She said keeping a dog like that was too much of a chance to take. One time I saw her kill a hen that crowed. Another time she threw out a perfectly good pot of soup she was cooking because she kept seeing things, like faces, in it. And she knew signs for bad luck that you never heard of. We made fun of her, but all the same a little of it rubbed off on us. I'm still wary of a screech owl, and a black cat crossing in front of me.

Of course, a whole lot of what Mama told us about her girlhood wasn't mixed in with what she'd learned from the old folks. That was when you could get glimpses of what it was really like for her. With times getting harder and harder for farmers and all the young people leaving out for the towns and cities, that old life her mama and daddy had was just about clear gone. I'm sure it was lonesome for her, lonesomer than she ever would let on.

But you could get glimpses of something else in what she told us. To me, finally, it was like she was leaving out some mighty important things threading its way in a kind of dark between the parts of what she was telling. I noticed it so many times. Mama didn't have a happy face, but when those times came I'd see, or think I did, and always feel a little twist at my heart. Some secret, sad, sad thing. Dorcas and Mabel were always wanting to hear about her courting days and whether she had many boyfriends and what they were like, and such. She'd give about the same answer every time. She had a boyfriend named Ed and another one named Foley. She wasn't pretty enough, she said, to have a whole lot of boys running after her, but she had several. I got in the way of thinking that several was more than two, but she never named any others. Once I straight-out asked her if, besides Daddy, she never had but just those two. The question gave me back one of the kind of glimpses I remember so well.

When I got older and came to look at Daddy in a way I hadn't looked before, I began to wonder why Mama had married him. It's not that she didn't tell us the plain facts in the case. When her little brother finally got married and she was the only one left at home, she decided it was time she did something, too. She couldn't get a job anywhere close around, so she came down to Riverton and found a place working at Mr. Tomlin's little grocery store.

It was a grocery but it had some chairs and benches for people that wanted to sit down and drink a Coca-Cola and talk to each other. She said Daddy was working for the timber people off and on that winter and it finally got to where he was stopping in at the grocery almost every day to sit and drink a beer. She said it wasn't long before she noticed him eyeing her and she wasn't surprised when he started making a play for her. She hadn't wanted him to, at first, and snubbed him. She wanted somebody who would be more polite to her and come around fixed up, instead of in old torn overalls and with his face not shaved.

Pretty soon, though, he changed. He would come in just before closing time as clean as a whistle and talk to her like she was a real lady too good to work in a little grocery. He started bringing her candy, caramels, and peanut brittle. After that she would let him walk her to the boardinghouse where she lived and stay a while on the front porch talking to her. It wasn't long before he asked her. She thought about it for a few days, the way a girl ought to. Then she said yes.

Of course by that time Mama wasn't exactly a girl anymore. She never made it clear to us but she was around twenty-five, which back then was getting along for a female wanting to marry. She probably thought this might be her last chance, even if the man wasn't the kind she was looking for. Not that she was any more high-born than he was, but all the same she was above him. She just plain saw a lot more and felt a lot more than he did, and I know it was a trial for her when he started showing her up close how true this was. Probably in the beginning his owning the farm outright gave her some confidence. She must have counted on his doing something with it, some real serious farming instead of just puttering around and finally selling off a couple of big pieces of the place. After the first few months of her marriage it was probably downhill for her all the rest of the way. At times when she comes back clear in my memory, I always think what a lonesome-looking face she had.

But I finally learned something about her I hadn't known right up till when she died. Then I knew her marriage wasn't the whole reason for her lonesome look. In fact, remembering those glimpses I used to get sometimes, it seemed like I half knew already what she was telling me now, telling it on and on. It was that old matter she'd always skirted around, keeping it dark, never letting it show except by accident in her face. I finally got it from her without trying to, the main pieces of it, just a couple of days before she died. I was the one she felt closest to and nobody else was in her hospital room that afternoon. Even at that she was talking more to herself, or to somebody invisible, than she was to me.

What she told me was just pieces of it, all right, but those pieces finally ended up making a whole story in my head. But that came a long time later, years after, from my thinking about how it must have been, adding in from my own imagination all the details she had left out of her story.

It all finally came together for me one summer day when, feeling as lonesome as I could feel, I took it in my head to drive up to where she came from in Horn County. I walked all around her old homeplace where nobody lived anymore, went inside the rotting-down house and off in the woods and hills, too, till I found what I think was that hollow she'd talked about. Then I spent a while driving around in the neighborhood, in the late evening, till I came on Bethel Church and the old graves there. When I left Horn County behind me it was just like I was bringing home a memory of every little thing in what had happened to Mama.

She said his name was Clay. He was about a year older than she was, maybe seventeen, and a grade ahead of her at school. She said she'd never paid much attention to him except to notice he was a sickly boy and stayed off to himself and was absent about half the time. When she thought about him at all, she reckoned he had another reason besides his sickliness for being absent so much. It was the kind of folks he came from. They had a name for shiftlessness and not caring about anything. And the father had been put in jail two or three times for making whiskey. They were the kind that Mama's father called "plain trash." Most likely Mama never would have got to know any more about Clay than she already did, if it hadn't been for a sort of accident you might call "fate."

Mama was one of three children but her older sister was already several years married and gone, and her little brother was too little to be any company to her. She had some social life, all right, but especially through the long summers she had to be her own company most of the time. She said that till she was twelve or thirteen she was still playing with the rag dolls her mother had made for her when she was small, making up lives for them that were a lot like the fairy tales and old folk stories she'd heard. When she put her dolls away, she was still making up stories in her head, with herself the main person in them.

Of course, there were other things, more and more of them, to take up her time, chores in the house and the barnyard. She churned and helped her mother with quilting. She fed the chickens and finally had to milk the cow every morning and evening. But there was still time left over for thinking, dreaming, I guess, in the still summer afternoons under the apple trees. She was plenty old enough by then to yearn for something more.

There were miles and miles of deep woods around in those hills, and she got in the way of taking long walks through them. She said she'd climb to the tops of different hills and sit down in places where she could see forever and ever out ahead of her. That special day she told me about — it was in late springtime, I think — she set out and walked all the way to and up Flint Mountain, which wasn't really a mountain but just the biggest hill around. It was a hard climb; I know because I climbed it myself. And sure enough, just like when she saw it, all down the other side of that hill were thick patches of bright, bright green laurel. I don't wonder she liked the look of it enough to walk down through it, having to pick her way, clear on till she came out in the hollow —— with me the same as tracking her, feeling what she must have felt.

The hollow was full of big tulip and beech trees that shut out all but patches of sunlight here and yonder. It had been sweating-hot coming down, but the air here was almost like in a cave. A clear branch ran between big rocks. I could see minnows and crawfish in it. I walked a little way up the branch, just like she had, and all of a sudden the air was cooler than ever. There it was. I was looking at a rock bluff with a hole in it as big as a room, and inside the hole a pool of water that the branch came from. She said that for a little while she didn't have a notion of anybody else being there. She said she jumped enough to lift her off the ground when she saw him.

It was a boy. He was sitting down, she said, on a rock against the bluff, looking at her like somebody who had given up on finding a way to rescue. After Mama got her breath back, she recognized it was Clay, and after that she wasn't scared anymore, just uneasy and flustered. But not as much as he was, she said. His hand with a pocketknife in it was still shaking a little bit. There was a piece of carved wood, the shape of a tiny dog, that he had dropped on the ground in front of him. When it looked like he never was going to say anything, Mama finally said the first thing to mind — something about school, as she remembered, and never seeing him there anymore.

But he just sat on with his lips clamped like he was meaning to keep quiet forever. She remembered how thin and pale his lips looked. So did his face, but she never had seen it any other way. His long hair was a sort of flax color, more yellow than it was white. It was almost like her own hair, that she was proud of because it was gold. Both of them even had the same kind of blue eyes, too, near as dark as a gander's. She said that when she noticed that, it came in her mind they could have been brother and sister, and all of sudden this thought stood up against what her father would've thought about her standing here out in the woods talking to this trashy boy. After that, she wasn't even uneasy with him anymore.

He got easy, too, after a while . . . or almost easy. After she called his name and got him to say he knew hers was Omie Walls, she got him kind of opened up. Praising the little dog he had carved, which he finally gave her to look at up close, brought him almost all the way out. He carved things all the time, and not just dogs. He made cows and sheep and chickens and such, that he kept in the barn at home because of his brothers, who mocked him. That was why he came here.

It seemed to Mama that once he started talking his face changed. His eyes went a lighter color, she thought, and his lips had stopped being tight and thin the way they had looked before. She said that sometimes when both of them quit talking for a minute she would hear, like a little silver bell that never hushed, the sound of water falling. That sound, plain as plain, had stuck with her all these years. So had another sound. It was the cry of a hawk, "kree-kree," coming down from the sky. She left him with her promise to come back the next day if she could. She hadn't had to ask him for the wooden dog she carried in her hand.

She kept the dog well hid, and everything else, too, though it took some managing. She had to lie to her mama and daddy pretty often and was always sorry afterwards, but she never gave a real thought to mending her ways. Never once to get caught that whole summer long she must have got as clever as a fox. But it was such a summer. She would think and think about meeting him next time, and dream about it in the night. She would wake up in the dark from seeing his face, still hearing that tinkle of water from the pool, and maybe that hawk's cry. She remembered people talking about how hot it was that summer. It wasn't hot to her, or cold or wet or dry or anything else but just all part of what kept the blood always churning around her heart. Climbing the slope of Flint Mountain was nothing to her either, except for that light, bright feeling in her head when she got to the top. And she had made a path straight as an arrow shot down through those laurel thickets, into the hollow where he was waiting for her. There were times, just a few, when she didn't find him there. Those times, her climb back up that hill was pure misery working in her breast.

But those little times were nothing worse than toothaches compared to what was waiting for her. On a morning in the fall, right after she got up, she was all of a sudden sick. She was sick the next morning, too, and having a country knowledge of such matters she started right in worrying. A few days more and it wasn't just a worry, it was sure. I don't know how she could have missed worrying before it happened, but it seems like she did, somehow. I guess it was just the spell that whole summer put on her, shutting out everything else but the way she felt.

She couldn't keep it hid for long. Her mother had sharp eyes and after several times catching her daughter being sick, she came right to it. For a while Mama tried lying, but it wasn't any use. The thing they couldn't get out of her, though, was who the father was. "Never," she said, screaming it, even when her daddy stood over her with a cane that he kept threatening to use on her but finally didn't.

They found out, though. She never knew exactly how, but she thought it had to do with them finding in her room the little wooden dogs and sheep and things that Clay had carved for her. After that it was worse than before, especially after she screamed out to them that she didn't care, she was glad, she was going to go to him. They made her sleep in the loft at night and there was hardly a minute in the day when her mother didn't have a watchful eye out. Even so, she ran off once, one afternoon at the hour when she was not likely to find him there. He wasn't there, and she came back crying all the way.

In November the weather made a sudden change. There was day after day of rain, and wind that lashed it against the roof and turned it to ice sometimes. Between chores, in the silence that had got to be her habit, she would go to her bed in the loft and lie there under the roof hearing the wind and rain, thinking about him. For a long time she had held on to a kind of a dreamy hope that one dark night he would some way signal to her from down in the yard and she would slip out and he would take her off to a far, far place that nobody else knew about. There was a high front window to the loft and she would stand there in the night and make herself think she could spy the shape of him under the plum tree down by the gate. But that was before she overheard her daddy talking quiet to her mother in the kitchen. He had been to Clay's house. He said she needn't to worry. She could evermore, her daddy had said, put that boy clear out of mind. Evermore. Mama said that then she was finished hoping, or thought she was.

But one night Clay's ghost came to her. It was raining again, after stopping for a week near the end of the month, and the wind was lashing the roof. She woke up and saw it, pale in the dark. It paled clear away when she sat up, and left nothing where it had stood. She might have sat there a minute or two. Then she was up, dressing herself, putting on her coat and a rag around her head. She went as quiet as another ghost, down, and out of the house.

She said she didn't know how to go by road but she thought she knew how through the woods. In the dark, though, with the lashing rain and the trees and bushes heaving and whistling around her, it was hard. The vines and sawbriers grabbed her and pulled her off her course, and water from that headrag, sopping wet, kept her eyes half blind. She had to stop and stand, searching for which hill was Flint Mountain. By this time she would be shivering, shaking in her clothes. Till finally, because it was coming daylight, she could see the high ridge of the hill against the sky. It was full dawn when she got to the foot of it and started climbing, miring and slipping in the soggy loam, heaving for breath, blinking back the streams of water that ran down in her eyes. When she got to the top she had to sink down for a spell, resting her head against the trunk of a tree. She said that was when she first felt the baby moving in her belly.

After that it wasn't as hard, though the rain and wind never slacked. From down in the hollow she knew the right direction, from Clay's pointing it out to her. That hill was not so hard to climb. And along that ridge it was easy, because she was walking a path. Easy except the wind was so cold. It blew her sideways off the path sometimes.

Halfway down the last hill she saw what had to be Clay's house. She said that at first she thought it must be seeing it through all that rain that made it look so fragile and sad and like nobody lived there. But even when she got close it kept on looking that way, except that somebody did live there, because smoke was coming out of the chimney. That was when she stopped. She said that all of a sudden she didn't know how she could just walk right up to that house and knock on the door. She didn't think she could. She was standing not far away from a ramshackle barn and she was so cold and hard-shivering that she turned off her path and went in it.

But somebody was in there. He was staring at her, holding a milk can, and for what was like a whole minute while her heart didn't hit a beat, she thought it was Clay. He looked like Clay but he wasn't. He was bigger and stronger and older. He finally spoke to her, asked her what she wanted. She made herself come right out and tell him, she wanted Clay, and she stood there waiting, finally wondering why he didn't answer. Then he answered.

She said that for a while it was like he had answered her in some kind of strange talk that she couldn't fit with any words she knew. She said it was like it didn't come really clear to her till she was already out of the barn and walking up the slope toward the road on the other side of the house. That was when she all of a sudden felt like she was going to have to sink down and lie there balled up in the mud and rain, wailing and wailing till she couldn't anymore. But she didn't. She went on like somebody blind and being led, and got on the road headed the way she thought would take her to Bethel Church. That was where Clay was, in the graveyard.

She remembered just pieces of that long walk. She said it kept raining all the way, soughing and sluicing down through the bare tree limbs she passed under. She didn't think she ever saw more than one or two people. A man she knew but couldn't name at the time talked to her and took hold of her arm, trying to stop her, but she fought him loose and went on. She never stopped once, no matter her feeling all the way that one more step and she would have to sink down in the muddy road and lie there wailing. And no matter that that baby kept struggling and struggling in her belly.

She was on the right road and finally through the rain she saw Bethel Church up close. It was no matter that there wasn't any headstone yet. A fresh grave was easy to find. That was where she sank down at last and put her cheek in the mud on that grave and let go with her wailing.

It couldn't have been very long before they found her. That man on the road must have gone straight and told her father, and there were people that lived near Bethel Church. Her father took her home and put her to bed and she had that dead baby a few hours later.

She was sick for a month and for a long, long time after that she didn't have anything to say to anybody. Except to Clay's ghost, that she said she kept seeing in the night. But finally she got to talking again and went on with her life, the way people do. They say time heals everything, and that was something that happened to her forty years before she died. But there she was, on her deathbed telling me about it, telling me what had been in her heart the biggest part of all her days. So that saying's just not true.

Five

J ust about all times were hard times for our family, and that was why
one or another of us was always cooking up some new scheme for
making money. At least once, though, we got an idea for a money-
making enterprise that didn't seem cooked up at all but just handed to us
fit and ready to go. It was plain from the start that Mama was set against
it, but she was that way about most of our ideas. When even Coop showed
signs of interest, I completely quit worrying about Mama's attitude.

The idea came from two things adding up together. There weren't supposed to be any bears in Clayton County, not for the last fifty years and
more. But one day in early spring Stack came in with the tale that this
wasn't so. He had a lot of traps and was always setting them in the woods
and along the banks of Stump Creek, catching coons and muskrats and
such. He said there wasn't just one bear, there were two, a she-bear and a
cub. He had been seeing their tracks along the creek bank and hadn't
been sure what kind of tracks they were. But just that day he had seen the
old she-bear herself. He said he saw her through a lot of brush but there
wasn't anything else in these woods that big and black.

Of course, this excited us boys, especially me. I started thinking and
talking about catching the cub and having a pet bear and maybe even taking him into town for people to see. Daddy said a bear could be bad
news, 'specially if you tried to catch her cub. That didn't scare me off,

though. I went looking the next day and I did find some big tracks on the creek bank. Stack said he figured she had a den in one of the bluffs along the creek, and we made plans to go hunt it out the next weekend.

The second thing happened that same week. I was in town late in the afternoon waiting for Dud and Stack to finish some business of theirs, when I looked up and saw my loony brother Bucky across the street. He was standing on the courthouse lawn next to where the steps came down to the sidewalk, holding his hand out, palm up, to one of two men who weren't looking at him. What the men were looking at was a good-sized wooden box on the ground. I could see that Bucky, with his head jerking back and forth, was saying something to the men, or trying to. After a minute I saw one of the men and then the other one reach in their pockets and come out with what had to be coins and put them in Bucky's outstretched hand. After Bucky had the coins settled in his own pocket, he leaned down and, almost like he was a magician or something, yanked the top off the box. Both men kind of jumped. They stood staring down into the box, till pretty soon I could tell that one of them was trying to ask Bucky questions. I knew what kind of answers he was getting, the kind that made him give it up after a minute or two. Then all of a sudden Bucky leaned and shut the top down quick. I saw why. A man coming down the walk was just barely a step away from a free look inside.

I know I stood there for a half hour watching Bucky take in the customers, wondering what it was in the box and what kind of coins he was getting for a look at it. As bad as I wanted to know, I was too ashamed of Bucky to go and see. At least I was till the customers quit coming and I saw the square had about cleared out because it was after quitting time. I crossed the street and climbed up to where Bucky stood by the box. His shirt was even more ragged and dirtier than it was the last time I saw him. He rolled his eyes at me and kind of smiled. "What's in there?" I said.

He held his hand out.

"Your own brother?" I said. "I ain't got any money anyhow."

Bucky blinked and his head jerked. "O-kay." He leaned down and opened the box. I jumped, myself. It was the biggest dang cottonmouth I ever saw in my life. It was as big around as man's arm and something between black and mud-colored and had a head that looked like it would do for a woodcutter's wedge. "How'd you catch that thing?"

"In m-m-my fish box."

I looked at the ugly thing a minute more. "How much you get for a look?"

His mouth worked, then said, "Du-dime."

"How much you made?"

He patted a bulge on the hip of his overalls. Then he reached in the pocket and took out a handful of coins, some of them quarters, that didn't leave that bulge on his hip much smaller than before. "Damn!" I said. "You going to get rich."

Just then Dud and Stack pulled up to the curb in Dud's old car and sat staring at Bucky's box. They had to come up for a look, too, which they made Bucky give them for free, and they asked about the same questions I'd asked. The thing different was that Dud wanted to know how much Bucky had made in all, and he wouldn't let him alone till Bucky got down and laid all those coins out on the walk to be counted. It came to six dollars and eighty cents, though I reckoned he hadn't made it all in one day.

"Goddamn," Dud said. "It's money in snakes, ain't it? You better go catch some more. Start you a snake zoo."

It was that word zoo that got things started. On the way home Stack, after being quiet till we crossed the bridge, said, "What if we started up a zoo? I don't mean just snakes, I mean all kind of wild critters. Maybe we could catch that bear, even. Else her cub. Maybe a bobcat, too. And a deer. And shorely such as coons and foxes."

"That'd be something, wouldn't it?" I said from the back seat. I was excited. Dud didn't say anything for a minute, just stared at the road in front of him. I knew how Dud liked to be the one to think of a thing and I was beginning to be afraid he was going to say it was a dumb idea. Then I saw him nod. "Ain't one zoo in this whole county," he said. "People likes to look at wild animals. Like that cottonmouth. We could shore catch a bunch of them."

"Rattlers, too," I said, leaning over the back of the front seat. "I killed one down in the hollow Sunday. Could of caught him. And copperheads, too."

"We need more than just snakes," Stack said. "That bear's what we really need. And a bobcat."

"Snakes is a good starter, though," Dud said. "Look at Bucky. With one dang snake."

That was how it started off and kept right on after we got in the house and settled down at the supper table. After I watched Coop for a minute or two, I was reassured. He didn't say anything at first but I could see him listening, like he was getting interested in spite of himself. Daddy didn't say anything at first either, just went on shoveling the food in, and I was getting uneasy for fear he was going to come in against us. But that was before he got it clear that Bucky was making real money off that snake.

"And he could of got a quarter easy as a dime," Stack said. "He had a bunch of them, folks'd pay more than that. Specially if snakes was just one part of it all."

"We could put a sign up on the road," I said. "Moss's Zoo."

That was the right thing to say because, I could tell, Daddy liked the idea of having his name up there on the road. I watched his jaw slow down and for a space there he didn't take another bite. When his jaw finally stopped all the way he said, "I'm kind of leaning to the notion it just might work. I even knowed a man made money charging to look at his nervous goats. Folks like that."

Dorcas and Mabel both looked at him with their mouths open and then at each other. It was easy to see they hated the whole idea, but it didn't matter about them. What did matter was what I could see in Mama's face, in the way her shut lips made a tight straight line. Then they came open. "Where you mean to keep these snakes? In the house?"

"Make a cage for them, o' course," Stack said. "A good tight one."

"What about the bear? And the bobcat?"

"Cages, too," Stack said. "Make a log pen for the bear, though."

"I hate a snake," Mabel said, screwing up her face. "What if they get out?"

"They'll come right for you," Stack said.

"When you going to build all these pens?" Mama said to him. "And you with a good job, for a change. You going to quit?"

"I can find the time," Stack said, cutting his eyes away. But I could tell that was what he was aiming to do.

Mama shook her head and drew a long breath. Then she looked up, like up to heaven. "I seen a lot of foolishness in my time, but not nothing like this before. And tobacco to set and corn to plant." She looked down again, looked at Daddy who didn't look back. In fact, he had the expression of a man doing some hard thinking. Mama said, "I ain't having one wild animal anywhere close to this house. Put them off in the woods. I ain't going to get caught like poor Mrs. Noah on the Ark."

Considering all the work we knew we'd have to do, and Mama so strong against it besides, it's a real wonder the whole business didn't just blow on over. After a couple of days when nobody did anything but talk about it and I saw Mama getting more comfortable-looking all the time, I was afraid it was done for. After all, there wasn't a one of us who was much for hard work except Coop, and he didn't get in on the talk like I wished he would.

How we did finally get started was another accident, kind of, with Bucky the reason for it this time, too. We had stopped by and told him to catch some more snakes for us, but we had about forgot it. Then, on Friday afternoon, he came puffing out of the woods with a box bigger than the other one. It had five grandaddy cottonmouths in it, all knotted up together like big old mud-colored ropes, the ugliest sight you ever saw. He said he had found a whole nest of them where we could catch all we wanted. In the meantime, we had to do something with these snakes.

Stack started right in that evening after super. He found enough wire on some banged-up chicken crates, and boards off the old falling-down shed out back. He worked by a lantern on till midnight, with Dud and Coop and me finally falling in to help him. It turned out big enough for a man to walk around in and looked so nice that when Daddy saw it in the morning, with the snakes crawling around in there, he got caught up, too.

For the next couple of days, with all the banging and sawing and cussing, that was the noisiest place in the county. We pretty soon ran out of boards and wire and nails and stuff, and Daddy had to go to town and buy everything except for some slab boards he scrounged off Mr. Cutchins at the saw mill. It took more money than Daddy had, but Stack was right there with his last week's paycheck.

By Sunday afternoon we had four big cages finished. With all the odd-shaped slabs on them the last three didn't look as good as the snake cage, but they looked strong. Daddy said they'd hold anything up to the size of a bloodhound, so we could get started catching coons and foxes and such. "What about the bear?" I said. Stack had several steel traps big enough for one and we were planning on setting them out that evening down along the creek. What if we caught the bear tonight?

Daddy thought for a minute, rolling his lips in and out. "Th'ow ropes around her. Tie her all up and drag her up here. Put her in the mules's stall."

"Ain't got no ceiling," I said. "A bear can climb."

"Make one. We got some more slabs. Anyhow, we ain't caught her yet."

I had some more questions — like, How would you ever get her out of there? — but I let them go for the time being.

Daddy was always quick to get enthusiastic about a new project to make money, but usually he got over it in a couple of days. Not this time. Every once in a while, when he should have been out in the field with his mules and plow, I'd see him standing there admiring those cages and those cottonmouth snakes that, for all the moving they did, might just as well have been dead. By the time he got through, he'd be standing up straighter than was natural for him, and he'd walk away with a kind of step that made me think of that big old red rooster we had. Pretty soon I could tell what was going on in his head. It was the same thing that made him, way ahead of time, paint those signs I saw in the barn. There were three of them and they said "Mosses Zoo" and "See Mosses Wild Animals" and "See Mosses Dedly Snakes." Standing there by those cages he was already seeing himself, with paying customers all around him, showing his animals off and explaining about them.

But it was the best part of a week before there was anything at all except snakes in the cages. We boys, including Stack who hadn't gone back to his job on Monday, were out in woods just about the whole time sneaking around and poking in holes and hollow trees that might have animals in them. Daddy didn't come along, but not because he didn't want to. Mama wouldn't lay off him. The tobacco plants in the plant bed were ready to draw and he hadn't even got the ground all worked up yet. Mama worked harder than he did keeping him at it, and even then she'd look out in the field sometimes and see the mules and the plow standing there but no Daddy in sight. He'd all of a sudden remember a hollow tree or something in the woods beyond the field and step off over there for a look. For all of Mama, he just couldn't keep his mind on farm work. When she'd start in on him at night he'd tell her again about the money we were going to make off the zoo. "Fifty cents apiece," he would say. "You add that up twenty times, you got ten dollars. Suppose you got a dollar apiece. You add that up twenty times. . . . "

"They ain't hardly twenty people goes up and down that road every day," Mama said, cutting in on him. "Much less twenty that's going to pay you a dollar to see a bunch of cottonmouth snakes. Or fifty cents either. Or ten cents."

"Ain't going to be just snakes. Take a little while to get us stocked up. They'll come. People likes wild animals."

"They already stinking," Mama said, meaning the snakes. "When the wind gets east I can smell them plain." She had tried hard to make him put the cages farther away, down in the woods, but he wouldn't do it. She said, "They going to die anyhow. Even snakes got to eat."

"We'll catch them some frogs," Daddy said.

Toward the end of the week we began to have some luck. The first thing, which I caught, was just another snake but this one was a copperhead, pretty big. We were uneasy about putting him in with the cottonmouths, for fear they'd kill each other, but we couldn't use up two whole cages on snakes. They didn't fight, though. The cottonmouths didn't even move a twitch, and the copperhead, after crawling around over the top of them for a little while, ended up lying there just as dead-looking as the others. But the day after that Stack caught three little coons in a hollow tree. That was pretty good, especially because the sow coon turned up and climbed around on the cage till we finally managed, through a hole we cut, to get her in there, too. Then we had a family. We caught a possum and, because of the way the snakes had got on together, put it in there with the coons. We weren't so lucky this time, though, because the big coon killed it. But this wasn't much of a loss. You could pick up a possum out on the highway just about any night. We kept hoping to find the bear's den but we weren't even seeing her tracks anymore.

The next week we really had some luck. First we caught a little fawn that couldn't get out of a thicket quick enough. Just like with the coons, the doe followed us. She hung around in the edge of the woods and, that night, came out and butted and pawed at the cage till we finally heard her and ran her off. She kept on hanging around, getting bolder every day. She got where she'd come out in the daylight, too, even when there were people around, and circle the cages and stamp her feet when somebody came too close. Then we caught a red fox. It was in one of Stack's big steel traps and by the time we got it out it didn't have but three legs left. There was nothing wrong with its mouth, though. It bit the daylights out of Stack and he went around for a week with a bandage on his arm, cussing that fox everytime he looked at it. "You son of a bitch," he'd say.

Two days later we had our best luck yet. Bucky turned up all excited, babbling about a "bu-bu-b-bob-k-cat." I had to get him off by himself before he could come out with the details. He'd been hearing it squall and taken note of where the sound mostly came from. He found the den about halfway up on the river bluff, a hole under a rock ledge that you could put your head and shoulders into. He said he knew that was it, because he could "s-m-m-m-mell" the cat.

That called for a conference. How did you get a bad bobcat out of a hole? Everybody kept talking about smoke . . . but how did you get smoke back up in a hole that probably ran twenty or thirty feet under a ledge? And what if you did make him come out? What were you going to do then . . . grab him? Daddy and Dud and Stack all had one or two opinions but Dud's was the dumbest. He had it from somewhere that a cat hated the sound of a bell, so we could take the dinner bell down there and reach in the hole and ring it till it drove the bobcat crazy. Everybody else thought that was foolishness. Nobody had ever seen any of our cats buck up when Mama rang the dinner bell, and a cat was a cat. Daddy thought we ought to pour the hole full of water. But how were we going to get that much water up on the side of a bluff? And what if the hole didn't go downhill? . . . which, running under a ledge, it probably didn't. So, finally, we all got quiet, just looking at one another. As usual, it was Coop who came up with something sensible.

To get what-all he needed Coop had to go to town, so it was the next morning before we got to the business. We all ate breakfast fast, with

Mama glaring at first one and then another of us. Nobody would tell her what was up. The only answer she got was when she said to Daddy, "Them tobacco plants is past ready. And you ain't even got the ground made up."

"Be on it by noontime. If not sooner," Daddy said.

We went in the truck down to Bucky's shack on the river and he led us along the foot of the bluff to a place where it wasn't so steep till pretty near halfway up. Just the last ten feet or so were straight-up climbing where you had to find hand and foot holds in the rockface. Bucky went first, and Stack, standing on Dud's shoulders, handed our stuff up to him. Except for Daddy, who had to take it careful because he didn't have enough fingers, we all got up there pretty quick. It was a ledge plenty big enough for the six of us and you could see the bobcat's hole back up under another ledge pretty near shoulder-high. When I leaned down under, I got the scent in my nose. But that didn't mean the cat was in there now and I said, "What if he ain't home?"

"He's in there," Daddy said. "Bobcat's a night hunter. Don't like daylight."

Coop was down on his knees, getting things ready. He had a tin can half full of gun powder he had got out of maybe fifty shotgun shells, and ten or fifteen feet of fuse he'd probably swiped from somewhere. He tied the fuse with a string to the bale of the can, then buried the end of it down in the powder. After that he crawled in under the ledge and set the can as far back as he could reach in the hole. "Now, hand me the pole," he said. It was a long stiff fishing cane with a screwhook in the end of it. In just a second he had the bale hooked, and the can, swinging just a little bit, moving on back and out of sight in the hole. When he finally couldn't move it any farther, you could just see the butt end of the pole.

"By God, if that don't get him," Daddy said. He looked as proud as if this whole thing was his doing. "Bring on the seine. Going to be the first dang bobcat ever did get seined."

Stack had it partly unrolled and was standing there holding one handle. It was Bucky's seine. From what I could see, it looked kind of worn, with a couple of tears in the netting. I hoped it was strong. I was getting more nervous every minute. For the first time I really noticed how high up we were, looking down on the treetops and the river out beyond them, standing on this little ledge with no place to run to. I remembered our old dog Lump, and how he looked after he tangled with a bobcat.

"Double it," Coop said. He meant the seine, to make it stronger. Dud and Stack, down under the ledge, had the seine in place across the hole already, but they minded Coop. A minute and it was done and Coop, crouched down about two good steps out from the hole, was saying, "He might hit it going fast. Roll him up in it quick as you can."

Coop had the fuse in one hand and a match in the other. Nothing left but to strike that match. What if all that powder went off like in a shotgun and blew rocks out of that hole? Coop started to strike the match, but he stopped. Over his shoulder, because Daddy was standing behind him, he said, "Don't step back off that edge, Daddy." Daddy had his attention fastened too tight on the match to even think about answering. Coop struck it and lit the fuse.

"Look at that," Daddy said, pretty near in a whisper. "Like a little old fire snake crawling." It went kind of slow, in a hissing flame, and after it passed under the seine it was still in sight for a little space crawling on in the dark.

"Get ready," Coop said.

Vro-o-o-m! The noise rushed out of that hole in one big, bright orange flash, sucking smoke behind it. If everybody jumped like I did, it didn't make any difference in the way they all looked afterward, posed stiff and maybe expecting to see the devil himself step out of that black smoke.

"Hear that?" Coop said, real quiet. I thought I heard something, too. But that was when I lost track of exactly what happened. Everybody was yelling and bumping into each other, and the snarling, screeching noise from out of that bouncing net made me think maybe it really was the devil caught in there. All I could see was something big and yellow that had white teeth going crazy under that ledge, and then, all in a blur, a paw with claws raking the air fit to leave scratches in it.

That was when somebody yelled louder than anybody else, but I didn't see for a couple of minutes that those claws had hooked on to more than just air. It was Dud they had hooked. He was dancing around holding his just-about-naked leg, with blood running out between his fingers and cusswords out of his mouth at a rate mighty near enough to drown the bobcat's noise. Coop, the only one who looked like he wasn't clear out of his head, had hold of Dud's end of the seine now, pulling it around, wrapping the cat up in it.

I guess it was just a couple of more minutes before we had the thing really caught and the noise on that ledge quieted down. Of course the cat was still snarling and spitting and struggling in the net and Dud was still cussing, though not as loud. But you could hear now, and Coop, still holding the seine by one handle, was saying, "How 'bout that. Look at the size of him."

"Bu-bu-b-big," Bucky said.

"Bet he'll go thirty-five pounds," Stack said.

But there was another sound I couldn't place. When I looked to find where it came from, I saw Daddy wasn't around anymore, and right quick I stepped over to the edge. There he was, four or five steps down the slope from the rockface where he must have rolled to after he hit. But he was sitting up, groaning, with his head lolling around and his legs stretched out down the bank in front of him. I let out a yell. Coop came up beside me and it didn't seem like more than a few seconds before he was down there leaning over Daddy. By then I was on the way down too, and so was everybody else except Stack. Stack kept yelling, "Is he hurt?" but he wasn't about to go off and leave that bobcat a chance to get away.

If you measured by Daddy's groans, he was about killed. He was hurt. What looked like a broken arm turned out to be one and he had all kinds of cuts and lumps and bruises. But after his head cleared up he could limp along. I walked down with him, holding to his good arm, while the others climbed back up on the ledge to help Stack bring the bobcat. I could still hear that thing up there spitting and snarling when we got back to where the truck was parked.

I'd seen Mama mad a lot of times, but this was it. She came out and took one look at Daddy in the truck and one at the bobcat in that seine on the truckbed and turned right white in the face. She didn't say a word, just showed us her back and went into the house. When we got Daddy inside and he started groaning for Mama to come doctor him, we found out she wasn't there. She was way down the slope out back, sitting on a stump near the hogpen. She stayed down there a long time. I reckon maybe she was afraid she'd kill him if she had him in reach.

It was a bad day in the house on till bedtime. Mama didn't use any cusswords but she talked rougher than I'd ever heard her. She wanted those varmints turned loose and the pens torn down, but most of all she wanted that tobacco ground plowed. For once it was true that Daddy wasn't able. His arm was wrapped up with tobacco sticks for splints and he was so sore all over he could barely get around. Dud couldn't do it either, because his leg where the cat had clawed him hurt him too bad. Stack just plain wouldn't do it. He was all taken up with the bobcat, because it was about to tear the cage down, and he had to keep nailing on more slabs and wire to stop it from getting out. To quiet Mama down, Coop finally said he'd do the plowing. He hadn't ever plowed much and wasn't very good at it but pretty soon he was out there with the mules doing his best. That made things some better around the house, but not enough.

After what had happened, and with Mama mad as she was, you'd have thought Daddy would at least keep quiet about his zoo for the time being. He didn't, though. In a couple of hours when he got to feeling a little better he started talking about how it was time now, what with the bobcat out there, to put up his signs on the highway. We didn't have no bear yet but we had enough to start with. That bobcat was "sump'm." And all them bad snakes. And a baby deer, with the doe hanging around there so you could see her.

"And a three-legged fox," Mama said. Her voice had an edge to it I never had heard before. "And then there's all them rats in the barn. Don't forget about them."

Daddy kind of blinked, but he went right on. He wanted to make another sign saying "Fierce Wildcat" because he thought wildcat sounded fiercer than bobcat. "One dollar," he said. "That's what I'm going to ask them. If we catch that bear I might ask them two."

For half a second there, I thought Mama just might hit him. All she did was turn around and walk out of the room.

Daddy made me go put his signs up. I put them like he said, on the highway shoulder nailed to posts on both sides of our turn-in. When I got through and came back, he had limped out to the yardgate and was sitting just outside it on a stool, already waiting for customers. He waited there till suppertime but that was just a couple of hours and he wasn't discouraged that nobody had showed up yet. He said you couldn't expect customers to come just as quick as you put your signs out.

Our luck wasn't any better the next morning, but up in the afternoon we had two customers, two grown-up boys together. I could see them looking down there toward the cages and saw one of them shake his head when Daddy asked them for a dollar apiece. He settled with them for fifty cents each. Then he got up and tried to go with them so he could tell them about the deadly snakes and the fierce wildcat. But he was too sore to do better than creep and the boys were through looking and were heading back to their car before he got halfway there. He turned around to ask them how they liked it, but they just went on without saying anything.

That was it for the day but Daddy wasn't discouraged. He held up the dollar bill to us and told us that was just the first of many a one to come. He said it would take a while for the word to get around. He said we needed to make them signs bigger. Mama, who was watching him, said, "It was a bill in the mail today. It was for fifteen dollars and sixty cents you been owing for two months."

"It'll wait a while longer," Daddy said and put the dollar in his pocket.

"How much you spent on the cages and stuff? And feeding our good chickens to them varmints."

Daddy looked away from her, and after a second Mama did what she usually did, walked out of the room.

But the next day was the big day, early on, at breakfast time. Stack wasn't there. He always went out long before breakfast to check on his traps but this was the first time he hadn't got back to eat with everybody. It wasn't a thing to take much note of, though, and we were halfway through when, just a minute after the dogs started barking, we all heard Stack's voice. "Look-a-here!" he was yelling. "By God!" He was on the front porch. There was some kind of a scuffle going on and a kind of strangled squealing noise.

We all jumped up from the table but before any of us could get into the front room Stack had already opened the screen door and was dragging something in off the porch. It was a bear cub! Stack had it roped around the neck and under its front legs.

"God-dang!" Daddy yelled. "Talk about a zoo! Look at that!"

With us prancing around and all talking and asking loud questions at the same time, the poor little bear, humped down in the middle of the floor, looked like it had given up on the last hope it ever had. It was just some bigger than the stuffed toy bears I'd seen girls have and looked a lot like them, except for the little red mouth that was open and slobbering and panting so hard its head bobbed up and down. Everybody wanted to touch it, and did, and the poor thing looked like it didn't even notice. It must have noticed when Stack caught it, though. There was blood all over Stack's hand and wrist — on the other arm, this time. Even his face was all scratched up.

We finally quieted down enough for Stack to answer our questions. "She's still down there in the trap. Caught good. You ought to see her, she's big as a growed bull calf. Bad, too."

"We got to get her," Daddy said. "Lord . . . Talk about a zoo!"

"I chased that thing in a brier thicket," Stack said. "Jumped right on top of him. Hadn't had that rope I never would have got him up here."

"We can th'ow a lot of ropes around her. Hold her in between us and drag her up here. Lord. . . ."

Mama, who was standing in the kitchen door, hadn't said anything till now. I think even she was kind of taken up with the cub. "You leave that bear alone, she'll kill you. That little one's plenty." Then she said, "You got to take it out of here, though. If you got to keep the poor little thing, put it in with the coons."

"He's too strong," Daddy said. "Put him in the mules's stall. We got to build a log pen anyhow, to put that big bear in."

"You the one ought be put in a log pen," Mama said and turned back into the kitchen.

Stack was getting ready to drag the cub out of the house but the girls wanted to pet it. "He can bite," Stack said. "See my hand?" They all drew back. Mabel was saying, "He's so furry and cute. Can't you just hold . . ." when all of a sudden everybody stopped. It wasn't just the dogs out there yelling blood and murder, it was the chickens and even the two cats under the porch. Before any of us could get our mouths shut and make it to the door, we were hearing something else through all that racket, a kind of clanking sound.

"God-a-mighty!" Dud yelled. Then I saw it, too. It was the old bear, black as Satan and big-looking as a dray horse, standing right there in our open yardgate swinging her head back and forth, with the dogs going crazy all around her. That clanking sound came from the steeltrap and chain on her foot.

"Shut the damn door!" Stack yelled.

But Coop had the wits, "She'll smell that cub in here. Get it out the back door quick!"

In one way, though, that was a mistake. When Stack yanked the rope tight to start dragging, the cub let out another one of those squeals. The old bear heard it, and her head went up. That was just a half-second before somebody made another mistake, which was slamming the door shut. It was like that noise told the bear just exactly where to head for.

"Get out of here!"

That probably was Coop's voice but it wasn't needed because everybody was already lunging for the kitchen. The jam of bodies between the doorposts took several seconds to work itself out, and it was lucky the bear had to stop and figure before giving that front door a bashing. On the way through the kitchen somebody grabbed Mama, who looked like she was ready to fight, but after that there was another bottleneck at the back door. For those few seconds, with the girls and maybe some of us screaming, and the bear and the dogs both in the house snarling and baying and turning things upside down, I guess there was more noise made than ever will be again in one little place.

As quick as we got untangled and out in the backyard, we all headed straight into the smokehouse and shut the door. It wasn't all of us, though. We saw that right off and opened the door part-ways to look for Stack. The first thing we saw was the bear coming off the back steps of the house. She hit the ground and reared up and knocked a dog rolling. Right after that was when she saw Stack. He was halfway to the barn still dragging that cub and it squealing. The bear gave a kind of a grunting roar and, dogs swirling and screaming around her, took off after him three-legged, that trap and chain clanking on the loose leg behind her.

It was a good thing she had that trap or she would have caught him sure. Stack meant to keep that cub and he got clear to the barn, his hand reaching for the door, before even he couldn't doubt the bear was going to catch him. He gave up with a sideways lunge right out of the bear's mouth. He hit rolling and didn't stop till he came up against the fence and heaved himself headfirst over the top of it.

After that the bear was too busy with the dogs to think about Stack. She was back with her cub, snarling something awful and rearing and stroking at them, all the time working her way past the barn and on toward the woods. A couple of more minutes and the whole uproar was out of sight, if not out of hearing. It didn't get clear out of hearing for another ten or fifteen minutes.

Where we were, though, and everywhere this side of the woods, those minutes must have been the stillest ones ever before or since known by our family. You couldn't look anywhere and see a dog or a cat or a chicken. You couldn't look down at the hogpen and see one hog, or out in the lot beyond the barn and see a mule or a cow. The fact was that the fence on the far side of the lot had a big torn-out place in it where the mules had hit it at a dead run. It took us two hours to round up them and our three cows out of the woods.

But the quietest minutes of all were the ones after Mama went back in the house to look around. When she came out she didn't much more than resemble herself. She just stood there on the steps with her face the color of fatback and her mouth so tight you couldn't see her lips. She didn't say a word, and neither did anybody else except Eve, who whispered to me, "Mama's awful mad, ain't she?" For a minute or two Mama didn't seem to be looking at anything, but then her eyes fastened on Daddy and kind of lighted up more than they were before. I saw Daddy turn his face away, blinking. When I looked again, Mama was on the way back into the house.

We were all shuffling around starting to talk to each other when we saw Mama again. She had come out the front door and was walking toward the zoo. I saw right off that what she had in her hand was a shotgun. Daddy saw it, too. He gave a kind of a grunt and then a little muffled shout and started after her in a hurry. He didn't get halfway to the cages, though, before he slowed down and then stopped and after that just stood there like he was hanging by a string tied in the top of his head.

I heard him say something just one time, right after Mama fired the first shot. It sounded like, "Lord God-a-mighty, help us."

Mama went right on shooting, stopping twice to reload. When she got through she had shot every one of those snakes all to pieces. She put the shotgun down and opened all the cage doors, the bobcat's last, stepping back away from it. In a minute or two there wasn't a thing left in any of the cages except a bunch of snake meat.

Daddy stayed down around the barn all morning and didn't come to dinner. While we were eating we heard his old truck cough and sputter and then start up. When he didn't come back by suppertime we figured he'd gone off on one of his drunks. Mama said she reckoned that was it. She didn't know how, though, when he didn't have but that one dollar left to his name. A second later, sounding like she really meant it, she said she hoped they put him in jail for something, anyhow.

Six

I think of my thirteenth birthday as a dividing line because about all the really unpleasant and bad things that happened to our family came after that. For a long time it looked to be just a drawn-out run of bad luck we were having, but later on, in a way that wasn't clear to me yet, I started thinking of all our misfortunes as somehow connected to each other. The first big one was Dorcas's doing, though now I can't much blame her for it.

I haven't said much about my sisters. Really I never did think of them that way, as "my sisters," all grouped together. Dorcas and Mabel were my older sisters, like a pair even though Dorcas was so much prettier than Mabel ever thought about being. Then there was little Eve, four years younger than me and all by herself. She's who I think of right off when I hear the word sister. I loved her better by far than either one of the others. I guess I loved Dorcas and Mabel on and off, but I never felt very close to them, especially Dorcas.

When Dorcas was sixteen she had hair that was almost gold, just like Mama said hers was when she was young. Her hair was the prettiest thing about Dorcas but it wasn't the only thing. By that time she was all bloomed out into a young woman with more than she really needed in those body parts that boys like to look at. And Dorcas made it worse by the way she was always wearing dresses too tight for her and fixing herself up with lipstick and rouge and stuff. I don't think she ever thought about anything but boys and making them look at her and whistle at her. After a while I caught on that both Mama and my brothers were worried about her and I got to worrying, too. I started noticing whenever I saw her in town. She walked with a lot more of a switch than she needed to, and several times I saw her change her direction just so she could walk close by a bunch of boys standing on the sidewalk. They weren't only boys her age, either. Some of them were the same as grown men and one of them I saw whistle at her had on a college T-shirt. I remembered him later. He was one of those Burford boys that had put the feathers on Dud.

It wasn't anything new that boys ran after good-looking girls. The new thing, because of what was happening to the town, was how much more they could get away with. Riverton had been growing for a long time but up till the last couple of years it wasn't something you noticed very much. The big difference started when they put in the tire plant out on River Road, and since then another, littler factory for making boxes right on the edge of town. It wasn't just that you kept seeing a lot of faces you never had seen before. The faces were a different kind of faces, because the people were a different kind of people from what the town was used to. They didn't care about a lot of the things the old people cared about and before long there got to be so many of them that old ways started breaking down. Pretty soon you could whistle at a girl on the street and nobody but a few grayheads would turn and glare at you.

But, of course, there were a lot of people who were glad to see this happen, because it brought money in and made the town livelier. There were more jobs to be had and more things for people to do, especially young people. Dud and Stack and Coop all had some of these jobs off and on, but the one in our family that got the most out of what had happened was Dorcas. It had used to be that she would come home around 3:30 every school day on the bus. Eve and Mabel still did but Dorcas was hardly ever with them anymore. There was a big new ice cream place in town, all shiny white and silver with chrome, that was where a lot of kids from the high school, and some older ones besides, gathered every afternoon. You could just about always find Dorcas in there, with two or three boys buying her ice cream. She started getting fat and had to go on a diet, but that didn't stop her from being there every day after school.

But an awful lot of girls did just the same way as Dorcas did, and so for a long time it didn't seem like something to worry too much about. Mostly we just made fun of her for all her primping up and wearing tight dresses. Coop, who was the worryingest one of us, would give her the hardest digs. "There she goes," he would say so she could hear him. "Going out of here looking like a milk cow." Dorcas's face would get fire-red and she would come up with the ugliest answer she could think of. Like, "You dirty little snake." Then she would storm out of the house.

All the cuts she got didn't make any difference and after a while things started getting worse. It got to where the boys around her weren't just high school boys anymore. There were more older ones, including some college boys who were in town all summer and came home besides for holidays and weekends. I, or one of us, was always seeing her in the ice cream place, the only girl in a booth with two or three of those grown boys. The Burfords were among them. We saw her with them several times, once in a shiny red car without any top on it. That was when we first got really upset.

But worse was yet to come. It wasn't long before a boy we never had seen till now, a tall, lean dangerous-looking one, moved in and took Dorcas over. He was college, too. His name was Mason, we finally found out, and his daddy was somebody big at the tire plant. The car he had made the Burfords' car look like a tin lizzie. I saw Dorcas two times myself, riding with him, her gold hair flying in the wind. Finally she was going out with him at night sometimes, though he never came to our house to pick her up. She would meet him up on the highway, leaving Mama with a dumb lie, like maybe it was a girlfriend she was going to meet.

Mama did what she could. One day when she didn't know there was anybody else around I overheard her talking to Dorcas in the kitchen. She wasn't getting anywhere. She was saying in that flat voice, almost her regular voice, that didn't sound like it expected anything, "He ain't looking to you for nothing but his pleasure. Our kind, we. . . ."

"It ain't true!" Dorcas said, hot like but maybe with some tears about to get into it. "He's sweet to me as sweet can get. He bought me that new dress I got."

I'd wondered about that dress, where she got the money. For a space Mama didn't say anything. It was like I could see her face, with that level far-off look turned toward a window maybe, not taking anything in. Then she said, "That dress weren't nothing to such as him . . . big folks like what he is. Folks that won't even come to your house to court you."

"I told him not to! He would if I wanted him to!" Dorcas made a little choking noise. "He says he wants to marry me . . . when he can."

Mama said, "When he can," in a voice that put me in mind again of that look on her face. "Marrying you ain't nowhere but in his mouth. Not with the likes of us, child."

I heard the choking noise again, just ahead of Dorcas's words: "The likes of you all, you mean. Not me, he loves me. He wants to marry me." Then her steps in quick retreat and the slap of the back screen door.

I think Mama's saying those things did more harm than good. Dorcas shut herself up in her room and wouldn't let even Eve and Mabel in, though it was their room, too. She let them in to go to sleep that night but she didn't come out to supper or to breakfast the next morning either. She went on off to school, looking straight ahead, without one word to say.

I know it wouldn't have helped any if Daddy had done what he should've done: come out strong against her, too. But when he found out who that Mason boy was, then for sure he couldn't bring himself to do it. Just because of Mama he made a kind of a try once or twice, but anybody could see how his heart wasn't in it. A boy from such big folks to court his daughter! Sometimes, times when he saw her go out the door looking the way she looked, I would see him swell up with pride till his face got red as a berry. I'm sure that at least part of the time he really did believe his daughter was on her way to a rich folks' wedding at the church. Once when he let that notion slip out, Mama called him "fool." She never had said that to him before.

Mabel, the only one real close to Dorcas, kept her mouth shut tight through the whole thing, and Eve, who was just nine, didn't half understand what was going on. For the rest of us, the one that stayed the most worked up about it was Coop. He couldn't sleep nights and he kept saying we had to do something no matter what Dorcas said or wanted. He said that bastard Mason was making a whore out of our sister. He said it was a goddamn shame for us to just sit by and not do anything. What he wanted to do was catch that bastard waiting for Dorcas up there at the highway and make damn sure he never came back again. On things like this Coop was always the hothead among us. Dud and Stack, seeing how Daddy was acting and how Dorcas wasn't about to listen to anybody, including Jesus, said it wouldn't do any good, she'd just meet him somewhere else. Coop would get still madder and call them "yellow" and tell them they weren't fit to be in our family. Once when Stack, who was working at the tire plant just then, said something about how he might lose his job if they did that, Coop got so mad he hit him in the mouth. Stack didn't hit him back. It wasn't because, being bigger and stronger than Coop, he knew it wouldn't be a fair fight. It was because, like the rest of us, he respected Coop. Besides that, he was already feeling ashamed of what he'd said.

Dud and Stack weren't even at home on the evening when Coop decided he would do something on his own. If they had been, I kind of think they would have gone in with him. Anyhow, Coop could tell by the way Dorcas was fixing herself up that this was to be another one of those nights. She stood there, in that stiff haughty way she had got into, in front of the mirror over the wash basin combing and combing her hair. She must have pulled that comb through it a hundred times. I said, "You're going to wear it plumb out, Dorcas. Then what'll your big shot fellow think?"

"Mind your own business." She said it low and mean.

When I turned away and didn't see Coop in the living room any longer, I went out on the porch looking for him. It was only just getting dusk and after a second my eye picked him out. He was on the road walking pretty fast up toward the highway. I ran and caught up but he didn't look at me, just kept walking. "What you going to do, Coop?"

"You go back," he said.

"You going to fight him?"

"Go back."

I didn't. I followed along a step behind him till we reached the highway. Mason hadn't come yet and Coop, without one word, squatted down on his heels to wait for him. I said, "You ought to hold off till you got Dud and Stack with you."

"Shut up."

Squatted down there on his heels he looked awful little to me, especially when I thought about Mason being pretty near the size of Dud. Coop was quick, all right, but that wouldn't be enough. He ought to have brought a stick. He didn't look worried, though, squatting there, just listening. Dusk was closing down and there wasn't anything to hear but a couple of bobwhites whistling.

Then we both heard it, the swishing sound of a car climbing that long hill, getting louder. Coop came onto his feet. He was standing on the highway shoulder when a bright yellow car with no lights burning yet and no top on it and one head showing through the windshield came around the curve. There was something flapping. It was a white scarf around the fellow's neck.

The car slowed and turned, coasting into our road, and stopped with the driver closer to me than to Coop. That scarf was slick looking . . . silk, I reckoned. Then I had to move to see, because Coop was standing between me and that Mason's head. Coop said, "You get the hell out of here. And don't come back no more."

Even sitting down in the seat Mason didn't have to lift his face but a little to meet Coop straight-on. He didn't look bothered, just stared steady in Coop's face with hard, slate-colored eyes. You couldn't see his ears for the long black hair. He finally said, "Who the shit are you?"

What I could see already happening to Coop didn't have anything to do with getting scared. The way Mason was looking at him and saying those words was why Coop's arm, the one I could see plain, had got tight and trembling. It was crooked a little and the fist at the end of it turning white. But his words came steady enough. "Coop Moss," he said. "Dorcas's brother. And there's two more of us a lot bigger and meaner than me. You come after her another time, we going to bloody up this highway with your ass."

Mason's face didn't change. His first answer wasn't with words, it was a little noise like spitting something out his throat, scornful. He said, "Thought her name was Caress." Then, "I go where I goddamn please, you dried-up little redneck. Go fuck one of your sheep or something."

I saw Coop's arm give a jerk that crooked it all the way and set it off like a snake striking. Mason didn't have time to more than get his hands off the steering wheel before Coop's fist hit him square in the nose. He took a second punch in the face before he could get hold of Coop's arm, and one or two others before he managed to get Coop by the hair and pull his head down on top of the door.

After that, Coop wasn't able to make any show against him. Mason came out of his car like he was jerked on a string and right quick he had hold of both of Coop's wrists. Then, just as quick, he pushed Coop back and stepped into a long mean swing that caught Coop square on the side his head. It knocked Coop down. When he tried to get up, Mason just reached out with his foot and kicked Coop down again. That was when I went crazy. I went for him with all my might, butted him in the belly and grabbed him around the waist trying to throw him. It wasn't any use. About a second later I was flying through the air and landing in the ditch by the road on my back. I was just getting up when I heard a kind of shrieking noise.

It was Dorcas. There she was, all got up in her tight clothes and lipstick and stuff, struggling to keep Coop from going for Mason again, sort of wailing and blubbering at the same time, "Stop it! Stop it!" And, for a wonder, she did get it stopped, even though Coop kept right on glaring and showing his teeth like he was getting ready again to spring at Mason's throat.

For just a second, before Dorcas turned around to look at Mason, I was sure she was going to come down on our side. It was those tears in her eyes that I thought were for Coop. But then she saw — what I just now really, and with pleasure, noticed — how Mason's nose was bleeding. Blood was all over his mouth and chin and dripping down on that white scarf. She just looked at him, watched his hand take the scarf and hold it up against his nose. When she turned back around, her eyes were bright in a way tears couldn't make them be. She said, "You all are hateful! Hateful! I hate you!"

Then she showed us her back and went to Mason and, taking the scarf out of his hand, started dabbing at the blood on his face. Mason said, "You tell them, if they ever come after me again I'll break their goddamn dirty little necks."

Expecting something, I glanced at Coop. He didn't have that cocked look anymore. Instead he looked like the last little whisp of wind had gone clean out of him. And Dorcas went right on dabbing at Mason's face.

It was only another few seconds before Coop turned around without a word and started walking back down the road toward home. I followed him, not saying anything either, and pretty soon we heard that car start up and drive away. Coop stopped and looked back up the road. It was still plenty light enough to see by, and the whole road up to the highway couldn't have seemed any emptier. Coop sat down against a tree trunk. I sat down with him. There was a big red knot still rising on his cheekbone.

◆

Dorcas didn't come home that night, or the next night or the third night either. My brothers all went looking for her. Coop spent the whole second night hiding across from Mason's house, which was a great big, new stone house overlooking the river several miles down from town. He saw some people go in and out but none of them was the right Mason and for sure none of them was Dorcas. He thought about going over and talking to those people, but he couldn't. None of us knew any other likely place to look.

By the third day we had almost quit talking about her except in a kind of secret way, when there were just maybe two of us together. The only one to speak right out, at the supper table that night, was Daddy. I think that off and on he still believed what he said then, what he stopped eating to say, which was, "It's still my judgment they's run off and got married secret. Few days more and you'll see them turn up man and wife. You just wait." Nobody said anything. Mama didn't call him "fool" but it was all over her face to do it. Mabel looked down at the plate, at the food she'd just pushed around a little bit. It was nature for her face to be red, to go with her red hair, but now it was the kind of red you get with a swelling. She had kept on keeping her mouth shut. I overheard Coop try her once, but if she knew anything, she wasn't telling. I don't think she really knew anything, not till later when Dorcas told her what had happened and wouldn't tell anybody else.

Dorcas came home on the fourth night. We didn't know it till in the

morning, because she came in quiet through the window. Even at breakfast we didn't know she was there in her room till Eve, not Mabel, told
us. We let her stay there, and later on Eve took her a plate of food Mama
had fixed. Along in the morning when I got a chance I tried to get something out of Eve. She didn't know anything. She said Dorcas wouldn't say
one word to her or do anything but just lie there on the bed with her eyes
open, even when Eve brought her breakfast in. That wasn't the only time
Eve tried to talk to her. It was always the same thing. Eve had tears in her
eyes. All of a sudden she was the one I felt sorry for.

I'd been noticing off and on that this business wasn't all going over
Eve's head. She had big, pretty, round eyes, a kind of gray-blue, that had
always looked at everything like it was just exactly what it ought to be.
But lately, sometimes, I'd been noticing a different kind of look in them.
Somebody would be talking, Mama or Coop maybe, and she'd be watching that person's face like it was new to her, like it was a face she needed
to figure out. One afternoon when I was sitting on the edge of the porch
by myself, she sat down beside me and picked up my hand. For a minute
neither one of us said anything. We both watched, or acted like we did,
an old red hen scratching and pecking around in the grass a few steps
away from us. In a real quiet voice, though there wasn't anybody but me
around, she said, "How come everybody hates Dorcas?"

"Nobody hates Dorcas," I said.

"They act like they do."

I could see her eyes getting wet, tears about to come. I said, "They
don't, though. It's her boyfriend they hate. They don't want her to go
around with him. Because he's bad."

After a little, seeming to watch the hen, she said, "Will he get her in
trouble?"

Of course she didn't know what that meant, had just heard it said, but
it gave me a jolt. "He might. Some kind of trouble. Because he's bad."

Another little space and she said, "Will it make our family trash?"

That gave me a bigger jolt. Who had she heard that from? Dud or
Stack? Maybe from Mabel, who had an ugly mouth sometimes. "What
you mean, trash?" I said. "Trash is low-down folks. Is Mama low-down
folks? Any of us? We got this nice farm. Daddy's pa was knowed all over

the county. We ain't any trash. Don't never think that. You hear me?"

"I won't."

I took my hand she was holding and smoothed her hair. It was silky fine, not gold like Dorcas's but a pretty dark-straw color. It came down onto her shoulders now. I put my arm around her and squeezed her a little bit. But I saw I wasn't able to squeeze all of the worrying out of her. I kept on noticing the signs of it now and again, and it got worse after Dorcas ran off.

Dorcas didn't come out of her room for a whole day and night, and when she did she wouldn't go back to school. She wouldn't say anything either, except in secret to Mabel, who finally gave in and told Mama. I know Mama didn't want to but she had to tell Daddy and that was the end of its being a secret.

Right straight that first night Mason had taken Dorcas to a fancy motel clear down at Nashville. She told him she didn't want to but he wouldn't let her say No. She said when she tried to he treated her in a way that made her kind of scared of him. After they got there he started being sweet to her again. He bought her things, like a pretty nightgown, all silky black, and took her out to eat at places like she never had seen before in her life. But after the second night he wasn't the same anymore. That morning he went off somewhere by himself and stayed a long time and when he got back he just barely spoke to her. A little later, when she came out of the bathroom, he was gone, gone for good. She found twenty-five dollars on the bed table. There was a note that just said he was sorry but something had come up he had to tend to, and that the room was paid for till tomorrow, and that this money would pay her bus fare home. He didn't even write goodbye or his name on it. She stayed on till the next day because she was ashamed to come home. She was afraid about catching the bus, too, but she finally managed it. Then she had to walk all the way from Riverton in the night.

After all this got out in the family, there was a day or two when Dud and Stack, and Coop up to a point, went storming around yelling about what they were going to do to that low-down bastard. They were going to go to his house and bust right through the door, if they had to, and drag that son of a bitch out by the heels. And then, by God. . . . They

73

couldn't think of anything bad enough, short of killing him. Daddy got into it sometimes, but pretty soon he got an idea he was proud of for a little while. It was about lawyers and going to court and stuff. But, of course, he didn't know the first thing about lawing, and all he knew about lawyers was that they always got a bunch of money out of you. So, since he didn't have two thin dimes to rub together, as usual, what was he going do? Sheriff Tipps kept getting brought into it, but everybody knew he wouldn't raise a hand against big folks like that.

But this was all just talk that never went anywhere and after several days everybody ran out of breath. I don't mean the thing was forgot, it was just kept kind of buried. For a long time I held to the notion that Coop, especially, had something secret running in his head, but he never did anything. Nothing, I mean, except act different to Dorcas. Now he was always being nice to her, doing her favors. Sometimes he would bring her ice cream from town and once he brought her a pretty blue hat with a wide brim to keep the sun off. She appreciated it, too. She got where she'd stay close by him whenever she could and she talked to him a lot more than she did to anybody else. That wasn't really very much, though. She went around quiet and hardly ever far from the house and stayed in her room every chance she got. She sure wasn't the same old Dorcas. It was the last thing I was looking for when, one morning several weeks later, we saw she was gone again.

She was gone for a whole week this time but it wasn't the same for us as before. That was because she left a note saying not to worry, she had something to tend to, she'd be back in a few days. It never even came in my head but I could see that Mama knew right off. She took that note and went out in the back yard and sat down on a washtub. Watching her from the back door I could see her kind of shaking, crying, her head bent down. I finally figured out what it was I heard her saying to herself over and over: "Poor child, poor child."

It was a late afternoon when I saw Dorcas coming down the road from the highway, walking slow, looking sick. She never said, but it had to have been Mason that arranged the whole ugly business and brought her back and let her off up there, which was like him. She came in the house without saying anything, and nobody could think of anything to say to her except "Hello" or something — the same way it would have been if she had just walked in from school. After that, we all went back to acting about the same as we had before she went off this time. Only a little more so, maybe, like everybody was hiding something from everybody else. Or everybody but Eve was. She just looked worried, studying faces, near to crying sometimes.

Things didn't stay like that, of course, but I always felt like what had happened left a sort of a lasting shadow with us. And something else I might have just imagined. It didn't seem to me that Dorcas ever got back again to being as pretty as she used to be.

Seven

That business with Dorcas happened in the fall. Except for a grinding close call getting our taxes paid, we got through the rest of the year and most of the winter without anything else bad falling on us. But trouble to beat by far anything we'd had before was setting up. It came, or the start of it did, in early March, in the last hard spell of a winter that seemed like it never would break.

It was just getting dark when a car came down our road and stopped in front of the gate. That was something that hardly ever happened unless it was Dud's old car, which it wasn't, and the surprise was all the more for us when we looked out and saw it was the sheriff's car. Really what we felt was more than only surprise. Everybody, except Mama and Eve who were in the kitchen, looked at one another. Had anybody done a thing to bring the law down on us? That's the way we were. I can see myself, even as a small boy, kind of halfway ducking when one of those patrol cars went past me driving slow.

It was Sheriff Tipps himself, just him, who got out of the car like a man in no hurry and came and climbed the steps. Daddy already had the door open for him and was standing bent over a little more than usual. The grin on his mouth didn't look real and kept dying out and coming back. "Come in, Sheriff. Cold out there," Daddy said. Even his voice wasn't his regular one.

Sheriff Tipps stepped easy through the door, just far enough so Daddy could close it. He was a fairly tall man and thin everywhere except in the middle. His thick strap of a belt, with a shiny buckle to match his badge, rode high across his belly and sagged down to the big silver pistol hanging on his right-hand side. He wasn't an old man but his face had a lot of creases and wrinkles, and the ones around his mouth gave it a kind of a twisted look. I noticed those hard green eyes that shifted around and took us all in. It would've made me a little more comfortable if he'd taken that big hat off.

"Set down, Sheriff," Daddy said. "We be having supper here directly."

"Just come to ask you something." He was looking around but now he wasn't looking at us. He wasn't looking at Mama and Eve either, who were standing there inside the kitchen door. For a couple of more seconds there wasn't a sound in the house.

Daddy said, "Ain't none of us done nothing, has we, Sheriff? We a family keeps to the law."

"Naw." Sheriff Tipps's eyes stopped on Daddy's face. "Just looking for somebody. Anybody come around here lately, don't belong here?"

"No sir, Sheriff. Ain't been a soul on the place but just us. Not in a long time. What kind of man you looking for?"

"Fact is," Sheriff Tipps said, his eyes straight on Daddy, "he's your brother. Clarence Moss."

Daddy's face went through a slow change that ended up in a sort of striken look. You might have thought he was that man, himself, caught red-handed in his crime. His jaw worked two or three times before he could make a word come out. Finally he managed, "I ain't seen Clarence in thirty-five years. Seen nothing nor heard nothing. Figured him dead, likely as not. Naw." Daddy began to turn his head back and forth in denial.

"He ain't dead," Sheriff Tipps said. "Ought to be, though. Wanted for murder and more besides. Police wants him in Texas and Nevada both. He's back in these parts somewhere. They like to caught him three weeks ago up in Kentucky."

Daddy was still shaking his head, with the same guilty look on his face. "Naw. Been thirty-five years and more. Ain't seen nor heard of him."

"A hunted varmint is liable to come back to his old den, finally. I know he's your brother, but if he shows up here you're bound by the law to come tell me. You don't, you're in it, too."

Daddy had stopped shaking his head but now he started again. "He'll never do it, Sheriff. Not never. Biggest fool there is knows better'n that. Naw."

"If he does, you just be sure you come tell me. Be a reward in it, too. A big one."

This was Sheriff Tipps's last word, but in turning to leave he did one little thing that made me feel maybe a shade better. He didn't lift his hat but he did give the least bit of a nod toward Mama in the kitchen door. Then he was gone, driving away in his car, leaving us all standing there as quiet and unmoving as that many gateposts in the living room.

It seemed like a long time before anybody, even Eve, said anything. Then it was Daddy, just saying again, like saying it to himself, the same things he'd already told the sheriff. "Naw. He won't never come here. He never was the biggest fool in world."

Our supper that night was one of the quietest I could remember. It was the same way on till bedtime, except for one little minute. Then it was Eve that said it. "Clarence is our uncle, ain't he?" Everybody in the room looked at her and then at each other like her words had fallen on us out of the sky. Finally Coop said, "Yeah," and after that we all got up pretty near at the same time and went off to bed.

We did talk about it some the next day and for another day or two, and everybody had a kind of a waiting look, like maybe it was about to happen. But it didn't, and before long our nervousness was pretty well worn out. Being no fool, he wouldn't come here. By now they might have caught him anyhow, we wouldn't know. In a week or so, we'd got to the point of looking back on the matter as nothing else but just a false alarm, like something we'd cooked up for the fun of only scaring ourselves. Several days later when it really did happen, we couldn't believe it at first.

We were still waiting for spring weather to break through, but up in the third week in March it was still like January, with ice in the morning and bitter wind and a little snow one night. Except for the one in the kitchen, the wood stove in the front room made all the heat we had, and on that night everybody was sitting around it, putting off going to bed in the cold. The first thing we heard was the dogs. But they made rows about nothing all the time and nobody wanted to think it was anything more than a possum, maybe, got too close to the house. The noise didn't move quite like it ought to, though. It made a slow half circle around the house and never did move on from right out back. That was when we really started to listen.

I think that faint knocking was going on for a while before any of us would let ourselves think we heard it. We could see into the dark kitchen from where we sat, but not all the way to the back door where the knocking was. It wasn't locked, we never locked a door. I think we were all thinking about this when the cold draft hit us. That was when Daddy got up from his chair. So did Coop, then Stack and Dud, but Mama hissed them back.

I can still see how Daddy moved, getting dimmer beyond the kitchen door, slow like a dream, almost. Then we heard a low voice, not Daddy's, that kept on for a minute. Then, just a little louder, Daddy's voice with a kind of pleading tone and once or twice a break in it. A few words got to us. ". . . can't stay here." And then, ". . . That sheriff. . . ." Then nothing for a little while. Daddy's voice sounded loud enough to make us jump when we heard it again, but all it said was, "Omie. Come in here." The back door went shut and for a minute there, while Mama got up from her chair and walked slow into the kitchen, we thought maybe he was gone.

He wasn't gone. Before Mama got the lamp lit we could see him like a shadow standing close to the kitchen table, wearing a hat. Then the light came, but a low light because Mama didn't turn the lamp up. This and the hat kept us from seeing anything about his face except that he had a stubble of white whiskers. That he was a slim man and wore a long dark jacket was all else we could see. Or was till he turned his head and the light struck his eyes. He was looking out at us in the living room, staring at us. It was the light that made them look so, but I was thinking his eyes had that hot glare in them because he was a murderer.

There was mighty little said in there and we couldn't hear any words. Most of the sounds were from Mama's putting a plate and a glass on the table and getting butter and the pitcher of milk out of the icebox. He was sitting down at the table now, with his hat still on. In the same second Mama put the loaf of bread in front of him, his hands were at it, tearing off chunks and stuffing them in his mouth, gulping them like a starving hound. That kept on for a while, making all the noise there was in the house, with Mama and Daddy, never moving a finger, just standing watching him.

He finally got finished. Wiping his mouth with the back of his hand he got up from the table. This time we heard what he said, "I thank ye." After that the talk was too quiet again and lasted till Mama turned and came out of the kitchen and went in her room. But just for a minute. She came out carrying the folded quilt with the blossom patterns on it and a blanket and took them in the kitchen. Without a world she handed them to him. We heard him again, "I thank ye." Then he and Daddy went out the back door, and Mama shut it behind them.

She put out the kitchen lamp and came in and looked at us all, like looking us over. "You chaps get to bed. And stay there," she said, as flat as you could say a thing. "He'll be gone 'fore daylight. And don't never say nothing to nobody."

Just above a whisper Eve said, "Where's he going to sleep?"

"In the barn. Get to bed."

Later I heard Daddy come in and I tried to hear what he said to Mama in their room, but I couldn't. For a long time I lay there in the dark wanting to get up and someway lock the doors, put chairs against them. I finally fell asleep and when I opened my eyes it was first blue daylight.

My first thought was that he would be gone by now. As usual I could hear Mama in the kitchen about her morning business, and I got up and went in there. She was stacking plates to put on the table. "Is he gone?" I said. It didn't sound loud enough but she heard and after a second said, "He's going to stay one more day. 'Cause he's sick."

"What about the sheriff?"

She didn't answer. She was putting the plates on the table.

"Won't we get in trouble?"

She still didn't answer. Like always she put just nine plates on.

It was Saturday and everybody was around most of the time all day. There was a little snow on the ground and bitter wind blowing and there were always at least two or three of us sitting by the wood stove, not saying much. The barn, whenever I looked out at it, someway seemed like a different place, unfriendly, maybe like a fort with enemies in it. Daddy went down there a couple of times carrying hot coffee and food in a bag, and stayed a while. I could tell everybody was watching, listening. Coop kept getting up and going outside and finally it got so he'd stay out there standing in the road for half an hour at a time. When he came in it was just long enough for him to get warmed up a little. But I was thinking it wouldn't do much good if Coop did hear them a minute sooner than we did, coming down the road.

It was during one of Coop's spells inside when Dud said what he said. There were just us boys and Dorcas at the time, around the stove, saying nothing. Dud kind of mumbled it out. "It ain't no sense in it. What if they put Daddy in the pen?"

Everybody looked at him.

"Maybe some of us, too. And him done kilt somebody."

We were all still looking at Dud when I happened to get a side glimpse of Coop's face. It looked like it was drawing up.

"He ain't no real uncle," Dud said. "I never seen him in my life before. And a reward in it, too. . . . And us needing money bad."

"You sorry bastard!" Coop's voice wasn't any louder than Dud's, just cold and quick like a blade. His face was not only drawn up, it was getting right white. "You ain't no better'n old Judas. Not one little speck."

"Shit," Dud said. It didn't come out strong, though. I could see by his look that Coop had got to him.

"He's Daddy's brother, ain't he? He's blood and bone of us, same as you. How you know he killed somebody meaning it? Might have been a fight. You don't know nothing!"

For a second there I thought maybe Coop was going to go for him. Dud looked mad but not as much as he did just sullen. He found something on the wall to catch his eyes and didn't act like he even noticed when Coop turned and stalked out of the house. A little later Dud got up and went into his room. The rest of us kept sitting there just thinking, till finally Dorcas mumbled, "You think Dud's right?"

"That's our blood uncle out there," I said, but nobody answered.

It was the same kind of night as the one before. After dark when Daddy came back from taking food down to him, we heard him in the kitchen telling Mama, "Says he's going to leave 'fore daylight."

"That's what he said last night."

For a little while Daddy didn't answer. Then, as quiet as before, "I can't hardly run him off in this weather, Omie. And him half sick. Got no place to go."

"Seem to me he might as well turn hisself in."

"He ain't going to do that. Says he don't aim to never."

"You got this family to think about," Mama said.

After another little space, "Let's give him one more day," Daddy said and came in the front room and sat down by the stove with us. I could see his lips working, the way they did when he got nervous. Nobody talked.

Sure enough, he was still there in the morning and we all went back to watching and listening, talking when we talked at all in just a secret kind of way. But it was getting the best of us and that afternoon Dud and Stack went off in Dud's car — just to the store, they said, they'd come right back. Coop watched them, but he didn't say anything. Pretty soon afterwards I noticed Eve wasn't around and I figured she must have gone with them. That turned out not to be so. Dud and Stack came back by themselves and I put on my coat and went out to find her. She wasn't anywhere along the road. I looked in the outhouse and even the smoke-house and down toward the hogpen and the thicket beyond. But by that time I was already thinking, with a kind of tight feeling in my chest, where she had to be. I stood looking at the barn.

Then I saw her. She was coming out, stopping to push the door shut, then heading up toward the house in that shaggy old coat that came right down to her ankles. She was all right, I could see that, walking pert up toward where I was waiting for her. Her face was flushed with the cold but it had a smile on it. Before she got real close she was already holding up something to show me. "Look," she said. "Uncle Clarence gave it to me."

Uncle Clarence? I didn't know what to do but take the thing she was holding out to me — it was a gold writing pen — and look at it up close. Uncle Clarence. The name stuck in my head like one of those strange ones from a moving picture show.

"It's a real gold writing pen," Eve said. "He got it out West."

It had a silver clip on it and little grooves along the shaft. I thought about saying "You oughtn't have gone down there," but it wouldn't have made any sense now. Uncle Clarence.

"He's awful nice. I think he's got the whooping cough, though."

"It's cold," I said. "Let's go in the house."

She showed it to Mama first, then to Daddy and everybody in the front room. They all looked at it, looked hard, but never touched it. You'd have thought it was maybe something alive that they couldn't be sure was harmless.

"Uncle Clarence is awful nice," Eve said. "He told me all about out West." She was standing with her back to the stove, still wearing that big coat and looking down at the pen in her hand. When she lifted her face her eyes had tears in them. So did her voice. "Don't let that old sheriff get Uncle Clarence. I know he didn't do no murder. He's got the whooping cough so bad."

"You oughtn't to gone down there," Daddy said, but in a weak kind of voice.

"Can't he come in the house tonight? He could come eat with us, couldn't he?"

"Hush up, gal," Daddy said. "You don't understand about it. Go get your coat off."

I don't know how much Eve was the reason for what we decided to do, but just a little later when Coop came up with his idea everybody seemed to be for it. We'd make Uncle Clarence a little lean-to way down in the woods, clear off our land. That way, if they caught him, we could say it wasn't us hiding him. We could take him a bucket of charcoal for heat, and blankets and food and stuff. We could say he stole the stuff somewhere and we didn't even know about him. The only one who didn't look at Coop like he was old Solomon out of the Bible was Dud, but he didn't say anything against it. I reckoned he was just still mad at Coop. "Let's do it right now," Coop said.

Daddy, after waiting a minute to get things set in his head, got up and with Coop right behind him headed straight down to the barn.

It wasn't any big job. We got some rusty sheets of tin off the old animal cages and a piece of a half-rotten tarpaulin for a windbreaker. We took it all down in the woods a good ways past our line fence, to where there was a little open place under some thick-grown cedar trees. We had the lean-to finished before dusk. It didn't matter if it looked like it might have been dropped where it sat. When we got the bucket of charcoal burning in there, it was a little smokey but pretty close to snug.

Daddy had already gone to get Uncle Clarence and we stood around waiting, telling each other how, wrapped up in a blanket or two, he'd be plenty warm. We had just fallen quiet, hearing the wind in the cedars over our heads, when Dud said, "All right. They catch him, though, they going to know who to blame."

"They ain't going to catch him," Coop said. "All we got to do's keep our mouth shut. They couldn't prove we put him here anyhow."

"Shit," Dud said, almost under his breath. The cedar foliage was soughing, heaving in the wind.

It was still light enough to see when Daddy got there with him. "These here's my boys," Daddy said to him. "All but one that's tetched in the head."

Uncle Clarence looked at us one at a time, kind of careful, like to get us straight to start with. His eyes, paler blue than Daddy's, were the only thing about his face that looked alive for sure. His mouth didn't show he was glad or sorry or anything else while he looked us over, and the way the skin stretched tight across his brow and cheek bones made you think of a man who'd spent just about all his years facing into a dry wind. Finally, though, his mouth did move and spoke some kind of a greeting.

"You ought to be warm enough in there," Daddy said. "We'll bring you some supper directly."

Uncle Clarence watched us shuffling around, waiting to leave. "I thank ye," he mumbled. And then, surprising us, "You boys come visit with me."

In the next few days all of us except for Dud did come a time or two at least. Eve too, twice when Mama wasn't around and she begged me to take her. Mama acted kind of like Dud, worried the whole time, and you could tell she didn't really trust Uncle Clarence. Once I heard her talking to Daddy so quiet I couldn't get the words, but I knew it was against Uncle Clarence. Daddy kind of hummed and hawed like maybe he would run him off, but he didn't. I was hoping and hoping he wouldn't. Almost right from the start I had got to be special friends with Uncle Clarence.

To me, he wasn't like he seemed. About the second time I went down there he kind of opened up and showed me how much he liked to talk about his life. I never knew anybody before who had been anywhere, but where he liked to talk about most was out West and, some, way on up in Canada and Alaska. It wasn't all just about places, though. He told me about some things he had done that, if it hadn't been for his way of telling them, would have left me pretty bothered. Of course, the times I brought Eve with me he stepped way wide of such stuff. He was mighty sweet to her. I remember him rummaging through his old baggy clothes to find something else to give her, but he couldn't come up with anything but a couple of nickels.

What he told me about his life and travels made it all sound awful lonesome, but I came to think he liked it best that way. His talk was always coming back to that desert land and how it looked and felt to be out there. Squatting on his heels in the smokey little lean-to, he'd look out over the top of my head like he had it all in plain sight. "On and on," he'd say. "Nobody and never no end to it. Great old colored rocks and flat-top mesas reach up, look like, plumb to the sky. Even light ain't like nowhere else. Go up some of them canyons, it's like you're walking kind of out of your head. Straight-up-and-down red walls and nothing finally but blank dead end. Not one sound to hear. A rattlesnake maybe. You might look and see a buzzard or something high up in the sky. Nothing else, nothing to move." I asked him about water, wasn't there any anywhere? Like it wasn't a drop in the whole world, he said. A fool that didn't take along his own, you wouldn't look to ever see him no more.

He asked me early on what the sheriff said about him, though I reckoned Daddy must have told him. I didn't want to use the word, but he made me. "He said you was wanted for murder."

"Yeah. Murder." You could barely see the trace of a grin that bent his mouth at the corners. "One of them words they has. To paint a thing how they want it to look. Don't want to look straight at it, it'd put them out of bidness. I never done nothing to nobody, they wouldn't of done to me. Law's a word for lying without never feeling bad."

At the time I didn't rightly know what he was saying. I just sat there with my mouth open and his words tumbling around in my head. Later on I figured what he meant, or part of it, was that he had just killed somebody to keep from getting killed. He was gone from there before I ever saw what I think he really meant. In all my life I never had thought or heard of such a notion.

He had done some stealing, too, and other things, but it always sounded like what a man would do because he didn't have any other choice, like stealing food when you're starving. Some things he told would bother me for a little while, but not for long. It was sort of a magic about him that made me see him far off in those desert places, standing against a red rock wall, or somewhere in a storm or snow, or fighting with all his might to save his life. He knew things I'd never heard of, wonders . . . 90dogs that worked like mules, and houses made out of ice, and Indians that walked backwards all the time. If I could have I'd have stayed down there in that lean-to with him every day from morning till night.

It happened on the day the weather broke, after it had rained the night before. We were just out of bed in bare daylight when we heard it, cars coming down the road and not even stopping in front of the house. I had just finished tying my shoes and I ran out there and saw two sheriff's cars. They were stopped just beyond the animal cages close to the edge of the woods. There were half a dozen men with guns getting out of them, and then a dog on a leash, a bloodhound. Seeing that hound was what froze me where I stood. I heard Daddy behind me say, "God-a-mighty!" and then, barely, the sheriff's voice telling the men something. Right quick they split into two groups, the sheriff's group with the hound, and headed into the woods angling away from each other.

"God-a-mighty."

It might have been Daddy's voice that started my brains working again. They seemed to take up on a thing I had already noticed, that both gangs were headed in ways sure to take them all north of the mark. I didn't think to start running but I did, with Daddy's voice hollering after me. I went straight as a bullet into the woods past the big ash tree, dodging my way down the long slope without any mind for the thorns that grabbed at me. At the foot of the slope I ripped and tore my way through the brier thicket and came out where I could see the cedar trees. He was outside the lean-to, standing up like he smelled something. "They're coming!" I said before I even got up close, barely holding it back from a shout. His eyes went over my head, scanning the woods.

"Which-a-way?"

Stopping, I pointed back north, lining their direction. "Toward the river. Six of them. They got a hound."

"You get on home." He ducked into the lean-to and when he came out, with his hat and a rolled up blanket, I was still standing there. "I thank ye," he said, looking at me. "You get going." Then he was out of sight in the woods.

When I finally heard something and wheeled around, it was Coop coming up behind me. "Come on quick," he said. "We ain't supposed to know." So I went.

Everybody was outside, on the porch or in the yard, watching Coop and me come on. We were clear to the gate before anybody said a thing. Then it was Daddy, in kind of a shouting whisper. "They catch him?"

"He lit out," Coop said. "They hadn't found the lean-to yet."

"God-a-mighty."

Mama was looking at me from the porch. "Boy, you're all tore up, clothes and skin both. Come in the house."

"Tell them we don't know nothing about him," Daddy said. "You all tell them that. God-a-mighty." His mouth kept working but nothing else came out.

"Come on here, Chester," Mama said.

I didn't move, I was listening, listening into the woods. The sun was coming up.

"Somebody told them." This was Coop. I saw where he was looking, at Dud up on the porch. Dud didn't look back at him.

"Had to," Coop said. "They knowed right where to come."

Dud just stood there looking off toward the woods, kind of sucking on his lip. Finally he said, "It wasn't none of us," and turned and went in the house. Coop watched him all the way in.

A little after that the girls went inside, too, and Mama with them. But she came right back out with a cloth and bottle of medicine and started in on me where I stood. She dabbed and wiped my face and arms and made them sting but I was listening too hard to notice much. When I heard that hound I jumped clear out of her reach.

They'd found the lean-to and the hound was already tracking, baying. We could hear how it moved on down into the hollow and up the creek a ways and then up the hill on the other side. Then it hushed. For a couple of minutes there wasn't a sound anywhere, from the hound or us either. Uncle Clarence was sharp and knew a thing or two, I thought, and felt myself smiling clear across my face. But the hound took up again. Daddy gave a kind of moan. "Lordy mercy," he said.

This was the way it went for what seemed like a long time, with the baying starting and stopping again, sometimes so far away we could barely hear it and then moving closer. The sun came over the tree tops, warming us a little. Mama had stopped pestering me now, and the girls and Dud came back out on the porch. Coop kept looking at Dud. Dud just stood there, sullen.

There came a long spell when we couldn't hear the hound at all. When it all of a sudden started up again, it had a different voice, one that said the track was hot. It seemed to come a little closer and then, by another change of the voice, we knew the son of a bitch had treed. It went on a while, steady. Just so we could barely hear him Daddy said, "They got him. Over there on Bally Ridge."

But what we heard next, mighty clear, knocked our mouths open. It was a gun shot. A few seconds later we heard another one. The hound's voice died away.

I sat down on the ground and stayed there a long while, even though Mama kept calling me. Dud came out and got in his car and drove away to his job, but I didn't pay him much mind just then. When I finally looked, there wasn't anybody else around. I got up and walked down close to where the sheriff's cars were and stayed there on and on.

Finally I heard something. Then I could see movements down in the woods. A minute later I saw two of the men, with Uncle Clarence kind of hanging between them half walking and half dragging his feet, the others following. When they got close I could see blood on Uncle Clarence's neck and coat collar and all over one of his hands. His hat was gone. A week or so later I found it down in the woods.

The sheriff came around ahead of Uncle Clarence and opened the back door of his car. They were starting to put Uncle Clarence in when all of a sudden he kind of heaved himself back and turned his head straight toward the sheriff. I saw it plain as day. He shot a big gob of bloody spit smack in the sheriff's face. Right off the sheriff hit him hard as he could, in the mouth. Uncle Clarence went to his knees but the two men caught him up and heaved him into the back of the car. I couldn't even see him when they drove away, one car behind the other, without a single word to anybody. As far as I could tell, they didn't give so much as a glance at the family standing there in the front yard when they drove by.

Eight

Except for a few times when there was trouble, like that trouble with Dorcas, we had always been a noisy family. If it wasn't a quarrel or somebody complaining or something we all thought was funny, it was one of those endless, aimless conversations about any old thing that came to mind — including subjects our house cats knew as much about as we did. But after Uncle Clarence showed up, that changed. I mean, it changed in a way that lasted on and on, and not just for those two weeks or so before the law got him. I don't mean we never talked anymore. The difference was that it didn't come so free and easy like it did in the past. It was more like we were all trying to be a little careful how we sounded and had to think about which words we were going to use. You might say that those first few minutes after the law drove off with Uncle Clarence that morning kind of put us facing the way we were going to keep on following. Nobody said a thing. Not till Daddy finally did, long after we were all feeling that something had to be said. "It weren't none of our fault," he mumbled.

None of us went to school that morning and, except for Dud, all of us were around the house or somewhere on the place most of the day. Off and on Daddy would try to reassure himself, and us, that we were off the hook. "They wouldn't of just drove on off like they done, they'd of said something. Else the sheriff would of come back up here to get me by now. They ain't going to do nothing, Clarence not even on our place. Naw." Nobody ever said anything back but we all got a little more comfortable as the day wore on. Except Coop, I thought, and it wasn't because he was worried about the sheriff coming. Along in the afternoon when we were down at the pen feeding the hogs, he told me and Stack what I already knew he was thinking.

"Dud's the one done it. I can tell."

"How can you tell?" Stack said. He wanted to be loyal to Dud. "Could of been somebody hunting come on him. Could of been anybody, you don't know. Dud wouldn't of done that."

Coop poured his bucket of shell corn into the trough. He kicked a sow that was pushing in against him. "He's the one. Didn't you hear him that afternoon? Talking about Uncle Clarence wasn't no real uncle. Talking about a reward, and how bad we need money."

"He was just talking. Like he does all the time."

"How come he run off like that this morning? You could see it in his face. Sulking."

"'Cause he wants to keep that job he's got," Stack said. "That ain't nothing." But his voice wasn't all that sure. And his eyes were blinking the way they did when something was getting to him.

A couple of pigs fighting over a tit began to squeal. For a minute Coop seemed to be listening to them. "You seen how they come in here this morning, just like they had a map. Went pretty near right for him. And Uncle Clarence probably dead. You can still see his blood on the grass up yonder. That son of a bitch Tipps."

"Didn't have to be Dud, though." Stack's voice was almost too quiet to hear.

"I aim to find out for sure," Coop said. He didn't say how, he just turned and headed up toward the house.

At first Stack and I thought he was straight on the way to doing something, but all he did was turn off down to the barn to get chicken feed. A half hour later when we weren't looking for him to do anything right away, we heard Daddy's truck start up. It was Coop at the wheel and I ran outside to go with him, but he wouldn't wait for me.

When we sat down to supper he still wasn't back, and neither was

Dud. We were halfway through, eating quiet as we ever had before, when we heard the truck pull up. Coop came in the back door already looking at Dud's empty chair, then sat down in his own place without saying a word. I watched him put food on his plate like he was going to eat heavy but instead he just sat looking at it. Everybody was waiting. Finally Coop said, "Uncle Clarence is in bad shape. They sent him down to the prison hospital in Nashville."

After a pause, "Is he going to die?" Eve said. I could see her wide eyes getting wet.

"Sent him to the hospital, all I know." Another minute and he said, "They're all talking about it in town. Just talking, they don't know nothing. Saying he's a terrible murdering rascal, law looking for him everywhere." Coop speared a hunk of cabbage with his fork but he didn't lift it off his plate. I had seen him many a time with this same sideways look out of eyes, but now it wasn't aimed at anybody. "That skunk of a sheriff," he said. "Already talking hisself up to be a hero. To make sure he gets elected again. He's the one ought to been shot."

"You hear anybody say my name?" Even after the question, Daddy's mouth stayed open.

"Naw. He ain't thinking about us. You can rest on that."

I couldn't quite hear it but I could see how that long breath came out of Daddy. His head kind of lolled to one side. It was Mama that broke the quiet.

"Who they saying turned him in?"

"They don't know nothing. One said it was hunters. Another'n said, nobody, the sheriff scouted him out."

For a while everybody looked to be thinking and when we did start in eating again it was slow and careful, like not to miss whatever might come next. The question that did come was a surprise, even a kind of a jolt, maybe partly because nobody would've looked for Dorcas to ask it. Just partly, though. She said, "What about the reward?"

Coop turned his head to put his eyes straight on her. He might have been trying to figure out why she said that. "What reward?" he said, just like he didn't already know.

Dorcas kind of faltered and in a low voice answered, "The sheriff said it, didn't he? That day he come in the house?"

"I don't know nothing about it," Coop said and lifted his fork and finally put that hunk of cabbage in his mouth.

Later on Coop told Stack and me one thing he hadn't told at supper. He'd tried to see Tipps. He went in his office in the new municipal building behind the courthouse and told the man at the desk, a deputy, he wanted to talk to the sheriff. The deputy asked him his name and wanted to know what kind of business it was. When Coop told him it was private, the deputy looked him over for a second, then got up and went in the little office room behind him. Coop could see in there and see Tipps when the deputy spoke to him. Coop said Tipps looked out at him, kind of a close look, and then spoke back to the deputy. What he said, in the deputy's words to Coop a minute later, was that the sheriff was too busy to talk to him. And one other thing. He said for Coop not to bother him anymore about what wasn't his business.

"What'd he mean by that?" Stack said.

"I don't know," Coop said, in a way that left us thinking maybe he did know.

Dud didn't come home till after everybody was asleep. He ate breakfast like always next morning but he didn't have anything to say, about why he was so late coming in or anything else. He had the same glum look he had when we saw him last and nobody tried to push him. A couple of times I saw Coop eyeing him. If he had in mind to talk to him in private, he never got the chance. When Dud got up from the table, he went straight off to work.

It was the same way for the next several days, with him coming in late and going out early and having mighty little to say to anybody as far as I knew. If he was trying to keep us from knowing he was the one that had turned Uncle Clarence in, he was sure going about it in a dumb way. He might as well have admitted it straight out, because pretty soon everybody, except Daddy, was just about certain it was him. It was a show that raised Coop's hackles straight up, and he got madder every day. Then, right in the middle of breakfast on Saturday morning, he put a stop to it.

"I'm going down to Nashville to the hospital," he said. "To see Uncle Clarence. If he's still alive." Everybody stopped eating, though after a few seconds Dud's jaw went back to chewing, moving slow. Coop said, "You want to go, Dud?"

Dud's jaw stopped again. He didn't try to say anything. Then he shook his head. Everybody was looking at him. Coop wasn't about to let him up.

"You could tell him why you turned him in. Couldn't you?"

Dud swallowed. He looked down at his plate, half full of eggs and grits. Daddy said, "What you talking about?" His fist holding his fork straight up on the table top, he looked at Coop, then at Dud.

"Couldn't you?" Coop said.

Dud swallowed. "I never done it," he mumbled into his plate.

"You're lying."

Dud set his mouth shut but after a minute he opened it again. "He was fixing to get us in trouble. Wasn't no sense in it, him a murderer. What I been hearing, it wasn't just one time, neither. Wasn't no sense in it."

"'What I been hearing,'" Coop said, mocking him. "It was sense in that reward, though, wasn't it?"

"I never aimed to keep it for myself. God knows, this family can use it."

"Even if it's blood money," Coop said. "You got it yet?"

"You shut your goddamn mouth!" Dud's face had got a dangerous look and I was glad Coop was two places down the table from him, especially when I saw he wasn't going to shut up. But Mama came in, loud and sharper than I ever heard her before.

"Hush up!" she said. "You both! I ain't going to have it. I don't mean to hear another word."

She stopped them, all right, but she didn't stop them from glaring at one another. Eve, who was looking back and forth from Dud's face to Coop's, all of a sudden jumped off her chair and ran out of the room. Except those two, everybody just sat there with their eyes on the empty doorway where she had gone out of sight.

Nine

That spring after the business with Uncle Clarence was a time when it seemed like everything had got off track, starting with the weather. I never have seen it rain like that. It would come down like Noah's flood for two or three days running, then quit just long enough for the ground to start drying up before it did the same thing over again. On and on. I know it wasn't sent just to spite us, but it sure seemed that way. For once Daddy was telling the truth when he kept saying he couldn't get in to plow. Our two fields, where we always planted corn and tobacco, looked like swamps half the time, and it was about June before we could do anything at all. By then the tobacco plants were ruined and the corn was in too late to do much good.

Daddy cussed and groaned about it, but for a good while there I could tell he wasn't groaning like he ought to have done. Mortgage and tax time both were coming up in the fall, and we wouldn't have had money enough to keep us in such as salt and coffee now if it hadn't been for what little my brothers brought in from the off-and-on jobs they had. Daddy knew all this as well as I did, but all the same those groans of his didn't quite ring true to me. What was more, early in May he hauled off and bought, on time payments, a little TV set that would run on batteries. Even on days when he could have been outside doing something, he was more than likely to be sitting hunched up close to it staring into that little picture screen like it was showing him Jesus multiplying the loaves and fishes. Mama would fuss at him, but he'd just say there wasn't nothing else he could do, "what with all this dang rain." I was pretty sure Mama noticed what I noticed, but she wouldn't say anything to me.

I finally found out the cause of it . . . which I didn't know why I hadn't seen already. Dud had got to where he didn't come home more than a couple of nights a week, but one of those times, just about dark, I happened to be standing where I could hear without being seen. Dud had just then stopped his car and Daddy was there when he got out. I couldn't hear Dud but I could hear Daddy. "You got it yet?" The answer I couldn't hear was No, because then Daddy asked, "Ain't he never said when?" The next thing Daddy said was, "You got to keep on him. Don't give him no rest. We needing it bad." Dud said something else I couldn't hear before he stepped past Daddy and went in the house.

That cleared the matter up for me but left me wishing it hadn't. It didn't only tell me that Daddy, even after Uncle Clarence's dying made it real blood money, was acting one way and thinking another. It started me wondering how many of us were thinking like Daddy was, and just talking so as to suit Coop and anybody else that might be on his side. That was just plain lying, now that I thought about it. And after I thought about it still more and started watching faces, the feeling came on me that all this lying right here in the middle of our family was just about as bad a thing as what Dud had done. It was a kind of an empty, sometimes a kind of a sick feeling. Except maybe for Mama, who had kept mighty quiet lately, it was like Coop was the only one I could really trust anymore. But I couldn't even talk to Coop about it, because I didn't think he felt what I was feeling. Being so sure he was right had kind of sealed him off. That was how he seemed. It turned out later, though, that I had him wrong.

Maybe if Uncle Clarence hadn't died, Coop would have finally got used to the thought of Dud's doing that. But he did die and, to make it worse, he died just a couple of days after Coop and I went to visit him at the prison hospital down near Nashville. Even just going in the place was a flat kind of feeling I never had had before. All gray stone and concrete walls in a gray drizzling light, and barred windows looking out on a big old yard like the bottom of a quarry swept clean of all the chunk rocks.

Still more bars inside in one part we passed through, and men behind them looking all about the same in those white suits, eyes just alive enough to follow when we went by. And after that, in the hospital part, a smell like a little whiff of lye that you couldn't snuff out of your nose.

But the feeling was worst of all in Uncle Clarence's room. It was the only little room I saw, with just two beds and one high-up barred window facing the door. Walls with nothing on them, no color but that same gray. You couldn't tell if the man in the first bed was even alive, the way he was lying stretched out like a corpse, with eyes open just wide enough so you could see the whites. But Uncle Clarence, back under the window, didn't look much different.

Coop spoke to him but Uncle Clarence still didn't look at us for a while. A little tube ran up to the corner of his mouth — to help him breathe, I reckoned, because the sound of his breath had bubbles in it. A bandage that didn't look real clean was wrapped around his neck, and you could see more of it down on his chest where the bedsheet lay across him. Neck and chest, that was where those two shots went.

He was looking at us. I hadn't noticed because nothing except his eyes had moved. Then, for just the flash of a second, I thought we had the wrong man. Those weren't Uncle Clarence's eyes, without any pupils but only one-colored discs like dusky moons. They had that kind of a glow, like moons you could barely see through gray cloudbank. But it was him. Maybe he didn't know us, though.

"I never thanked you proper."

He said that, though his lips hadn't seemed to move. He said it to me, and afterwards I saw his eyes shift to take Coop in. Neither one of us knew anything to say.

"I don't know," he said, " . . . who done it. Spotted me for them."

It might have been a question and I couldn't keep my eyes meeting his. I looked at Coop. I saw him swallow and then, slow, like his neck just barely would work, answer No with his head. Uncle Clarence took it in, watched him a second more. Then he didn't seem to be looking at either one of us.

"Two times they shot me. Me down. No sense that second time." The bubbling sound rattled his voice. He coughed but it didn't help much.

"Way it is. Seen it all my life. Makes them feel still better that second time . . . more 'good.'" The twist he put on that last word made him cough again and keep on coughing for a little while. Then, in just that same way, he said it another time. "'Good.'" Then he fell quiet, even in his breathing.

Coop and I just stood there. We weren't even sure whether or not he was still looking at us. In an almost clear voice he said, "I'm heading back out there. Going up one of them long red canyons, on and on."

That was the last thing he said. After a couple of minutes we weren't sure but what he was asleep with his eyes open. We knew he wasn't dead, because his breath was coming regular and clearer than it was when we first came in. Before we left, Coop mumbled a few words like, "We hope you get to feeling better," but we couldn't tell whether he heard them or not.

Even after we heard that Uncle Clarence was dead, Coop and I didn't talk much about that visit. I wanted to and tried several times, but Coop wouldn't go on with it. The furthest I ever got was once when I asked him what Uncle Clarence meant about it making them feel "good" to shoot him that second time. At first I thought Coop wasn't going to answer. He stood there kind of squinting off toward the woods across from the house. He said, "Why else would they shoot him, and him down already?"

I said, "Just plain meanness, I reckon."

"Meanness is right. But he meant more'n that."

"What?" I said.

"You remember what he said before, down there in the woods?" I remembered. I had told it to Coop. "About law was a word for lying, so you didn't have to feel bad?"

I waited, but Coop just left it like that. I figured the reason was that he didn't more than half understand it himself.

What he did understand, though, which he let me know by and by, was that except for me, everybody else, maybe including even Mama, was waiting for all that money Dud was supposed to bring us. They were too ashamed not to keep quiet about it, but he could see it, just like I could. And the signs went on getting plainer all the time. One of the big ones was that little TV set that Daddy and, pretty soon, the girls were always watching, pushing one another to get where they could see it good.

Before long Dorcas and Mabel were pestering Daddy to take that one back and get a bigger one. It got where you'd hear mention of getting things that our family never thought of owning before. The biggest thing was a brand-new car. One day when Stack and Dorcas didn't know there was anybody else in the house, I heard them talking about how we needed one. I know Coop heard such stuff, too. Every day he got a little more tight-faced and a little bit quieter. He wouldn't even stay in the front room when they were running the TV.

Then, up in May, Coop left home. He did it quick and didn't even say why, even to Mama. All he did say, with that tight-faced look he had got into wearing, was that he had him a job at the box factory and was going to live in town. He already had his stuff together, most of it wrapped up in a bedsheet, an he had just got it all out on the porch when the taxi cab from town rolled up to the gate. So he had it planned to make it good and quick. Even I hadn't known.

Of course, everybody, except maybe Eve, knew why, but afterward Mama was the only one that said anything at all. She just said, standing there in the front room looking out where the taxi cab had stood, "That's how Coop is. He'll be back. Give him a week, he'll come back." Everybody seemed like they were trying to keep from looking at one another.

I didn't think he would come back and I doubt that Mama or the others did either. I know Mama had been wanting to talk to him and tell him, probably, such as that you had to be practical in this hard world and not to keep blaming folks for giving in to the ways of human nature. But Coop wouldn't ever give her the chance. He was such a proud boy and stiff-necked and stood by what he thought. I was too big to cry anymore but in our room alone that night I wanted to. Coop gone was like the heart being snatched right out of our family. It was like we had lost what held us up and tied us all together.

Ten

I knew I had to get used to Coop's being gone but it was like I just couldn't do it. At night was when I missed him the most, in what used to be his room, too, where he would talk sense to me in a way nobody else in our family could. But I missed him pretty near as much at mealtimes, especially some of them. For the first couple of days everybody was trying too hard to act like there wasn't anything different. You could see them being careful to say the same kind of things they would have said if Coop had been there. But that wore off. In a week they were back to talking about whatever came natural to them, including kinds of foolishness that in front of Coop they'd have at least stopped to think twice about. But the thing that seemed to come most natural to them now, with him gone, was all that money we were going to get. Dud, who never had said exactly where he was spending most of his nights lately, started coming home more often, and those were the times when talk about the money didn't leave much room for anything else.

"Sheriff said when, yet?" Daddy would ask him.

"Said you can't tell for sure. Said a month or so, maybe. Always take a while." It got where Dud would finish off with a blink of his eyes that I didn't much notice at first. Later on I got to noticing it more and more, and thinking about it, along with other things.

"You keep on him. We needing it bad," Daddy would say instead of pitching in eating as soon as we all got settled at the dinner table. He'd have his fork ready, holding it straight up in his fist on the table top, but at first it was like he'd completely forgot about his food. "Need the 'lectric to come in here, for one thing. Mama ought to have one of them 'lectric ice boxes. Plenty of things we needs. Two thousand dollars go a long way." That was the figure that Daddy, from no cause I knew of, had got fixed in his head. He kept coming back to it like it was a plain fact, and whenever he said it in front of Dud, everybody would wait to see if Dud backed him up. He never did. He'd always look like he hadn't even heard what Daddy said. It didn't seem to bother anybody, though, unless maybe Mama. Sometimes I'd see her mouth pucker a little bit and her gaze go someplace else away from Dud.

I'd found out pretty quick where Coop was living and after a while I went to see him. It was a sorry place to live, about the size of a henhouse, in a man's back yard that overlooked the river bottom. There was a cot and a table and a rickety chair, and a bathroom you could barely squeeze into in one corner. He had several wooden boxes, brought from the box factory where he worked, stacked on top of each other like a kind of a cabinet to keep his clothes and stuff in.

"It's as good a place as I want," Coop said. "For a while, anyhow. Till I get some money built up."

"Be a long time, won't it? With what you get for just loading boxes."

"I'll be moving up. You just watch."

He said it like he really meant it. He was sitting on the cot, giving me the chair, with his chin resting on the heel of his hand and his eyes looking out the window across from him. He might have been thinking more about what he was seeing, black cattle grazing the green bottomland and the river on beyond it, than what his voice was saying. It struck me that just these two weeks or so had already made a difference in the look of his face. Though it was hard to say exactly how. Some thinner, so it sharpened his nose and cheekbones a little. And hair that didn't need cutting now. But the real difference was something else, and I decided that the word dimmer was the one to describe it. It showed most in those dark, almost black eyes of his that before had always had such a quick, glancing way about them, but it showed in the rest of his face besides. It was like the cords and muscles in it had got too stiff to move and so didn't tell you anything about what he was thinking. Unless it was that he wasn't thinking at all. Knowing him so well, that bothered me. It put me in mind again of how smart he'd been at school and how high up he'd been in his graduating class. I thought a minute and said, "Well as you done in school, you could've gone to college. That's the way to get on. They all say that."

"They say a lot of stuff. Half of it ain't true. What's the difference? All they got to teach me worth knowing I can learn on my own."

Watching him sit there with his chin propped on his hand, still looking out the window, I finally said, "Ain't you ever going to come live at home again?"

Coop didn't stir for a minute and then just his mouth did. "Time for me to move on anyhow. I ain't going to hang around there like Dud and Stack. Not a bit of use in the world. Getting little odd jobs here and yonder that never come to anything."

"Looks like Dud's gone for good, too," I said. "Except he comes home some nights. You seen him around?"

Coop's shaking head might have said No, but his mouth didn't say anything.

I didn't tell him that day what I was already thinking some about, but a week later, thinking more and more about it, I told him. Now that the rain had stopped it was too hot, even in the late afternoon, to sit inside, so we took to the shade of a locust tree on the bank looking out toward the river. I spent the first little while just prattling on. Finally I said, "The sheriff keeps putting Dud off. 'Bout the reward."

Coop looked quick at me, then off again across the river bottom.

"Keeps telling him it'll be a while . . . be a while. All he ever says. Dud's got nervous, I can tell." I hesitated. "What you think, Coop?"

"I don't think anything," Coop said. "None of my business." He picked up a twig and put it between his teeth.

That wasn't Coop talking. It pained me to hear him. With my throat feeling tight, I said, "You're still in the family, ain't you?"

"Not anymore. After Dud doing that. And everybody getting behind him, licking their chops about all that money they're looking to get. For killing Uncle Clarence."

"I ain't behind him. Mama ain't."

"She never said she wasn't." He blew off his tongue a piece of the twig he'd bitten.

"And it wasn't Dud, it was old Tipps that killed him. He didn't have to. Dud didn't know he would." I waited a little space but I could see this wasn't making any difference to Coop. I said, "I'm thinking he ain't ever going to get that reward, either."

"I hope to God he don't." Coop threw the twig away.

I fell quiet and for a long time both of us just sat watching the sun sink, watching the line of shadow from the hills eating its way toward us across the river bottom. It was already late and I had to walk home. It would be full dark when I got there, and supper over with. What I said came out of me all at once. "What we going to do, Coop? With no tobacco crop. Corn in late. Daddy ain't got two dimes to rub together."

"Like usual," Coop said.

"Naw, Coop, it ain't like before. Daddy and them thinking crazy about that money. And debts already he can't pay. It ain't never been this way." I waited for Coop and when he didn't say anything, I let the rest of it come out. "They'll take the farm and all away from us."

The way Coop had bent his head down kept me from seeing much of his face anymore. When I started thinking he wasn't going to answer at all, he said, "Probably be just as good. A farm ain't anything anymore. Just scraping and straining ass to stay alive half-way. All it is. It ain't nothing . . . not nowadays."

If I'd had any words to answer him with, I couldn't have done it because of the lump in my throat. Even a few minutes later, when I got up to leave, my goodbye words were just kind of a croak.

My long walk home didn't do anything for my spirits, and right after I stepped in out of the dark they went down even lower. It wasn't because Dud was there in the front room. It was because of the way he only half looked at me when I spoke to him, like I was just a thought crossing his mind. I saw he wasn't going to speak, so I went on in the kitchen where Mama, washing up dishes, had left my supper on the table. She knew where I'd been and got a few quick answers out of me about Coop. But Dud was who I was thinking about. I could see him in his chair, sitting like he was listening to somebody who wasn't there. Then there was somebody — Daddy, though I couldn't see him — already talking when he came out of his bedroom door and settled down on the sofa across from Dud. I stopped chewing to listen.

" . . . pay for the 'lectric coming in," he said. "I already got that new 'lectric ice box. Out there by the back steps right now waiting. Just come today. You seen it? Let me show it to you." I could tell Daddy was starting to get up, but Dud, not moving, not even looking at Daddy, said, "I'll see it after while. 'Fore I go to bed."

"Well." The sofa squeaked when Daddy sat back down. He said, "It's some things folks has got to have. Lord knows, we ain't never had them. Might be I ought go see Tipps, myself. Me being older. . . ."

"Naw." Dud's voice came quick and kind of sharp, though he barely looked at Daddy. "Better not do that."

"Me an old taxpayer and all. I'm the one to get him moving."

"Naw you ain't. Don't you do nothing. You don't know what he's like."

It wasn't just the rude way Dud said it that took hold of me. He said it with his head down, like hiding his face so Daddy couldn't see what might be too plain in it. Daddy didn't come back at him, either, and for a minute or two there wasn't any sound at all.

Then I noticed Mama had stopped washing dishes. She was standing still at the sink, with her back stiff, listening. She didn't move even when we both heard Dud, mumbling something, get up and step to the front door and go outside. It was another minute, a long one, before the sound of his car starting up, and after that, like on purpose to put things right again, Mama making the dishes rattle in the sink. I was setting myself to have it out plain with her, but she let me know with that stiff back of hers that she didn't want to talk.

She talked later, though, but not to me. Everybody else had gone to bed and as soon as I heard her door fall shut, I sneaked out of my room to listen. She hadn't wasted much time getting to it, though I couldn't quite hear the word she was saying. But I could hear Daddy's, part of the time, rising up in that tone he got when good sense didn't suit him. "No such a thing! And him the law." And then again, butting right out through Mama's quiet voice, "No such a thing. It's taking a while, is all.

Law-doings work mighty slow." He said it again, in almost the same words, and then another time. Finally, after a pause, Mama must have said something about his needing to get a job, because the words I heard shutting her out were, "Sawmill work ain't nothing. Working for Cutchins ain't a thing but a way of starving to death." It was like Mama to hush when she saw her breath all going to waste. I didn't hear her voice another time, only Daddy's, running on, saying the same things over again till the streak of lamplight under their door went out.

Dud had been coming home a couple of times a week, but after that night he stopped. Just before suppertime I'd see Daddy go out on the porch and stand there watching till about the third time Mama called him. He'd settle down in his place and, holding his fork straight up in his fist like always, sit still for a minute like he was fixing to ask his question to the empty chair at the other end of the table. For more than a week Mama kept putting Dud's plate on, in case he showed up, which finally just made things worse. To me the empty places where Dud and Coop used to sit were like two big holes in our family — knocked out, sort of, in the way a rock hammer might have done it.

And before long, as it seemed to me, my feeling was one that everybody shared in secret together. There was still some talk among us, but it wasn't like before: it never seemed to come to much. And then, just all of a sudden, there wasn't anything more said, even by little Eve, about stuff we were going to buy. I didn't really know how it was that all of us, without its being a matter we talked out, had finally come to the same conclusion. I think bad news has its own secret way of travelling underground.

In those weeks there was just one thing that was better than I could remember it ever being before. For once, all my brothers had jobs and all of them, even Coop who said he wasn't part of us anymore, were bringing or sending a little money home. That was a help but it wasn't enough. What with debts I hadn't even known we had — like for a bunch of new clothes the girls had bought — there was less than no chance of saving up against the tax and mortgage times that were going to come down on us in the fall. The power folks put the electric wires in but then wouldn't turn them on because we couldn't pay for the service. Two men from the mercantile store came and took the ice box back, so we just lost that down payment. I thought the battery TV would go next, but Daddy wouldn't have it, no matter for all Mama's fussing at him, telling him there were things we really needed. He said he needed that TV. I hated seeing him sitting in there watching some fool show when he ought to have been out plowing the corn or doing something important. It seemed plain crazy to me at first, till I figured out what was behind it . . . though that was crazy, too. In his bone headed way he was making himself believe he didn't need to worry about work anymore because that reward money was still going to come in. It would just take a while, that was all. The money was going to come for the good reason that it just had to.

I was turning fourteen that summer and I started thinking maybe I could get a job somewhere and so help out a little. But Mama said I'd do better to stay home and do the things it looked like Daddy wasn't going to get around to. The corn was the big thing. Daddy had taken a few licks at plowing it out, but he hadn't got even near halfway through. I never had done any plowing but I had seen an awful lot of it, so I caught old Bell out of the lot and harnessed her and led her out to where the plow was standing in the cornfield.

Bell was an educated mule but I didn't have the feel of the thing, and up and down my first two or three rows I kept letting the plow sidle and root up three or four stalks of corn before I could right it. I hated that. It pained me to see those green young stalks, as long as my leg, lying flat and done for with their roots out of the dirt. I stiffened up on the plow and went on pretty well till I hit a buried rock. The plow bucked up and one handle caught me under the chin hard enough to knock me dizzy for a minute. I kept on, though.

After a while Daddy at least had the gumption to come out there and show me a thing or two, like keeping my point at a level depth by the feel of the handles' balance in my hands. I was glad when he left, though. The whole time he was keeping up a kind of an act. I could see him trying to hold on to the fool notion that plowing behind an old mule's ass was work a grown-up man with plenty of money wouldn't dirty his hands to do.

The longer I went on plowing, the better I did at it. Along up in the afternoon I was feeing like a real, old plowman and like I didn't want to ever stop. It made that day stick in my memory. Back and forth between the rows of green unfolding corn, and dirt looking almost black shearing and rolling like a wave across my bright plow blade. My plow, running deep, made the corn stalks tremble when it passed them, and later, when the sun got slant, made the leaves give off a greenish glitter. Rein in the mule, let her blow a minute. Then cluck her on, seeing the sunshine slip and slide on the sweat of her rump, and long ears dip and rise in time with her head working.

Once, halfway down a row, something made me stop her. I think it was just the look of the dirt. I dropped the reins and down on my knees cupped some of it in my two hands. It was damp and fine from the good season, made for corn . . . even for corn put in too late. At first I didn't know why I'd started crying. Then I knew it was because, come fall, this dirt wasn't going to be ours anymore. This dirt or any other, as far as I could see.

I didn't know Eve was there behind me. She'd followed me down the row and must have been standing there, barefooted, in a little soiled pink dress, for at least a minute or two. She had tears in her eyes but I think it was just because I was crying. I didn't ask, I only hugged her to me. I loved Mama and I loved Coop, but I felt then like I loved Eve better than anybody.

Eleven

Except for the details, Stack might just about as well not have told me. I was already sure enough to where my mind jumped right on past those first words of his to the main thing he was going to say. Stack had always been special buddies with Dud and after those first couple of weeks, when he couldn't decide how he ought to feel about Dud and Uncle Clarence, he found out where Dud was living and went to see him. I know he went other times, too, though he kept it quiet at home. Or did till the day he told me what Dud told him. The heart of it was the same thing all of us but Daddy had already about got used to believing. There wasn't going to be any reward money. Stack said, "Old Tipps telling him it was a mistake, never was supposed be any reward. Says he just had it wrong, so Dud better forget about it." Stack, leaning on the yard fence, spat straight down onto the ground. His voice was a murmur, though nobody else was close around to hear him. "Dud says he's a lying son of a bitch. Says he done put that money in his pocket."

With my voice as quiet as his, I said, "How does he know?"

"He says he just knows. For one thing, Tipps done bought him a new car. Dud said he seen it setting there by his house. Says he thinks it was a whole lot of money. Maybe two, three thousand dollars."

"That car don't prove nothing," I said.

"I reckon not." Stack spat again. "Dud says he can tell from how he talks he's lying. Says this last time and the time before both, Tipps been saying that one thing over and over. 'You better just forget about it.' And looking straight at Dud when he says it. You seen them hard green eyes Tipps's got. He's same as warning Dud to keep his mouth shut."

I thought about those eyes. I'd seen Tipps up close more times than once. I said, "Dud better look out for him."

"What I told him. But Dud ain't scared. What he is, is madder than I ever seen him. Got so mad telling me about it, he kicked a hole in the wall. Says he's going to prove it. Talking about maybe going to a lawyer."

"Lawyers is all crooks," I said. "Which one of them's going to go up against Tipps anyhow?" And I thought but didn't say, "For the likes of us."

"I know it. Told him so," Stack said. One of the dogs, Ham, came nosing up, pushing against Stack's leg. "Dud ain't going to do that anyhow. Telling people what he done to Uncle Clarence. . . . I don't know nothing he can do. There ain't nothing."

Ham was nosing me now. I put my hand on his head. A thought passed across my mind and then came back again. Without being sure it was worth saying, I said, "Unless he could get something on Tipps."

"Yeah. What?"

"I don't know. I've heard said he's a crook, a lot of times. Maybe find out something he did."

"How? You can't even prove this on him."

I didn't answer. I stroked Ham's head, making him start to whine. I was about to say, "What we going to do, Stack?" but just then Eve came out on the porch and called us in to supper.

I remember that time, that summer, as maybe the unhappiest time of my life, and the lonesomest. Coop and Dud gone — for good, it looked like — and Stack just there at night. Even Dorcas, who had got us started worrying about her again, came and went like home was nothing but a place to keep her clothes. That left Mabel, who never was any company, and Eve. Eve was a comfort, following me around, helping me some with my chores. When it came time to chop out the corn, she would pretty often go to the field with me and follow along, talking to me some but not a whole lot. She was feeling it, too, had probably caught it from the rest of us, maybe me especially. It was like a thought made out of something heavy, that everybody carried around and that left us too tired to talk to one another like we used to do. And it got to where, as the summer wore on, that the quietest one of us all was Daddy.

I think I liked it better when Daddy was still acting a fool, hanging blind onto his notion about the money coming. Till the day Stack made it so plain to him that he couldn't hang on any longer. It made him change, but it wasn't a change for the better. Instead of fighting back, like getting down to work, he just flat gave up. I was already doing the best part of his work for him, but after that I was doing just about all of it. He did come a couple of times to help me chop out the corn, but he didn't stay long and he barely said anything while he was there. He was like somebody else besides Daddy, who was a man that had kept his mouth running pretty near all the time. I knew his mind was on getting back to that TV. He still wasn't going to let go of that, payments or no payments. Without that TV to keep his head full of pictures, he'd have had to think about things.

My best times were the ones I spent with Bucky down on the river. We'd fish in that old boat of his, just stopping sometimes to bail when too much water leaked in. We'd mostly fish in the shade along the bank and in the mouth of Stump Creek. But again, when the sun wasn't too high and hot, we'd paddle out to mid-river and fish clear down on the bottom where the big cats would bite once in a while. I liked that best, though not for the fishing. I liked being far out from the banks that way, with slant sunlight lying like polish on the smooth water and no sounds but ones that barely got to us from a long way off. But just as much, I liked being out there with Bucky. He hardly ever talked and the expression on his face didn't express anything anymore than the river's face did. It was just there, taking the sun, not showing even a ripple. Off and on I'd spend a minute hoping it never would be any different for him.

I still visited Coop whenever I could, but that wasn't very often. Half the time he wouldn't show up and I'd be left sitting there in his little old outhouse till it got too late for me. But I saw him often enough to know he hadn't changed his mind. He wasn't going to move back home and he didn't want anything more to do with Dud, ever. He acted like he'd really got interested in the box-making business, and the day he told me about getting a promotion his face lit up in a way to almost make me think he wasn't only acting. "You just watch me," he said. "I'll be a supervisor before you know it."

I didn't want to stop thinking he was the same old Coop, but after that I wasn't as sure anymore. It didn't help, either, that little by little I started feeling like we weren't the friends we used to be. I'd notice how much of the time he left me in the dark about his personal doings.

But I hadn't even laid eyes on Dud since that last night he came home and left pretty soon after supper. Siding with Coop was mainly what kept me back and kept me trying to stay mad at Dud. Now, though, with the way Coop was acting, I got to thinking about how Dud had always been good to me, helping me out and taking me places. Then I could see I wasn't really mad at him any longer. Anyhow, I had got curious. After that one time, Stack wouldn't talk to me about Dud anymore and before long I started wondering if something was going on. So one Friday night, I took Daddy's truck — which lately, since nobody stopped me, I had taken to driving any place I wanted — and went to town. I thought afterwards what a wonder it was that I hit on that special night and time for my visit.

Stack had mentioned where Dud lived. It was a little way north off the square, in a room upstairs at the back end of Berry's department store. I parked on the street and walked up the alley to the back corner of the building where a night light was already burning. Dud's car was there, the only one in a little fenced-in lot. There was a window high up in the wall and a door under it at ground level. I opened it and climbed steps into black dark till I touched another shut door. I couldn't hear a sound in there but I knocked anyway, several times. Then there was light under the door.

Dud, in nothing but his undershorts, was looking down at me, blinking. It was like he didn't know me right at first, but I guess he'd been asleep. He just said, "Chester," and stepped back to his bed and sat down on it. There was no place else to sit on but a keg, so I took that and said, "Hadn't seen you in a while."

"Yeah." He sat slumped with his elbows on his knees, his fingers kind of stroking his scalp under his long brown hair. He'd always been skinny but now he looked like his body didn't have any meat at all left to it except the kind that made up all those cords and strings of muscle under the skin. He looked like starving. So did his whole room, for that matter. Besides his bed that sagged like a hammock, and my keg, and his clothes lying scattered around, I couldn't see a thing in the room. Yellow paint had just about all peeled off the walls and the only light was the bulb hanging over my head. Finally I said, "Just wondering how you was getting on."

"All right." He looked up just long enough for me to notice the dull look in his close-set eyes. "How's Mama doing?"

"Fairly well. She ain't sick or nothing." He might have been waiting for more family news but I was uneasy about going on. I was afraid he'd think I meant it was his fault. But he said, "Eve all right?"

"Yeah. She's fine. Nobody sick or nothing."

He didn't look up at me when, after a space, he said, "I been seeing Dorcas in a car with them Burford bastards."

I didn't know what to say. I just kind of nodded. He didn't know what to say either and, turning his head a little, he looked toward that one dark window. To break the silence I asked, repeating myself, "You getting on all right?"

He didn't answer. I could see he was thinking, though, and it came on me now to ask him my question straight out. But I was still shy and only said, "What you been up to?"

When he looked at me this time his eyes had sharpened up. "Wait and see."

"See what?" I managed.

"I'm going to nail him."

I hesitated. "Tipps? How?"

"You wait and see."

"Have you got something on him?" I whispered.

Instead of answering, Dud just looked mysterious. I was still waiting, hoping, but all he did finally was lie down and put his hands under his head. A minute later, "Tell Mama hello."

He wanted me to leave. I got up, but then I stopped. "Don't get in no trouble, Dud."

"You can come back again if you want to."

"All right." Then, "You want the light off?"

"Yeah."

I reached and switched it off and felt my way out the door.

I hadn't much more than stepped into the little parking lot when my eyes caught something. It was a man standing across at the fence corner where some bushes were, with his hands on the wire like he was getting ready to climb over. I couldn't see him plain. He was just a man, kind of big, with a hat on. I could tell he was looking at me, so I turned and walked as natural as I could around the corner into the alley. It didn't feel right, and I stopped and stood behind the corner out of sight, listening. I'd waited long enough to start thinking the man had probably gone away, when all of a sudden I heard the fence creak. A minute later I heard his steps on the gravel. Not to let him catch me spying, I turned to start back down the alley. Then I heard that door pushed open. My glance was just in time to see him hesitating there before Tipps stepped into the dark. That something on his hip was a pistol.

My heart was hammering like it was going to bust out through my chest bone. It couldn't be that he — it was Tipps for sure — would go up there and shoot Dud, Bang, right in his own room, right here in the middle of town! He'd never do it! I was too scared to move, but then I found out I could. I stepped slow and then faster around to the door and found it left wide open. I couldn't hear anything up there, not for a few seconds. I barely heard a voice. It died out and came again, a little louder. It wasn't Dud's voice. It came and went another time or two, and if Dud ever answered him I couldn't hear it. What I did hear, finally, was footsteps, and bolting out of there I was around the corner and all the way to the street before I stopped.

When — it must have been several minutes — I was pretty sure he had left by the way he came, I stole back up the alley. There was nothing, nobody in the lot. I stepped quiet to the door. There was light from under the door at the top of the steps, but not a sound. I climbed, still quiet, and with my hand shaking took hold of the knob. "It's me. Chester," I whispered, and whispered again louder, before I pushed the door open.

Dud, standing up in the middle of the floor, was staring straight at me. Or not staring at me, I wasn't sure. He had a stony look, even in his face that was white as a hunk of granite. "Dud," I said.

He blinked. Then he was seeing me . . . in a way. He said, "The stinking son of a bitch."

"It was Tipps, wasn't it?" I said.

"Yeah."

That stony look, like his muscles and joints were locked up hard as ice, still hadn't turned loose of him. But now I could see it wasn't from being afraid. It was the way he would look once in a while when he was too mad to settle for just hurting somebody.

"What'd he want?"

"Me to mind my bidness."

I waited.

"'Cause I done lucked up on his goddamn tracks, is what."

"What tracks?"

"Said things happen to folks with long noses. Stood there resting his hand on his pistol . . . kind of working his fingers on it. That's one mean bastard. He figures I ain't nobody he can't step on any way he wants to."

"What'd you say to him?"

"I didn't say nothing." Dud drew a long breath that lifted his shoulders. I saw one of the hands at his side clench tight and then unclench, stretching the cords in his arm. The he turned and stepped to the bed and sat down.

"What tracks?" I said.

"It's none of your bidness, Chester. You just keep your mouth shut good. You hear me?" His eyes stopped for a second on my face, then settled on the wall across from him.

"Tipps is dangerous," I said.

"Shit."

A minute later Dud settled back on the bed and put his hands under his head again. "Turn off that light 'fore you go. And keep your mouth shut."

I hesitated, then reached for the switch. But I stopped short. "Why don't you come on back home and live, Dud?"

He didn't answer. After a minute I switched off the light and left him.

I sat in the truck for a minute or two, then cranked it up and drove straight to Coop's place. I parked a little short of the man's yard and, like I needed to be secret as a robber, walked along under the hedge back to Coop's little house. I could tell he had just got home from someplace . . . some fancy place, it crossed my mind, because he had on nicer clothes than

I'd ever seen him wear. When I stepped through the door he looked at me in that way I couldn't get used to. "Something wrong?" he said.

"It's Dud. I'm worried about him."

"I ain't." Coop, seated on his cot, bent down and took off a shoe.

"He's our brother, Coop. I think he's in trouble. I think he's in danger."

Coop just watched me.

"Tipps came to see him while ago. Up there in Dud's room over Berry's store. Came just to warn him off. Kept his hand on his pistol the whole time. He told Dud, things happen to folks that get nosey. Dud's got something on him. Tipps is a dangerous fellow."

Coop watched me for few more seconds. "What's Dud got on him?"

"He wouldn't say. He just said he lucked onto his tracks. He meant it was something bad. Bad enough to make Tipps come sneaking in the dark."

Coop stopped looking at me. He bent and took off his other shoe. "How come Dud could find out what nobody else could? Dumb as he is."

"I don't know. He said it was luck. It was enough to make Tipps come up there, though."

Coop leaned back on his elbows and thought for a minute. He looked at me with his dark eyes and said, "Likely some little moonshine whiskey thing. Half the sheriffs in the country make a few bucks off 'shiners. Ain't any big deal, nobody much cares but preachers. It sure ain't something to shoot somebody about."

"Tipps is mean, though. I heard it said a lot of times. Plenty of people are scared of him."

"He ain't that mean. Who'd believe Dud anyhow, even if he had something? Tell him to stick to his business . . . before he makes a bigger fool of himself than he already is. If there ever was any reward money, it's gone by now." Coop sat up an took off one sock and then the other. They were thin, slick, black ones.

I felt a good deal better but not quite all right yet. "You know how Dud is. You can't stop him."

"Yeah, I know."

Coop got up and stepped out of his pants, then took off the sky-blue shirt that I hadn't looked close at before. It had some kind of a little shape sewed onto the pocket. I watched him put the pants and shirt both on a coathanger and hook it over a nail in the wall. I was still thinking about Dud, but I said, "I never did see you all dressed up before."

"Moving up in the world. I'll be getting out of this dump before long."

I thought of things to say, about home, about Dud again. But I didn't say them. I said I had to be getting on now and left him washing his face in the little sink. Back in the truck, driving along, I hadn't got across the river bridge before I started all over worrying about Dud.

Twelve

When I told Stack about Tipps coming up there in the night, it worried him, too. Like me, he had the notion that Dud was onto something a lot bigger than what Coop said it was. He said Dud wouldn't talk about it to him, either, just told him the same as he told me: to keep his mouth shut. Stack said, "First time I ever knowed Dud to keep anything to hisself. It ain't like him. And Tipps sneaking up there that-a-way. It don't sound like Tipps neither."

It was enough to start us keeping check on Dud, and for the next week or two one or the other of us would go every night to see about him. We didn't have to go up to his room. His car in the parking lot would tell us, and his light in the window, most times. Several nights, watching on the sly, we finally had to give up on him and come home worrying. But then, the next morning, he'd turn up at the tire plant where I'd be waiting to spot him. So when nothing happened, it got to where we stopped worrying as much and just went around there once every two or three days. Knowing Dud, we started thinking it likely he had just got a bug in his head and had been blowing off his mouth enough to make Tipps, or anybody else, good and mad at him.

Besides, there was more than just Dud to worry me. One big thing was Dorcas. It had been bad enough for the last month or two, but now, into August, it got about as bad as it could . . . bad enough so I'd catch Mama with tears in her eyes. Dorcas, who said she was a grown-up woman now, didn't seem to care a hoot what Mama thought of her doings. She said she would do as she pleased and if she didn't come home nights, that was her business. A couple of times already it had been two or three nights running, and when she finally did come home, looking pale, with her long yellow hair mussed up, she'd have that bold hot light in her eyes that dared anybody to say a word. The only sign she felt any shame was once when she lied about where she'd been. Out at Blue Stone, she said, staying with a girlfriend. I already knew better; Stack had told me. She had been the whole time at a camphouse the Burfords had down on the river. If Mama didn't know that fact, she still knew what was what. I was sure Mabel could have told her that fact too, but she never said a thing. Even Mabel was getting restless. I noticed how she had taken to mooning around and fixing herself up, like she was dreaming about following in her big sister's footsteps.

And Daddy. For all the attention he paid, you'd have thought Dorcas's comings and goings were nothing but the natural thing. But it wasn't only the TV anymore that had hold of him. That was too bad, because at least the TV had kept him out of trouble for a good many weeks. Till one afternoon he got in his truck and went on a tear of his own for two nights running. This time, though, it was worse than just a drunk. I'd already had a forewarning. A few days before, when he thought he was all by himself in the house, I saw him take a pair of dice out of his pocket and, stooping down, pitch them a few times against the wall. He was already thinking about that game that went on all night every Friday and Saturday in the back of Hailey's Garage. After that it was just a matter of finding where Mama kept the little stash of money she got every week or two from my brothers.

It might have been all right if, that first time out, Daddy had lost. As it was, he brought home, on Sunday morning, $53 he had won with just the $14 he stole out of Mama's fruit jar. He gave the $14 back to her and sat down at the dinner table to count out the rest of it over again. A big lot of it was change and he separated out the nickels and dimes and quarters and laid them down together in three squares, like fancy paving blocks, till they covered pretty near half the table. It had been a long time since I'd seen his face alive like it was, his eyes lit up. "Hot damn!" he said. "Look at that. I was feeling old Lady Luck on my shoulder the whole dang time."

Mama didn't say anything. She stood there holding the $14 in her fist, looking at Daddy's face like it was something she was too tired to look at much longer. I think it was right then that Mama gave up hope of stopping him, even though she tried later on, without any more success than she expected, to make him give her the rest of the money. He hid it where neither Mama nor I could find it, and the next Friday evening when he went out to his truck she didn't even look up from her sewing. She did say something to me, though. She said, "It ain't no telling what he'll put up to borrow money on."

But far and away the worst thing that was going to happen that summer got started without us even hearing for a day or two. I'll get to that in a minute, but first I need to mention something else that had to do with it . . . really set it up, in a way.

Till that time I never had heard of motorcycle gangs and marijuana and stuff before. I saw my first real gaggle of bikers, with their long hair and ratty clothes, back in May hanging around on the square but specially around the town monument that stood on a little walled-in island off a corner of the courthouse lawn. They didn't seem to do anything much but just sit on their bikes at the foot of the monument or perched on the wall like that many big old buzzards.

Why they came to Riverton was a mystery to me. They didn't seem to care that the town didn't like them, or even that Sheriff Tipps kept hounding them. Tipps was at them one way or another all the time. It was good publicity for him and, careful as they were, he'd now and again catch one of them with or doing something illegal. He'd charge them with that and whatever else he could cook up, and he finally managed to get two of them sent down to the pen for long stretches. And that, his success at it, is why I mention them here in my story.

It had been a few days since either Stack or I had gone to check on Dud, and the night I finally went by, he wasn't there. But that wasn't scary till the next morning, a week day, when I went out to the tire plant and waited to see him come to work. He didn't show up. I waited out on the road an hour or more, then finally walked in through the gate to where three men I never saw before were loading bales of tires onto a trailer truck. They knew Dud and said he hadn't showed up yesterday either. That was all they knew. Stack was working at Casey's Garage out on Highway 10, and I drove out there and told him. "You can't tell about Dud," he said. "Could of gone off somewhere and got drunk. Found him a gal." It scared Stack, though. A shiney smear of grease made wrinkles show up plain on his forehead.

I didn't say anything at home that day, but after supper Stack and I went back to town to check again. He wasn't there. His door was unlocked and everything looked just the same as it had the last time I saw it. Stack stood by the window thinking, his face knit up. "Wherever he's at, he's got his car. Maybe we can spot it parked someplace." So we drove around town in the night for a long time peering up driveways and unlighted sidestreets. When we finally stopped, we were at the place both of us had been thinking about all along. It was the new municipal building behind the courthouse, where the sheriff's office and the jail were now. We sat there for a minute or two before we got up the nerve to go in.

There was a hallway and then a door with a glass in it and "Sherriff" painted on the glass against the bright light inside. The man sitting at a table, with his back to a wall that had two shut doors in it, was already looking at us before we got clear across the threshold. I'd seen him a lot of times, strutting around town with that badge riding high on his big barrel chest. I'd seen him look at people the way he was looking at us now, like they'd be safer if they explained what they were up to. He didn't say a thing when we stopped in front of him, just sat there waiting. On top of a long counter beside us there was a radio playing country music you could barely hear.

"We can't find our brother," Stack said. His voice sounded ragged, forced out of his throat.

"What's his name?" The man's eyes catching the light were a cold steely gray. They made Stack blink before he answered.

"It's Dud, Dud Moss. Real name's Dudley."

The man —— Deputy Willis, according to a brass bar on the table —— pursed his lips, showing pink. "We got him back there."

Stack blinked again. Still in that voice that might have belonged to somebody else he said, "In jail, you mean?"

"That's right."

"What for?"

"Possession of marijuana. Sale of marijuana. Resisting arrest. I forget what else." His flat gaze never left Stack's face.

Finally, when it looked like Stack wasn't ever going to come up with an answer, I said, trying not to sound like a kid, "Dud don't fool with no marijuana."

Willis just looked at me the way he had been looking at Stack. Then he said to both of us, "Anything else?"

"Can we talk to him?" Stack had got use of his voice again.

"Jail's closed tonight."

"In the morning?"

"Talk to the sheriff." Willis stopped looking at us and bent forward over some papers on his desk. The song I could hear getting sung on the radio was "Blue Eyes."

"Is he here?" Stack said, glancing at the two shut doors.

"Nope."

We stood waiting for Willis to look up again, but he didn't. Pretty soon Stack moved, starting to turn, but the anger I all of a sudden felt kept me standing there. Though not very loud, I said, "Nobody told us."

Willis still didn't look up. "Nobody supposed to."

It wasn't any use. Finally Stack touched me. We turned and went out without saying anything.

We drove around through the alley along the back of the building, but the windows were all high up in the wall, and dark. We stopped just long enough to see that the old car parked back there was Dud's, then drove on to the street. We stopped again and sat for a minute with the motor running. "We better go see Coop," Stack said.

"He don't like Dud no more."

"He's still family, though," Stack said, and put the truck moving again.

But we didn't see Coop, though we waited in his room for a couple of hours. Mama was long asleep when we got home, but we didn't tell her the next morning either, or anybody else. Stack, who had to go to work, left it to me to tell Coop. I left home early but the truck kept quitting on me and I didn't get to the box factory till a while after opening time.

Even with Dud so heavy on my mind, I was noticing enough to be surprised. I went looking for Coop in the big long tin building in back of the little brick one where the offices were. My surprise came when he turned out to be in one of those offices, the one at the end of the little hall straight back from the front door.

It was a nice bright office with a couple of pictures on the walls. It had two shiney desks with nobody at one of them and Coop at the other one sitting there in clothes like nobody in our family ever had worn to work before. He even had an ink pen in his hand, and when he looked at me I felt for a second like he was somebody I didn't know. I'd always thought he was far and away the handsomest boy in the family, but now, with his dark hair all combed so smooth and his face not sunburnt anymore, he was the kind of handsome you'd see on somebody working in a bank. His voice straightened me out, though. "What you want, Chester?"

"It's something bad. They put Dud in jail. They're saying for having marijuana, but Dud don't. . . ."

"Shut the door."

I did, quick, and faced back to him. "Dud never has fooled with no such stuff. Saying he was selling it. And 'resisting arrest.' And talking like it was more besides. They wouldn't even let me and Stack go talk to him."

Coop's mouth was open a little way but he didn't say anything for a space. He was rolling that ink pen in his fingers. "It was Tipps said that?"

"One of them deputies. Willis. He's mean, too. I bet he's a crook just like Tipps is. I bet he. . . ."

Behind me the door opened. It was a woman with her hand on the knob, a mighty pretty red-headed woman dressed up finer and smoother-looking than Dorcas ever had been. But I didn't like the cool way her eyes took me in, kind of in passing, and skipped on to Coop. Coop was already halfway out of his chair when she said, flashing him a little smile, "Excuse me, Coop. I'll see you a little later," and drew the door shut behind her.

Back in his chair Coop mumbled, "Boss's wife," looking at me like he needed a minute to get his eyes focused again. This bothered me in the back of my mind some way, till he said, "All right. What're you betting?"

"I'm betting he's in it with Tipps. Whatever it is Dud knows on them. Something bad. That's why they made this up on Dud, to shut his mouth. Stack thinks that, too."

Coop's lips opened again like he was starting to say something, but he didn't. He looked past me toward the door. Directly he put his hand on his head, stroking with his fingers, messing his hair up. "How do you know it's not true?" he said. "About the marijuana. Dud's been wanting money bad, hadn't he? You know how he is. He could have done it."

I felt like sitting down in the empty chair beside me. It was like I had to think back on those words to be sure it was Coop that had said them. It was then I noticed, what I should have noticed from other times through the summer, that even his talk wasn't quite like at home. It was better, school talk, the kind he never had bothered about before. When I got my head cleared up, I said, "He's still our brother."

Coop didn't answer that, he just said, "He did worse with Uncle Clarence."

For a spell I didn't know what to say. He was looking down at the papers on his desk. Then I said, "Ain't you even going to try to help him?"

"Yeah. I'll go see Tipps. And talk to Dud."

But even after he said that he didn't look at me. For the first time in my whole life, starting slow, a mean feeling toward Coop was rising up in me. It got so strong I found a mean thing to say. "You ought to wear your nice clothes . . . so he'll think you're somebody big." Coop's eyes snapped up at me, but I even added, "'Cause he thinks we're all just trash. That's how come he can kick us around."

Coop was looking at me in the same hard way when he finally said, "All right. I will."

That was all. I didn't even say goodbye when I went out.

I thought about going home and telling Mama but I didn't have the heart to. I thought about going to see Tipps, myself, and asking him to let me talk to Dud. I almost did, but then I backed off and drove on past the municipal building and headed out Highway 10 to Casey's Garage. Standing in the hot sun outside of where Stack, greasy all over now, was helping work on a car, I told him in a kind of a whisper about Coop.

"When's he going to do it?" Stack said.

"He didn't say. Just said he would." Then, partly repeating myself, I said, "Coop ain't like he was, though. Like he don't care much anymore. Saying Dud might of done what they say. You ought to see him in that fancy office . . . all shined up. Done got all over being like us. Going to be a big businessman." I could hear how the tone of my voice had got. I could see it, like I had said something wicked, in the hurt way Stack looked at me.

"He's going to do it, though, ain't he?"

"I reckon so."

Driving back into town I had Dud so strong in my head that I turned onto the street in front of the municipal building. Right off, I saw him. He was coming out of the courthouse across the street, handcuffed to a deputy I couldn't remember seeing before. They were crossing just in front of where I'd stopped, and Dud, though he'd had his head down till now, looked up and seemed to say something to me with his mouth . . . a swollen mouth. A bandage, too, on his cheek. He did the same thing with his mouth again before they got to the sidewalk and went on into the municipal building. For a couple of minutes I sat there stopped in the middle of the street, thinking I'd get out and follow him in and make them let me talk to him. It wouldn't work, it would have to be Coop . . . whenever that might be.

Driving slow I headed home, the only place I could think to go. For once I was glad when the truck quit on me and I had to get out and fiddle with the generator wires. Instead of the wires, I kept seeing Dud's face, the bandage on his cheek but mostly his swollen mouth making some words for me. What words? I tried but I couldn't read them. I was still trying when I got home and, to keep from seeing anybody, went straight to my chores of feeding and milking that I hadn't done this morning.

I thought I could feel Mama studying me when, so late up in the morning, I finally brought the milk in the house. She didn't ask me, though, and I figured I knew why. It was because she had got a sniff of something and, already having so many bad things to carry around in her head, didn't want to hear of another one. In fact, though I didn't know it yet, she was right in the middle of a new kind of trouble that had just got started while I was gone. My coming in had put a stop to it, but only till I went out to fix the hogpen fence. It starting up again was what sent Eve after me.

"What's the matter?" I said. She wasn't crying but her red eyes made her look like she had just now stopped.

"Daddy's so mean." Her voice broke.

"What'd he do?"

"Yelling and calling Mama names. 'Cause she's got his money we need so bad. Mama won't tell him where it's at."

No need for Eve to tell me any more. It was Friday, and gambling night coming on. He had lost last time but he still had some money . . . hid, and Mama had found it. I thought how she must be feeling, to stand against him this way. "He ain't hurt her, has he?"

"Him yelling hurts her. He quit when you come in. Come on back to the house."

I touched Eve on the cheek. "You stay down here."

All I could hear when I climbed the back steps was the TV blazing away. Nobody was in the kitchen but I could see Daddy in the front room sitting about three feet from the screen where those fancy folks were carrying on their monkeyshines. He wasn't watching it, though. He had his head in his hands, maybe not even hearing the TV voices bellowing around him. Till all of a sudden his head popped straight up. "God damnit!" he yelled, loud enough to blast those voices right out the room. "Woman!" He jumped up onto his feet and stood for maybe a second. "A woman to steal her husband's money! It's wicked!" He waited another second. "By God, I'm leaving! Ain't never coming back!" The only kind of an answer he got was a fluty TV voice saying, "I doubt that Dr. Goldman is back from Europe yet."

Daddy turned and saw me in the kitchen and turned back toward the front door. He walked fast out to his truck and cranked it and was turning around when I heard Mama behind me. "Go quick and stop him," she said, handing me the money. "Give it to him."

I hurried but I was too late. He drove past the gate without even a glance sideways and went on up the road.

Mama was on the porch. "Take it on to town and give it to him," she said. "Best he lose the money than something worse."

First I went and told Eve to come on back to the house, Daddy was gone. Then, taking the short cut through the woods, I walked to town. I couldn't think of anywhere to look except Hailey's, so I walked the two blocks along Main Street and up Beech to where the big garage building, with cars standing around in the lot, sat back from the street. There was a mulberry tree beside the building and Daddy's truck was parked under it. He was in the truck, his blue shirt-sleeved arm hanging out the window, set for his long wait till night.

The first thing I saw when I walked up to him was that he had a bottle of whiskey, because he had it turned up to his mouth. I wondered where he'd got it, with no money. When he looked at me his eyes were full of tears from that hot drink. Kind of choking he said, "What you want, Chester?"

"Mama said give you this." I handed him the money.

He looked at it like it was a miracle. "Lord, Lord," he said, taking it from me. "Old woman seen the light, huh? She going to be glad she done it."

A loud coughing motor started up inside the garage.

"What if you lose it, Daddy?"

"Ain't going lose it." Holding up the money, "You see that? Thirty-six dollars. Started out with fo'teen. Lost a little last time but I wasn't feeling my luck. I'm feeling it on me today, though." He pushed the money into his jacket pocket.

"You drink that bottle of whiskey, you won't win."

"I done it before. Make me see better."

I started to leave, but didn't. "Daddy." I got his attention. "Please don't bet no more'n that money. The mules or nothing."

"No need. Naw, don't worry."

I made to leave again but he stopped me. "Boy, you know what's going to happen if we don't get some money?"

"I know."

"You got any money?"

"Naw," I said.

"Well, then."

On that I started another time to leave, but some way a thought had come in my head. It was to tell him about Dud. That held me a second, then let go. It wouldn't be any use, and mumbling something I turned and went on off.

It just past noon by the courthouse clock, and I thought it could be around this time that Coop might come looking for Tipps. I put myself where I could see the entrance to the municipal building and waited under a tree. It wasn't many steps from there to the monument, where a few bikers were perched around in the shade my tree cast on them. Two or three of them were smoking. It couldn't be marijuana, I reckoned. I figured they were likely doing it just to torment the law, thinking maybe it would get Tipps's hopes up so he'd come and make a fool of himself.

After a while I did see Coop. He was coming out of the building up there and I had to hurry because I could see he was fixing to get in a car. He had started up the motor but he saw me and waited. In the window across from him I said, "Did you see him?"

"Just that deputy. Willis. Tipps wasn't there."

"You didn't even see Dud?"

"He said I couldn't till Tipps was there."

"Why?"

"Said it was a rule." Coop wasn't exactly looking at me . . . seeing me, I mean. It was a distant kind of a look.

"What'd he say about Dud?"

"Said he was in bad trouble. He said Dud fought them. Pulled a knife. Said he had marijuana in his car trunk . . . a lot of it. He said Dud could get ten years."

I couldn't even speak for a second. Then, bursting out, I said, "Dud never pulled no knife. Dud don't even carry no knife."

Coop kept looking at me the same way.

"They making it all up. Dud wouldn't of fought them, neither. Specially with a knife." Then I said, "Dud's the one's beat up. I saw him this morning, his face, when they was bringing him back from the courthouse. He wanted to tell me something. They're lying, making it up on him."

Still looking the same way, Coop said, "I wish we could know it for sure."

"We're already sure," I said, raising my voice, "I'm sure." I didn't say, ". . . even if you're not." I noticed how, since this morning, Coop's hair was all combed back in place.

"He's going to have a lawyer. They're getting him one," Coop said.

"Lawyers is all crooks. They won't go against Tipps . . . not for the likes of us," I added.

Coop's eyes kind of snapped again. "We'll have to wait and see. There's nothing else we can do."

Trying to think what, I stood looking back at Coop, seeing him put the key in the switch. "Can't you make them let you talk to Dud?"

"When I can catch up with Tipps, I guess I can. I've got to go." He started the car and drove away. It wasn't a new car but it was all shined up like one.

I decided to wait and try to see Tipps myself. I sat by the same tree again and waited an hour, then two by the courthouse clock.

I saw the sheriff's car drive up to the municipal building. I got on my feet but then I couldn't do a thing except just stand there straining against my nerves. About the time I finally managed to take my first step, I saw I'd waited too long. Tipps, in a hurry, came out of the building and drove away again.

I still didn't give up. I killed the whole afternoon walking around and then coming back, stopping sometimes in front of the courthouse where the old men sat talking and whittling the time away. Once I walked around behind the municipal building, but those barred jail windows were a lot higher than my head. Tipps never came back. Neither did Coop. Traffic had just about stopped crossing the square when I finally gave up. I thought about Daddy waiting in his truck, but think was all I did. I headed back for home.

Thirteen

ecause she figured there would be just the five of us, Mama held
back supper that night for me to get home. Stack had done my
chores already, and we sat right down as soon as I got there. We'd
had a lot of quiet meals lately, but this one was the quietest yet. I don't
think Mama said one thing but "I don't know," when Eve asked her
where Dorcas was, and Mabel, even to talk about getting a job and living
in town, never opened her mouth except to eat. Once in a while one of
us would ask for a dish or something, but that was about it. I'd even have
welcomed the sound of the TV mouthing away in the front room.

I reckoned that if Mama or anybody else but Stack and I knew about
Dud, there would have been something said. I was wrong. Stack had told
Mama before I'd got home . . . because, he said, it was high time she knew.
Thinking about it, I stood where I could see her in the kitchen cleaning
up, the lamp beside her showing me how slow her hands picked one dish
and then another out of the sink water and wiped it with her rag and set
it down without making any noise. I never saw her once lift her head.

Going to bed as tired as I was, I thought I'd fall asleep like falling into
a black-dark hole. Instead I spent the whole night in and out of dreams,
the worst of them being the one that made me think I was all by myself
in the house, everybody but me dead and the silence ringing and ringing
in my ears. Finally, though, even that dream wasn't the worst of the lot.

At first daystreak I waked up sudden with the thought that something awful was going to happen. I got clear out of bed to throw it off, and right in that same second I knew I was hearing a noise that wasn't the dogs barking. It was heavy feet out on the porch. Then somebody was pounding on the door.

I was the first one there, ahead of Stack and Mama. I thought, Daddy, but I knew it wasn't Daddy even before I pulled the door open. The beam of a flashlight hit me square in the face.

"Your brother here?" a voice said, ugly-like.

It was Tipps, and somebody right behind him. I couldn't say a thing.

"Is he here?"

Kind of quavering, I managed, "Ain't he in jail?"

"Not no more." He stepped right into the house, with Willis behind him, saying, "Got to have a look," scattering me and all the rest of us out of his path. He, and Willis with him, went in every room, even shining his flashlight under the beds and in the corner closets where our clothes hung, while we all stood there in the front room gaping after them. Finally, from the kitchen door, sliding his beam around over the ceiling, Tipps said, "You got a loft?" But right with those words his beam stopped, shaping the shut square hole above his head. He made Willis hold him up while he knocked the little door out, and then, head and shoulders up through the hole, searched the loft with his flashlight. There was nothing up there but broken things, no place for a man to hide.

Finally, so you could barely hear her, Mama said, "You mean he's broke out?"

"That's right," Tipps said when his feet came down on the floor already walking, with Willis behind him, straight on back out of the house.

In that first blue early light we all stood looking after them, seeing two other men out there in motion by the car. Till then it was like we had fallen stone deaf to the racket the dogs were making. Now we could see them swirling around and the men kicking at them. Then a low voice among us, Stack's voice right behind me, said, "They got that bloodhound in the car." Nobody else said anything.

We watched them from the kitchen windows. They went around and into the smokehouse and the henhouse after that, and finally down to the barn. We could see their light through cracks in the barn wall and flashing in the high-up window to the loft. Back at the car, kicking off dogs, they took the hound out on a leash and in full light of day headed for the woods.

We stood on the porch. Directly the east got bright as a flame. We heard, now and again, the faint voice of the hound in cries that died off into quiet a second later. Nothing but that and the purring sound of chickens in the yard.

"It's like with Uncle Clarence." Eve said it, in a whisper. We all looked at her, seeing how white her face was. Then we watched the woods again.

We must have stayed there an hour and more, because the sun, well up over the treetops, was shining strong in our faces. All but Mama's face. Sitting on the steps with her gray head bowed, she looked like she was too tired ever to get up again. But we heard a voice, finally, and saw the men, the hound with them, coming out of the woods. Right quick Stack and I helped Mama onto her feet. We were in the house with the door shut before they got back to the car. But they didn't stop for even a look to see if we were around.

Till that one, I can't remember a day in my life when Mama, well or sick, didn't fix breakfast. Now she stayed on the sofa while Mabel and Eve did it, and only came late to her place at the table and sat like she might have been made out of wood. Just once she came to life and said something, though she said it like she didn't expect anybody to pay attention. "Daddy ought to be told." Nobody answered, but I thought maybe I would do it . . . if I could find him.

I finally went about my chores and when I got through I saw Stack about to crank up the ratty old motorcycle he'd had on loan for weeks now. I'd been thinking, and I hurried to catch him in time. "Wait a minute," I said. He settled back on the seat. "How come Tipps to come up here like that? Ain't nobody dumb enough to bust out of jail and head right straight for home. Tipps bound to know that."

Stack looked away and let his eyes wander for a second. "I reckon he couldn't think of no place else. Thinking about Uncle Clarence."

"How'd Dud bust out of there anyhow? Through all them bars."

"I don't know," Stack said. "I don't know."

"It don't make any sense."

Stack drew a long breath and let his eyes wander some more. "I got to go." He cranked the thing four or five times and got it started popping and drove away. After a little while I left, too, walking the short cut through the woods.

I went straight for Coop, but he wasn't there. "He should be back around lunch time," a man that wore gold glasses told me. He was the one in the first office along the hall, with his door open and his long polished desk between him and me. He didn't have a coat on but he had the kind of slick look that woman yesterday had, all clipped and close-shaved and like his clothes couldn't fit on anybody else in the whole world. He even had that way of looking at me, taking all of me in easy before he got around to saying anything. It made me nervous and left me feeling like he thought there wasn't much worth taking in.

"You're Coop's brother?" he said. It was just barely a question.

"Yes, sir."

Afterward it struck me that maybe he already knew about Dud. So maybe that was the reason he looked at me like he did, down at me. But I didn't have the heart right then to think any more about it.

I got it in mind that Coop being gone might mean he was seeing Tipps, so I walked as fast as I could on up to the Municipal Building. Coop's car wasn't there. After a minute, though, getting up my nerve, I went on in and as far as the door that had "Sheriff" on the glass. I could see a deputy inside at the table talking to a woman, and another woman behind the counter running some kind of machine. That was all. I took a breath and another breath, feeling my heart get tighter in my chest. I'd only wait till that woman came out.

But I never went in. I was set to go and I would have, I think, except for the picture that came up in my mind. It was a picture of me, a kid not even quite to size for his age, with "poor" spelled out all over him from hair down to raggedy shoes. I looked down at my shoes and at my breeches, all dirty and with cockle burrs stuck on them. Even my shirt sleeve had a tear. What came over me, stronger than ever before in my life, was a feeling of shame. I couldn't face those eyes, cold eyes from across that table. It would have to be Coop. I hurried on out of the building.

What I felt most like just then was heading for home, sneaking so no eyes would see me pass. Not yet, though, not without knowing something. It was a thing surely for people to talk about, and pretty soon, standing where I'd stopped on the courthouse lawn, I thought about the old men sitting along the walk down front.

There were five of them and I picked the one on a bench across the walk from the others. For a while I reckoned he didn't even see me standing beside him. He was a gaunt old man with a face all lines and creases and a stick his hands were holding between his knees. I was feeling the other ones starting to look at me when my old man said, "You want something, boy?"

His eyes, all pale and melted-looking, must have been hard to see out of. I made myself say, "It was somebody broke out of jail last night. I heard that."

"Yep. Sho' did. Got plumb away, too."

"'Less they catch him," a toothless man across the walk said. "They likely catch him. Tipps a tough one."

They all nodded. In the pause I said, barely loud enough, "How'd that fellow get out of there?"

One of them not much bigger than me said, "Grabbed that deputy th'ough the bars. That Billings. Knocked his head on them. Taken his key."

"Like in one of them Wild West pi'ture shows," the toothless man said to him. "I seen it done in one of them."

"That weed makes them wild," the little man said. "Try anything."

"Old Link Moss pretty wild, too, when he gets in his whiskey. I reckon that boy's like him. Tipps says he's a bad one."

It seemed like all my blood had jumped up into my face. I turned it away from them and then, making myself move slow, headed down toward the street. Behind me I heard, "What boy's that?" and another one say, "Beats me. Come from way back, I bet."

Before I stopped I was off the square and headed toward the bridge. At first I couldn't even think why I'd stopped. Daddy was why. I finally turned around, but I walked slow, trying to think what to say if I even could find him.

At first I thought he was gone from there. Even when I saw his truck back behind the garage, parked under a different tree, it looked like it was empty. Then I saw a knee sticking up. Daddy was lying across the seat with his head and shoulders propped against the far door, and one little ray of sunshine the size of a quarter resting on the crown of his bald head. There was an empty pint bottle on the seat between his legs and another one up on the dashboard. I'd thought his eyes were shut, but they weren't. Like the rest of his face they were just shade-colored, and they didn't change when I looked straight into them through the window. "Daddy."

His eyes moved a little bit, away from me.

"You all right, Daddy?"

"Boy . . ."

It looked like that was going to be all of it. I said, "You want to go home? I'll drive the truck."

"Naw." After a minute, "Not never."

"Where you want to go?"

I could tell he was thinking about it, but nothing came out when he moved his lips. Then he moved them again, saying, "Want to stay here."

I stood there. Back inside the garage, something like a tire iron hit the concrete floor, ringing. "You ought to have something to eat," I said.

It was something else for him to think about. Finally, just in a mumble, he said, "Get you a hamburger." Then his arm moved, and his hand, the one missing his first finger, worked slow into his pocket and dug around. When it came out it held two dollar bills and some change. It was all he had left, I knew. He said, "Up there at the King. Got good 'uns." He held out his shaking hand with the money. "Make them put you plenty onions. 'N' cheese."

I reached and took the money but I said, "I mean, for you."

"Naw." His eyes fell away from me. "Naw," he said again, though he looked like he had forgot what he was answering to. Finally he said, barely so I could hear, "Had my boy up there locked up. Say he busted out last night. That Tipps said."

It took me a second, made cloudy in my head by the sound of somebody laughing inside the garage. "You went up there . . . to the jail?"

"Told me get my drunk country ass out of there. Else't he'd lock me up."

I waited and finally saw his lips move again.

"He ain't no bad boy. I hope . . . I hope to God he's got plumb away."
When his eyes shifted back to me again, they were wet-looking.

I said, "Dud didn't do nothing. They lying, Daddy. They trying to get
shed of him 'cause. . . ."

My words weren't getting to him. He must have been talking to himself, because his mouth kept moving without any sound. Till it stopped,
and then in a voice I could hear, said, "It ain't one thing in the whole
world a man like me can do."

"Let's go home," I said.

I guessed he had gone beyond hearing me. His eyelids started to drop.
I opened the truck door and crowded in against his legs to make room
for myself. After a space he gave way and, maybe already in his sleep,
moved so I could settle down under the steering wheel.

All the way home he never waked up, and I left him asleep in the truck
when I got out.

Fourteen

The feeling of that blank, empty summer afternoon, with Daddy asleep in the truck and Mama and even the girls all quiet as whispers in the house, wasn't something that went away just because of nightfall. It wasn't much different the next day either, or the day after that, or any one of all the days running on into September. There were times when the lot of us, even Mama, sat with Daddy in front of the TV, staring at it, mixed up on just exactly what was ailing those pretty people. Till a man with the news came on. I'd listen thinking maybe he'd mention Dud, tell about him. Dud far off someplace, hiding or running, Dud all by himself and never a soul to talk to. I'd think and think about him, and then, feeling my blood rise up, I'd think about Tipps and grind him between my teeth.

There was talk in town for a couple of days, then nothing. All else we'd ever heard was what Coop had come to tell us, showing up like a stranger on the evening after it happened. I went to the door and saw, there in the dusky light, Coop getting out of his shiny car. In the whole run of those empty summer days, there was just that one moment to make me feel like everything was coming back, crowding warm around my heart.

I saw I wasn't the only one to feel it. Mama came smiling and hugged him in the doorway. So did Eve, and Stack and even Mabel stood around with their faces lighted up. I wished for Daddy, still sleeping like dead out there in the truck.

But it didn't keep on quite like it had promised to. The news Coop brought, such as it was, I guess was the biggest reason. He'd seen Tipps an hour ago. Seated in the rocker now with the lamp burning beside him, Coop for a minute or so looked like he might have forgot about us. When it came, his voice was just flat, matter-of-fact. "Tipps says he just reached out through the bars and grabbed that deputy, Billings. Banged his head against them and got his key. Said he went out through the hall window right outside the cell block."

"Tipps is a liar," I said.

"Billings is wearing a bandage on his head. I saw him."

"It ain't nothing under it. Nothing but just his head." I couldn't keep my voice down.

"Hush," Mama said.

"We've got no way to know," Coop said in the same flat voice.

"We can catch him somewhere and pull it off. That'd show Tipps is lying. He wants shed of Dud 'cause Dud knows something on him."

"Hush."

"If he does, we don't know what it is. Why didn't he tell somebody?"

"'Cause he never had a chance to. They wouldn't let nobody talk to him." Coop's dark eyes were giving me that cool, level look. I took in his silky green shirt and his hair that must have had some kind of girl's lotion to keep it in place. I burst out, "Ain't you on Dud's side? Whose side you on? You scared them fancy folks going to look down at you? I seen them. I seen how they looked at me."

"Shut your mouth, Chester!" Mama said. "I won't have it."

I'd seen how Coop's eyes snapped at me, but I'd seen, or thought I had, something else besides, something that gave me a mean satisfaction. I thought he'd kind of winced, making the cords in his neck show through. And then, though his voice came out in the same flat way, there was another thing. He said, "I ain't worrying about them. I'm on Dud's side, same as you. I'm just trying to tell you how it is, plain."

It was in his words, dropping his school talk. All of a sudden I was sorry for my meanness.

"They think they going to catch him?" This was Stack. He never had sat down, though Mama and Mabel had.

"Tipps says they will," Coop looked down, seemed to be thinking. Finally he mumbled, "I don't know."

"He won't, 'cause he won't try to," I said.

A hush fell on us. Mama's eyes were on the lamp, showing the redness in them.

"He's so mean. Tipps is." Eve's voice was like a little, sad, quavering flute in the stillness. The next thing you could hear in the room was the lampflame's whispering sound.

Finally, "I reckon he's that, all right," Coop's low voice said. "He's got a way . . . the way he talks. It's kind of to the wall instead of you. Like hearing his voice through something. Like you'd better not not mind it. Something dangerous." He broke off.

Nobody said anything, but I looked at Coop with a feeling that was some way hopeful and uneasy at the same time.

When Coop said he'd stay for supper, I went to the table almost thinking it would be like it used to be. It wasn't, though, even with him trying to be the old Coop again. He answered Mama's questions about his job. Yes, he had come up quick from lifting and loading. Yes, a sort of a boss, he said, seeing after things, checking and ordering stuff. In an office, too, that he shared with another fellow. Telling about it sharpened his voice, brightened up his face.

Or did for a while, till something happened, a thought crossing his mind. It was when he was saying how nice his boss, Mr. Sherman and his wife, too, had treated him, even inviting him several times to parties at their house. Right there was where I saw the thought come on his face like a shadow. It stopped his voice and made him look down at the food he'd forgot about. You might have thought he'd noticed something hateful on his plate. But a minute later, the time it took him to blink and draw a breath, he said, "I ain't had any good turnip greens for a long time."

After that he was like the old Coop again, except not quite. He was Coop with something standing between him and the rest of us . . . like a pane of glass you could see him but not reach and touch him through. He asked about the corn crop, and the hogs and the mules and the cows, stopping shy of the heavy things we'd rather not think about. For sure he noticed Daddy wasn't there, but he stepped around that too. He said that from now on he was coming home more often.

I timed it so I'd be there by his car when he came out to leave. The moon made light enough for me to barely see his face, waiting there, inviting me to say what I had to say. Like telling a secret, I said, "Ain't there nothing we can do?"

Just as quiet he answered, "I don't know of nothing. But just hope he don't get caught, I guess."

He made to get in his car, then stopped again. "Chester." He waited a while, hesitating. "Mr. Sherman doesn't like for people to come visit me in work time. I wish when you want to see me you'd do it at my place. Any evening."

I didn't like the sound of that, and after he drove away I was still standing there thinking about it. I remembered the man with the gold glasses — Mr. Sherman, it would be — and how he'd looked me over, looked down at me. That made it clear in my mind. The likes of us. Not Coop, though. My feeling against Coop, still stronger now, came back and settled in me.

So when several weeks went by and Coop never showed up again like he'd said he would, I wasn't surprised. Who did show up, after being gone for pretty near that long, was Dorcas. She'd got a job at Corey's Dollar Store and said she'd be living with a girlfriend in town. She didn't say the girl's name. Stack said it wasn't a girl at all and wasn't even in town, it was out in the Burford's camphouse on the river. But whoever she was living with must have packed a wallop. Her lips were all bruised and swollen up and she had an eye as black as any I ever saw. She even had a broken finger. She came in before daylight Sunday morning, through the front door that we never kept locked, and straight on back to her room. She never came out till up in the afternoon, with nothing at all to say except that she wanted Mama to doctor her finger. Mama did, tying it up with a straight stick inside the bandage, making Dorcas squawl like a cat. Looking the way she did, she wouldn't go to work Monday morning. Mabel, who begged to, went in her place, but I don't think Dorcas would have cared if nobody went.

For the last few years I never had had much to say to Dorcas, but once in those few days while she was still around, I did talk to her. I guess you could say I jumped her, though I managed to keep it from seeming too much that way. I'd been watching her moon around with her black eye and her mouth tight shut and never even thinking she ought to apologize for the way she was doing. Then, one afternoon when I saw her get up from in front of the TV — where, along with Daddy, she had been sitting for three hours — and go outside, I made up my mind. I waited till she got a little distance from the house and sat down on the stump there. When I got close to her she looked around, not very friendly. Not wanting to get her raging, I made my voice soft. I said, "Dorcas, I wish you'd talk to Mama. She's all upset."

"What about?" She wasn't looking around at me now. Her voice didn't come as sharp as I'd been afraid it would.

"You can't blame her for fretting about you . . . the way you been doing."

"What way?" This time her voice had a real edge to it.

"You know. Fooling around and all." I finally added, "With boys."

Now she looked, even that black eye blazing at me. "How do you know?"

Feeling my way slow I said, "Just from hearing. Stuff like that comes back. Stack hears things."

"Stack's nothing but a dumb ass. I don't care what he hears. None of his business. Yours neither. I can do like I please." She turned her flushing face away from me again.

"Don't get mad." Then, stiffening up my nerve I said, "You shaming our family, Dorcas," and stood waiting for the blast to come. I saw her still-swollen underlip poke out, but for a minute nothing else happened. Her voice when it came didn't sound like I expected it to. It wasn't more than loud enough to hear.

"It ain't never been nothing but shame for our family. Us poor as a snake, not even no 'lectric lights. And Daddy . . . nothing but a old no-'count drunk. Everybody knows it. And all that about Dud, now. And Bucky, that don't even have any good brains. Living down there on the river like a wild man."

"It ain't true about Dud," I said. "They lying about him. He never. . . ."
She wasn't listening.

"Sometimes I wish't I was dead. Be better'n being trash."

"We ain't no trash," I said. "You know Mama ain't. And Coop, he. . . ."

"I be glad when they take the farm away from us. I'm going to Nashville. Live there the rest of my life. Where nobody don't know me."

"We ain't no trash. Don't talk like that. You don't want them to take our home away."

The tears running from under her eyelids glistened in the sun. Her hair, that was still all gold, was lit up too, and it came on me all of a sudden how pretty, beautiful, she was, and sad. I put my hand on her shoulder. "Please don't." And then, "We all love you, Dorcas."

She blinked her tears back. She reached across and touched my hand and then got up off the stump. I watched her walk away, the sun on her hair, till she reached the steps and went on into the house.

All the same, Dorcas didn't stay with us any longer than she needed to. She went back to her job and to living away from home, though we found out for sure that now, anyhow, the place she lived wasn't Burford's camphouse. We found it out from Mabel. That little taste of working at the Dollar Store had moved her to do what she'd been talking about for weeks. All red-faced and excited, she told us about the job she'd got waiting on tables at Jason's Cafe and that she and Dorcas were going live together in a boardinghouse on Gaines Street. Two days later she was gone, all moved out. Besides Mama and Daddy, that left just Stack and Eve and me living at home. It made me have that same dream I'd had before, about waking up scared with not one soul left in the house but me.

But come the end of the year, it wouldn't be our house, or our farm either, anymore. This was the thought that, just one day after Mabel left, got a still tighter hold on me, like on my throat sometimes. The bill for the mortgage came in. Mama left it lying open on the eating table and it stayed there till somebody finally put it on top of the icebox. Once I heard Mama talking about it to Daddy, who didn't seem to be the least bit interested. She mentioned, like it was barely worth her breath, selling off the mules and all. Along with the little corn we had, that might pay the mortgage. What was the use of that, though, with taxes still to come? And anyway, without the stock, how could we make a living? Daddy's only answer was to turn the TV up a little louder. More and more often I'd see Mama sit down there and watch it with him. I reckoned that now it was just about as well we had the thing in the house.

Along with that matter, Dud was always somewhere in my head, waiting to run away with my thoughts for long spells at a time. I'd think about where he might be, and was he starving or maybe dead. It was up in September now and never yet one speck of news. Every few days I'd go to town just in the hope to pick up something by accident or by reading through the newspaper. It seemed like I couldn't stop my thoughts anymore. They'd run right on through the chores I did and even through mealtimes and on after I went to bed. The day I plowed up the near-dead garden, I kept not noticing when the mule stopped because I'd run her up against the fence at the end of a row.

But early one Tuesday afternoon things started getting a whole lot worse. I was out back with Mama and Eve, helping them wash and hang up clothes. I looked around and there was Bucky, with his hands clenched and twigs in his hair and his stubbly face all working. He was sputtering to say something, but the only word that came out clear was "Dud."

"What about Dud?" Mama said, quick as a blade.

"Dud, Dud, he . . . . " We couldn't make out the rest.

Mama took his hand and held it. Making her voice soft she said, "Just tell it slow. Real slow."

Bucky got still, all but his little shifting eyes.

"Slow," Mama said. "Is Dud down there? On the river?"

"He run. Sheriff come."

"He run from the sheriff?" Mama said.

Bucky's head bobbed up and down.

I blurted out, "Did he catch him?"

Bucky looked surprised I was there. His mouth worked for a second before he started turning his head fast from side to side. Then, "Dud run." He lifted his free arm and pointed east. "Down." Then clearly, "Down the river."

We all got still, but Mama didn't let go of his hand.

Then I thought to say, "Did they have a dog? To chase him with?"

"No dog."

"Go down there," Mama said. She was speaking to me. "Go find out."

"They won't be there," I said, but I was already on my way to the truck.

"And go see Coop," she called after me. From in the truck, cranking the starter, I could see Bucky pulling and Mama holding on tight to his arm.

I drove that old weaving truck faster than I ever had before, and turning short of the bridge, went bouncing down that piece of a dirt track along the foot of the bluff. From where I stopped I couldn't see the hut through the tree limbs and the bushes, but I didn't need to. There wouldn't be anything to see. I listened a while and heard just a couple of birdsongs. But I got on the path and walked down there like I was expecting something anyhow. I saw the hut, beginning to lean, and the old boat with water in it pulled up halfway onto the bank, and two fishboxes floating lopside in the river. And trash, tin cans and bottles, paper lying around. Even the birdsongs now had hushed. All of a sudden in my mind I was standing in a place where something big and awful, something that couldn't be mended ever, had happened and gone and left its waste all scattered out behind it.

But a little later something caught my eye. It was lying in mud on the river bank, shining brassy in the sun. It was a shell casing, the kind for rifles, and when I put it up to my nose I could smell the burnt powder inside. So they had shot at him. Or shot him. For a minute or two I couldn't do anything but stand in my tracks on the bank thinking that somewhere out there, well downstream by now, Dud's dead body with staring eyes was drifting and winding on in the river's current.

"Dud run," Bucky had said, shaking his head for No to answer my question. Then Dud had run and they had shot and missed him . . . along the bank, and got away. Still running. I prayed to God for him to be still running.

I had to do something. Hurrying, I drove into town, straight to the municipal building. There wasn't even one patrol car parked in the space where they kept them. Stopped where I could see the entrance, I thought and thought about going in, and didn't. To wait, I cut the motor off and sat there fidgeting. Mama's "Go see Coop" came back to me, and then a rush of anger. Coop with every hair in place, Mr. Sherman watching. No help, not from Coop, who wanted just to be shed of our whole family.

I was there till nearly sunset, in and out of the truck, crossing the lawn sometimes to stand, none the wiser for it, in earshot of the old men along the courthouse walk. Around five o'clock one little happening made my blood jump. A patrol car came off the square and parked in the regular place. It was Willis, in no hurry, who got out. The same thing happened an hour later, except that this time there were two, one of them Tipps, in the car. When Tipps finally came back out of the building, I was still there in the truck all set and ready to follow him. I did, nervous, hanging far enough behind so he wouldn't notice me. But all he did was drive straight out to his house on Mill Creek Road. I drove on past and turned around and headed back for home.

Fifteen

Bucky, because he was afraid to go back down there by himself, was still at the house when I came in that evening. To make it sure, I pumped him. "They didn't hit him, did they . . . when they shot at him? They shot and missed him?"

Bucky's head went up and down. "Di'n't hit him." His eyes were getting wild again.

"He kept running, didn't he? Along the bank. And got away."

"Got away," Bucky said, nodding up and down. "'Long the bank."

"Did they go after him? Chase him?"

"They chase him. Dud . . . he got away."

"Did you hear anymore shots . . . more guns go off? After they started chasing him?"

Tears had come in Bucky's eyes. He seemed to figure out what I meant, though. His head turned from side to side. "No more guns."

"Leave him be, Chester," Mama said from behind me. "You all eat your supper." She brought a bowl of greens and set them down on the table in front of Daddy. Then she struck a match and lit the lamp.

"Lord, Lord," Daddy said, his face plain now in the lamp light. I didn't think he'd been drinking, but his eyes, kind of bleary and rolling slow in their sockets, made him look like he had. "It's more befalls a man than he can take sometimes. When the Lord's agin', you, what you going to do?" He forked out some greens and, slower than was natural for him, started eating them.

What were we going to do? Then I said it outloud to Stack, but I meant it as much for Mama. Neither one of them answered. I noticed that for once the TV was turned off and that except for Bucky chomping his food, stuffing it in with his fingers, there wasn't even the ghost of a sound to be heard. Till Daddy came out with a kind of an answer that didn't belong in his mouth. "Turn to the Lord. It's the Lord's wrath come on us all. For not never going to church or nothing. For all our wickedness."

I looked at him, thinking maybe he was drunk. I saw Mama looking at him, too, but just for a another second. She said to me, "How come you didn't go see Coop? Like I said to."

Looking away from her I said, "I told you why."

"It ain't the truth."

Her tone gave a little stop to my mouth, but not to my mind. "You don't know him no more, Mama. He don't care about us no more." My anger came welling up again. "All he wants is to be shed of the lot of us. So he can be. . . ."

"Hush up, Chester. I know my own."

I drew a breath and looked down and finally reached to put some food on my plate.

After supper I talked to Stack about my afternoon. "I seen Tipps when he come in," I said. "Not in no hurry, same as if nothing happened. Willis, too, and another one. Same way when I followed Tipps home. Might of been any old regular day."

"I don't know," Stack mumbled, sitting slumped on the porch steps beside me.

"'Cause they don't even want to catch him . . . just run him off so he won't come back." Then, all of sudden not so sure, I said, "I reckon." And finally, "They didn't come in till a long time later, though. Bucky says they went after him. He didn't hear no other shot, though."

"You maybe can't go by Bucky much. He gets mixed up." Then, "I don't know."

"I don't know." Stack was always talking that way now, like he didn't want to think about it anymore, just wanted to push it away. It was like with Dud gone he didn't have any spirit much left to him. I said, "He ain't mixed up this time. I got a rifle casing to prove it." I took it out of my pocket and handed it to him. "Laying on the river bank."

Stack held it, brassy-bright in his hand. "Might be a old one."

"Smell it."

He held it up to his nose. "I reckon so," he said.

I took it back and got up and went inside.

But I could see why Stack felt like he did. When all you can do is sit back like in a picture show or maybe a dream and watch and not see even half of what's going on or why it is, you're likely to finally get that way. Or else get like me, mad and nervous and worried all the time and not knowing anything to do about it. That was my fix more and more. The next day went by and then the next one. What if, not having any place to go, Dud made up his mind to come home in spite of all? It got to where every time I turned my head I was afraid of my eyes picking him up at the edge of the woods or someplace else like in the barn loft window. Nothing happened, nothing different. Both days I spent a long while poking around town with my ears and my eyes cocked, and never any better for it. Till I'd start to wonder if the whole story wasn't just something conjured up in Bucky's scrambled brains. Go to Tipps, face to face? I couldn't make myself do that. Or even go to Coop . . . for all he'd know about it, or want to know.

But Stack did, went to Coop. He went because Mama made him when she saw I wouldn't go. But I was right not to, which came out in Stack's telling about it. He'd blundered in there in just about the unheeding way I would have expected him to and, first thing, run straight into Mr. Sherman in the hall. The way Sherman had looked at me that day through his gold glasses was probably just a sampling of the look he put on Stack. What Stack said he said sounded like it wasn't too far from "Get out of here and don't come back."

Anyhow, it was just about then that the door at the end of the hall opened and Coop was standing there. Before Stack could say anything to him, Coop, with his mouth turned white, came and grabbed him by the arm and hustled him not only out the front door but on way clear of the building. He wanted to know why in the hell we couldn't come see him somewhere else besides at work, goddamnit. He said it was bad enough already, with all the stuff our family was bringing down on him. Stack said that for a couple of minutes Coop, looking mad as a snake, wouldn't even listen to what he was trying to say. When he did get through to him he still couldn't make Coop believe it . . . or look like he believed it. Coop said that if Bucky was all we had to go on, how did we know it was true? He said that rifle casing wasn't anything, it could have been lying there a long time, Bucky might have found it someplace. Besides, if a thing like that had happened, why hadn't the word got around? Stack couldn't think of any answers. Coop was still bristling when he turned away from Stack and walked back to the building. Stack said there was just one little second or two when he felt that maybe Coop was having another thought. That was when, just before Coop pushed it open, he paused with his hand on the door and seemed to draw a long breath that left his shoulders kind of fallen.

"I'd of told you not to go," I said to Stack. "Coop don't want no part of us."

So there wasn't anything to do but just to keep on like before, trying to tend to what little work there was and think about other matters. Maybe Coop was right, even, and this whole thing was nothing but Bucky's stuff. For any difference it would make, we might as well have believed that.

As it turned out, though, we didn't have even another whole day to wonder what was true. It was up in the afternoon, a Friday, and even before the thing happened I was already feeling something different and scary in a way. The cause of my feeling, the clear one anyhow, wasn't really cause enough. I was home by myself, that was all, not too unusual for me. Mama, just for the look and feel of that locust-humming, red-gold-shining September afternoon, had taken Eve and, instead of in the truck, set out on that long walk down the highway to Simmon's Grocery. A good while after that, when I heard the TV cut off, I knew what was coming. Since he lost all his money that night, Daddy missed a couple of weeks, swearing he never would go back, making holy noises. Till now. I think he'd sat in front of the TV calculating the time it ought take Mama to get inside the store, so she wouldn't see him go by on the highway.

That was when he cut it off and went and got in the truck. Did he have any money? Or planning to bet the mules or something? Hearing the truck go rattling up the road and fade clear away then down the highway slope, I almost didn't care anymore.

That was when the quiet in the house took hold of me all of a sudden. I sat on the steps in front of the door listening to it behind me . . . a sound like in an empty well when you put your head down in it, or a long-drawn thread of breath escaping out of a clogged-up throat. It was the same as having that dream come back when I was wide awake, about the house standing empty forevermore around me. It kept on till I had to get up and do something with myself, anything. Heading for the barn, I'd just stepped through the yardgate when a real sound stopped me, a motor popping. But the motorcycle coming in view didn't have Stack on it.

It was a boy with pale girl's hair and a band around his head, a blue-jean vest over a dirty T-shirt, coasting toward me now with the motor quiet. He didn't get off when he stopped, just put a foot on the ground. With a shaved face, I thought, he wouldn't have looked all that much older than me — me with a crooked nose.

"Your name Moss?" he said.

I nodded. "Yeah." Already I was watching for his mouth to move again.

"Got a brother name Dud?"

A nod had to do it, my throat had got stuck.

"Anybody else at home?"

I made "Naw" come out, and then, "What about him?"

"He's in bad shape. Real bad. Shot through the chest. He wants somebody to come get him." The boy looked at the house, and around. "You haven't got any car?"

I shook my head.

"We don't either. He needs help quick. We've done all we can. You don't want any doctor in it."

"Where is he?" I managed.

The boy pointed with his thumb south. "Our place. A couple of miles this side of Silver Hill. Can't you get a car somewhere?"

It came to me. "Can you take me to town?"

He looked at me, blinked a time or two. "All right."

I got on the seat behind him.

We went fast down that long slope, flashing past Mama and Eve on the road shoulder, his straw hair streaming and stinging my face and giving me little glimpses of the gold ring in his ear. Then over the bridge in slant sunlight and, slowing, up onto the square. Moving too slow for me to stand, almost, we crossed and got on Main Street and came to the turn-off at last and then the garage. It was there, the truck was, letting me finally draw my breath again. And the key in it too, like always, and Daddy not in sight. "You'll have to lead me slow," I said. "It won't go a bit fast."

The boy just nodded and sat there waiting for me.

We had to go back across the bridge and up that long, slow hill to the ridge again. Maybe ten more miles, I figured. I counted off two when we crossed Stump Creek and another one on top of a bare ridge where the sun was perched straight out in front of my face. After that I couldn't find any more marks to count by. Later we passed a farm or two, then hills with woods again. Going faster on the down slope made the boy's long hair stream out and shimmer in the filtered light. Then he was holding his hand up.

Where we turned at the foot of a hill was a track just barely worn through the underbrush. We bounced along through pine and sweetgum thicket, turned on a downhill slope fast getting steeper, and saw the river glinting through the trees. The shack, like something little kids had knocked together, stood in a thicket of loblollies high up from the river bank.

There seemed to be three more of them, boys, and maybe one of them a girl, that afterwards in my memory looked all about the same as one another. One in a sleeveless shirt with words I didn't take time to read, who got up off his boot heels when I stopped the truck, said, "He's inside, there," his thumb pointing. "We got him ready to go. Best we could."

I was out of the truck following him through the little door, stopping there to get my eyes sharpened in the bad light. The shape of Dud came into my view, wrapped in a blanket up to his neck, lying flat on maybe rags on the dirt floor by the wall. A couple of steps and I was looking straight down into his face. His eyes were open. "Dud," I said.

He heard me. He moved his lips like he needed to get them set. "Chester." He said it barely loud enough to hear. Then, "Glad to see you."

"I'm going to take you home."

"All right."

"Better get on with him." It was one of the boys standing behind me. I started to bend down but two of them beat me, taking hold of Dud, lifting him, blanket and all, slow till they had him cradled in between them.

"Goddamn Tipps." That was Dud, his voice wet-sounding.

Another voice answered, "Fucking son of a bitch ought to be hung by his balls."

They eased him sideways through the little door, with me and the others right up close behind. One of them in back of me said, "We got him wrapped around the chest tight as we could. We haven't been able to stop him bleeding, though."

I wanted to say "Thank you" but I was too fixed on Dud, reaching to help, watching his face. Out here in the sunset light his skin, even his lips, made me think of the skin a snake sluffs off. The same voice was saying, "We found him yesterday morning. On the river bank, a little way down. He didn't want us to get any doctor."

"Thank you."

We set him easy, easy in the truck.

"You better go real slow. So not to bump him."

"I will." I pushed the door tight shut against his shoulder. He'd broken out of his straight-ahead stare, had shifted his eyes to look not at me but at the boys behind me. I couldn't hear what he said, but it had to be a thanks or else goodbye.

I drove so slow up that dirt track, eyeing him half the time, that it was deep dusk when we got up onto the pavement. It had to be slow even then, watching for bumps and easing on curves that might have leaned him too hard. "You all right?" I kept asking. He'd move his head just a little. I reckoned it was just the growing dark that made his face look whiter and whiter to me, but it was still a comfort when he answered by moving his head. Now and then when we passed a car his face would bloom out staring into its headlights. Too bumpy, too bumpy, even where there weren't any bumps in the road. "You want to stop and rest?" He moved his head yes. I coasted down and easing onto the road shoulder cut the motor off.

We just sat there with the lights on, making me still able to see his face. Finally I got myself to say, not much over a whisper, "You ain't bleeding, are you?"

"Some."

That blanket hid everything. "Bad?"

"I'm all right." Just the least little bit he leaned his head back, and finally said, "He told me he would. Kill me if I ever come back."

"You ain't dead."

"Told him I knowed more'n what I did. Guessing right. About them cars."

"What cars?"

"Them folks stealing them. Cutting him in." His voice stopped. After a second, real slow, he let his head lean all the way back. "It wasn't no place for me to go. Mama be waiting for me, won't she?"

"'Course she will. Just be a few more minutes." I watched his white face, upturned by his head leaning back. My hand jumped straight to the key switch and I almost forgot to make it slow when I set the truck on the road again.

For a while I didn't look at him anymore. When I did I saw his head was leaned back in just the same way as before, but I was still glad for an oncoming car that let me see his eyes blink. Stump Creek was already behind us and I didn't look again. A few more minutes, we'd be at home, just over the crest of the ridge we were climbing now. Up and over and then the big beech with the turn-off just beyond it. "Two more minutes," I said outloud, searching ahead for the beech. It came up sudden and, coasting the truck, I turned down into our road.

The person framed in the lighted door was Mama. Even before the motor quit kicking, I was out on the ground with the words in my mouth. "I got Dud, come help me." Quick around through the head-lights to his door on the other side, I snatched it open. "Dud."

He was sitting with his head still back, except it had fallen sideways.

"Dud." I waited. In the backwash from the headlights I could see his open eyes. Open but not blinking anymore. The voice in my ear was Mama's, close to me now, her body pushing against me. Dud's blanket had slipped off, and his hand, all dark, was lying on it beside him. The dark on his hand, when I lifted it up to the light, was cool and slick and red instead of dark.

Then Mama was in my place. She had his head, had it up against her. It seemed to me a long time before she made even one sound I could hear.

Sixteen

I've had some bad, bleak hours in my life but never any, I think, that came up to that one. There were those first minutes beside the truck while Mama, not making even a sound, just stayed there holding Dud's head up against her. I heard a dog whining but not one other thing, and when I finally noticed, nearby, Eve's face like a dim white bloom in the dusky light, I had to turn my eyes away. Right after that was when Mama made her first sound, her only sound for a while yet, that came like something ripped straight out of her throat.

The two of us had to do it, take him in the house, Mama close to falling when we carried him up the steps. After that we had to put him down and let him lie there face-up on the porch for a minute or two. But we got him in and onto her bed at last, stretched out on his back, staring. With her hand and fingers not too steady Mama reached and shut his eyes. There were other things we'd have to do but we didn't do them yet. Not till Mama had spent a long while beside him holding his hand. The blood from his clothes had got all over the bosom of her dress.

If she ever broke and really cried outloud, the way she had to have done finally, it was after I left in the truck. Right before, in a clean shirt-waist, she was cradling Eve like a baby in her arms, almost crowing to her, the same as if she, herself, didn't look like she might have been lightning-struck. That was how she still looked when she told me, "Go get Daddy.

And Coop. The girls, too. Stack'll be coming in, hisself."

I didn't even rightly know where the girls lived, and the picture of me pulling Daddy, likely already drunk, away from that crap game was one I wished I could put clear out of my mind. And Coop. Driving along I thought at first I wouldn't even tell him, he could find it out for himself. But it came to me I wanted to tell him, wanted to throw it straight and hard in his face, be watching when it hit him. That was the thought that set me on my way to find Coop first of anybody.

Coop didn't even live in the same place but the woman in the main house put me right. It was north of town in a new district where the houses sat in big yards and had the look of money. He wasn't there either, not tonight, but the man I talked to gave me a notion. Dressed up like for a party. The man gave me Sherman's address out of his phone book and it didn't take me long to find the street and then the house where a lot of cars were parked.

Nice cars, shining in the house lights. I pulled up last in the line and, getting out, couldn't help thinking even now how the old truck looked like a pile of junk dropped down out of the sky. The thought stopped me for a minute. The house sat white and tall in the wash of its lighted windows and span of fresh-clipped lawn. I could hear the voices, somebody laughing, and for all the push of blood around my heart I knew I couldn't walk straight up to that door. But Coop was there, my eyes picked out his car. The back door, then, because, no matter, it was something I had to do.

I circled, passed under a tree and stopped where I could see people on a terrace in back of the house. Not many, and none of them Coop . . . including the man that after a minute came out through the big glass door. I saw another door in the side wall of the house.

A few steps brought me where I could see in through the panes. It was the kitchen, and a black woman in an apron was doing something at a counter. A few more steps and, slow about lifting my hand, I knocked on the glass. She looked, then came and pulled the door open. Words I could barely hear myself came tumbling out of my mouth.

"I got to see my brother. Name Coop, Coop Moss. He. . . ."

"What?" the black woman said.

"Coop Moss. I got to see him. Tell him come out here. He's young, got black hair."

She just looked at me, looking me over like she might decide to shut the door in my face.

"Please."

"Wait a minute." She was halfway across the kitchen when the swinging door she was headed for came open. It was a white woman, the one I'd seen my first time in Coop's office . . . Sherman's wife, it was. The black woman said, "Boy out there want something," and went to her counter again. It came on me to step back into the dark but I didn't let myself.

She was taller than I remembered, dressed up in blue fine as a queen. "What is it?"

"I got to see Coop. Please."

There wasn't shadow enough to hide the measuring look on her face. "Is it very important?"

"Please. It's . . . my brother's. . . ." I couldn't say it to her.

"Can't it wait till tomorrow?"

"Grace," a voice said. She turned around to look at a man, Sherman, in his gold glasses holding the swinging door. "We need some more ice out here."

"Guess who's arrived," she said, stepping from in front of me, motioning with her head. "He's come to see Coop. Very important. You take care of it." She stepped away to the big icebox.

"My God." He didn't say it quite outloud but that was what his mouth said. Just throwing a glance my way he said, "All right. One last time," and let the door fall shut behind him.

To wait, I moved a little back into the dark, feeling the blood still gathered hot in my face. "Dud," I said to myself, making come in my mind the sight of him stark on Mama's bed. But I was still standing so I could see when the swinging door there in the kitchen opened. Coop — for all his fancy get-up, it was him — came through it and on with barely a pause when he stepped across the threshold into the yard.

In the second his eyes turned on me, I saw how his face was. His squeezing his voice tight and low didn't make it any more gentle. "Goddamnit! I told you, goddamnit!"

A rage that made me hate him stopped my throat for a second. Still hearing that voice, I tried to make my own as ugly as his. "Dud's dead. Tipps done killed him."

"You know you're ru. . . ." His voice died out like a candle snuffed. "What?"

"He come back . . . like Stack told you. Tipps chased him and killed him." I waited for Coop's face to take some kind of shape, but it just looked blank in the bad light. I wasn't about to let up. "You wouldn't believe neither one of us. Wouldn't do a thing. In your fancy clothes." He was wearing a red-looking coat and a bright necktie.

"Where. . . ." His voice, just a whisper now, went out again.

"He's home. Up there with just Mama and Eve to watch."

There was a voice, not mine or Coop's . . . faint, from inside the kitchen. "Another one of the litter." It was her, Mrs. Sherman's voice, answered by the black one's throaty chuckle. Then, Mrs. Sherman again: "It's not going to happen anymore. That family . . . God!"

Coop's face, when my eyes came back to it, had the same blank look. Had he heard that? I hoped he had . . . or would find it later on stuck tight in his memory. I said, "Just thought I'd come tell you. I got to go get the others." I turned and left him, walking fast.

But almost to the truck I stopped and looked back. The dim shape of him was standing there yet. He moved. Three or four steps put him almost to the kitchen door, but he stopped again. He was still there when, a minute later, I got in the truck and drove away.

I didn't know how to find the girls but there was Daddy. So there wasn't anything to do but drive to that garage and walk straight into the shop where the game was, under a hanging bulb, on a stretched-out blanket with maybe ten men kneeling or squatting around it. Several of them looked up at me, but that was all. Daddy, next to the fat young man who was cussing about something, was the one with the dice right now, shaking them up beside his ear so they rattled in his hand. "Come on here now," he said and sent them flicking across the blanket. Then, "Hot damn, look at them snake-eyes. Men, I'm on a roll."

"Shit," somebody said . . . because, I reckoned, of what I saw for myself over Daddy's shoulder: that he had just a dime and two quarters lying there. I put my hand on his arm, my mouth close up to his ear. "Daddy,"

I whispered, "you got to come home. Something bad's done happened."

"Huh?" He looked around and up at me, breathing his whiskey breath in my face.

"You got to come."

His red eyes blinked. "What 'bad'?"

"Come on, please."

His eyes got almost steady on my face. "What's bad, boy?"

I barely whispered in his ear, "It's Dud. Come on."

"Dud," he said, too loud, drawing every eye straight on us. It was like a word he wasn't sure about. Finally, "Dud come home?"

All of a sudden I didn't care anymore. "He's dead," I said, not whispering, laying it out there for the lot of them to look at. Let them know. "That bastard Tipps done killed him."

There wasn't one sound in that whole place for a minute. Not till I said, "Mama's waiting for you," and took tight hold of his arm. His open mouth looked to have a question ready, but finally he didn't ask it. He let me pull him onto his feet, holding back just long enough to reach and pick up his bottle of whiskey. The stillness followed us all the way out the door.

Driving along I told him the rest, as much as I figured he could take in just now. I think it was more than he did take in, because, except for "Lord, Lord," over and over, he never said anything till we got home. Then, before I could get the truck door open, he said, "It was Tipps done that?"

"It was him for sure."

He had to have two more swigs before he'd get out of the truck, and I had a hard time making him leave his bottle behind. Later, after he'd spent a long time in there with Dud, just standing, holding to a chair, he came through the front room walking like a blind man and headed back out to his truck. When we went for him he'd finished off his bottle and we had to help him in the house.

It was Coop that helped me with him. Finding Coop there when I got home was maybe the one thing that could have given any lift to my spirit, even for the little while it lasted. He wasn't wearing his coat and tie anymore and he had the cuffs on that silky-looking shirt rolled back. His hair, too. I think he must have ruffed it up on purpose. And before long it seemed to me that if he still wasn't quite the old Coop come back again, the reason was a kind of difference he never had showed before. He was always a proud boy and pretty often quick and sharp with his tongue. He didn't seem that way now. I never had heard him speak so soft or look so much like he wasn't sure about what he was saying. Or all of a sudden come up with a kind thing to say or do . . . like making the coffee Mama set out to make, and taking poor little sleepless Eve in his arms. When Stack came in from trying to find the place where the girls lived, it was Coop's idea to go, himself, and see if he could find it. Which he did, and brought them back. I reckoned nobody could change this much so quick, not to really last. But I could see how he was feeling it, and for that night, anyhow, I just about forgot being bitter toward him.

On in the night, with everybody else asleep or nodding off in chairs or on the sofa, we talked in my room . . . that I hoped would come to be our room again. I told Coop everything, about the bikers and Dud and Bucky and all the things I could recollect they said. The rifle casing, too, and how Tipps and his boys, hours after that, came rolling in like nothing at all had happened. Propped against the bedstead, watching the lamp mostly, Coop just listened all the while. Till finally I ran out of words.

Then, "I guess it was just that one shot did it," Coop said. "When they couldn't find him, I reckon they thought they'd missed him." Coop studied for a while. "Could have found some blood from him, though, maybe. Either way. . . ." Coop thought some more. "Either way they must have figured they'd got rid of him. Better not to say anything unless they had to. Even if they did have to, it needn't matter much. Tipps could come up with reasons enough why he hadn't told it around . . . I guess." After a quiet minute he looked at me. "I bet he's worried, though . . . if Dud was right."

"Got to be," I said.

"Those bikers," Coop said, wanting to hear the part again about the stolen cars. I couldn't add anything, though, except that we'd have to go talk to them. After tomorrow . . . tomorrow afternoon, I thought. I thought about putting Dud in the ground, and sitting there on the foot of the bed, in quiet made even quieter by the lampflame's thread of sound, I kept thinking on and on about it. Till another thought came out of that one.

"What about when we're gone from here? Dud won't be lying in ground that's ours no more."

"We ain't gone yet."

It wasn't my little glimpse of hope in those words, it was because Coop said them, saying "we," that made my blood rise up. I think I might even have grinned at him. He didn't act like he noticed anything.

"I wonder how much it'd take. To pay it all off."

Still feeling that glow, I said, "I don't know. A whole lot. A lot more'n Daddy's got. He ain't got nothing. Never will have nothing."

"I could sell my car. It's a nice car."

Grateful, I said, "You need a car, though."

"Old piece of junk that'll run would do me."

Swimming in my gratefulness, I finally said, "Your boss wouldn't like that, would he? That woman, neither." When he didn't answer, I thought about saying, and then, hesitating, did say, "You hear what she said? In the kitchen there tonight? About us. Said it to that nigger woman."

Coop's dark eyes fastened on me. "What?"

"I was another one of the litter. How sorry our family was."

His eyes stayed on me for a minute and finally blinked. "I don't give a goddamn what she thinks. Not anymore."

Would he quit his job? I didn't ask him. And later I started wondering if, tomorrow or sometime after we got Dud in the ground, he would go back to being the way he'd been before tonight. I think what happened the next day, and what came of it, had a lot to do with Coop's deciding.

Seventeen

W hen I look back over the years to my boyhood, one of the things I think about is how much our family just didn't know about the world that had come to be around us. We children went to school and all our family went in to town a lot, but somehow we missed out on things we should have paid attention to. I mean serious attention, because we couldn't out-and-out fail to notice the changes taking place. I see now that it was a matter of what was really real to us . . . which was the way we thought and did, and down the generations always had thought and done. It was as if those changes we saw weren't anything solid enough to last long and would end up bringing the world back around to the way it was supposed to be. I remember well how the news on Daddy's TV seemed to us like reports of happenings so far off and unsubstantial that they couldn't have anything in the world to do with us. But plenty of things a lot closer to home seemed almost the same way. On Saturday morning, for instance, when we dug the grave and made the box to bury Dud in, we never thought of ourselves as doing what other people didn't do anymore. That a death in the family, no matter the cause, wasn't a thing you could choose not to report, came in the afternoon as an ugly surprise to us.

We'd set it for four o'clock but we had about everything already done two hours before time. The girls had picked bunches of the ginger lillies and tea roses Mama had growing out beside the garden, and because I knew where to look I'd taken them down in the woods for meadow rue and oxeye daisies and butterfly weed and Queen Anne's lace. They had them all around the room and on the half-open box where Dud was lying, pink and white and orange together, smelling so pretty and sad. Once in a while I'd go stand and look down at him. I'd feel my tears gathering, and if I stayed there long enough they'd get to be bitter instead of sorrowful tears. When that happened I'd go outside and sit with Mama on the steps in the fall sunshine. She wouldn't say anything and neither would I. Sometimes in the hope to see Mr. Beasly coming before his hour, she'd cast her eyes up the road. He'd come with his daughter driving because he was old and almost blind. It had to be him to say the words, though. Mama couldn't even remember the name of the preacher up there now at Shiloh Church.

But the car that came early wasn't Mr. Beasley's. Mama and I saw it at the same time, the red light on top and and two faces with big hats to shade them looking at us through the windshield. We were both on our feet when the car stopped and Tipps, taking his time, got out on our side. He came through the gate and stopped three or four steps away from us. His eyes, hard as a pair of agates, took Mama in and passing over me went to the door behind us. "Where's your husband?" he said, though he wasn't looking at Mama.

Mama, stiff in the face, looked straight at him and said, "He went off for a while." He hadn't, though. He was under the mulberry tree down back, consoling himself in a bottle of 'shine he had got someplace this morning.

Tipp's eyes just touched on Mama before they cut back to the door. "Hear tell you got your boy up here. Dead."

Mama didn't say anything.

"Need to have a look at him."

When she still didn't answer, he came on and without a word passed between us up the steps to the porch. The huddle of faces looking out parted when he pulled the screen door open. I followed him that far and from the threshold, along with the rest of us, watched him stand there looking down at Dud. It seemed to take him a long time, the hat brim shading his face. Finally he turned his head and took us all in, even Mama and me still standing just outside on the porch. "How come you never reported this?"

We kept on watching him.

"Got a man here dead and nobody said a word."

Instead of Coop, whose face I couldn't see, it was Stack that said, "We didn't see no need to."

Tipps eyed him. "The law says it's need to. You already broke the law." Then, "You didn't know that either, huh?" He was speaking to Coop. Even by a movement of his head, Coop didn't answer. Tipps, looking level out of those agate eyes, waited on him a minute. When he spoke again it was aimed at any one or all of us, in a voice that wasn't quite so flat as before. "He come up here and die?"

He had to wait another little space. I saw his eyelids twitch. This time it was Coop's voice, speaking in a way that told me exactly what his face looked like. "We found him down on the river bank."

"Where at?"

"Down a ways. I don't know. My brother found him."

Tipps hesitated. "Which one? That dummy?"

"Yeah. That dummy." The small quick movement of Coop's head warned me. His voice said, "He wasn't too dumb to see you shoot Dud."

Hard little knots of muscle took shape at the corners of Tipps jaw. Finally he got his mouth open and said, "That shot went wide, never hit him. Never even slowed him down. Had to be somebody else shot him." Then he blinked, blinked twice. "Don't matter anyhow. It was done lawful and that's the end of it. He hadn't broke out, he wouldn't have got shot."

Knowing Coop, I figured something was rising up in him, getting ready, and I was surprised when he kept on holding it back . . . till Tipps finally cut in on him, saying, "So that's the end of that." But it wasn't. A thought you could almost see working behind those eyes brought him right to it again. Tipps said, "He was down there on the bank already dead, huh?"

Coop didn't answer. I saw his head make the little movement he'd made before, but nothing came of it. Then I noticed Tipps's, the same knots of muscle standing out of his jaw, the way his eyes had got the look of somebody sighting a gun. He had to wait a while yet. Coop said,

"Naw. He lived on a good little while longer. Talked to us some."

Tipps opened his mouth, then shut it. I guess a whole slow minute went by before he got all the way clear on the fact that Coop had shut up for good. That was when Coop just flat turned his back and stepped between me and Mama out onto the porch. Tipps followed him with his eyes but that was all . . . till his head gave a kind of a jerk like waking up. Then he looked at Stack and then at me and then at all the rest of us. He ended by looking down again at Dud's still face in the box. "Coroner'll be along to get him after while. According to the law. Which you already broke."

He looked at us again, then walked straight through us and onto the porch where Coop was standing with Mama and me. It was Coop he spoke to.

"You got a permit to bury on the place?"

He knew we didn't. He'd put it in a question just for meanness's sake. Without a blink Coop shook his head and looked off toward the gate where the car was parked. I noticed that the man out there was Willis, propped against the fender watching us. Tipps said, "You can't bury 'less you got one. If they even allow it anymore."

"I never did hear of such." It was Mama, in a voice so faint I just could understand her. If Tipps heard, he didn't show it. In fact, for the next minute or so I couldn't figure what he might have in his head. I saw him look out toward the car, at Willis, maybe, who seemed to be looking back at him. Maybe, in some secret silent way they had between them, Willis spoke to him, told him to do what he did. It was to turn his eyes on Coop and say, "I reckon you're the one better come with me. I got to get all the details for the record."

Coop just looked at him. I saw his face change a little but I don't think it was being any afraid that caused it.

"He can't go now," Mama said, like a plea.

"Let's go," Tipps said.

"I won't be long, Mama." And then, before he followed Tipps down off the porch, "We got to put it off anyhow, you know."

Mama hadn't understood that yet, and she still didn't seem really clear on it an hour later when that black van stopped in front of the house. After they took him away, in the box, I had to keep telling her over and over that they'd bring him back, that it was what the law said do. But all she did was cry and cry and finally go in her room and shut the door. Except I was so nervous, I would have gone in and tried to comfort her. By now it was thinking about Coop's not being home yet that had got first hold on me.

I hung around the yardgate and finally walked up to the highway to wait. I kept thinking of how Coop wouldn't answer him, left him hanging, and how in that minute Tipps's face had looked. But when I got too restless to stand it and went back down to the house, the first thing I saw was Coop coming out of the woods. He had walked home.

"He made you walk?" I said, after I met him halfway to the house.

"He had to go out on a call," Coop said, but his voice said it wasn't true. We were close by the big oak stump and Coop went over and sat down on it. I thought he looked a little more pale than before, and his eyes darker.

"What'd he say to you?"

"It ain't what he said. It's what he meant."

"What'd he mean?"

"Tell me how to get to where those bikers live."

"I'll show you where. What'd he say, though?"

"Wanted to know what Dud said . . . for his record," Coop sneered. "I started to tell him, but I thought better." Looking off toward the woods, he said in a quieter voice, "I might ought not to have done him like I did, before we left here." After a second, "I told you if Dud was right, Tipps'd be worried. So he had to be right someway, 'cause the bastard's worried. Mean worried. It got kind of scarey."

"What way, scarey?" I almost whispered.

"His eyes say more'n he does. He saw I told him lies. He's got ways of threatening that you just catch on to, he don't come out and say it. He does it like with a question or something. You start to think he's just trying to get friendly, till a minute later. Said more than once what a shame it was for a young man like Dud, all the sudden gone from here. He knows about Dorcas. Said it was always some danger, living the way she did. Accidents and such. Asked me if the rest of us were keeping to the straight and narrow . . . 'cause he wouldn't want to see anything else like what happened to Dud. That's when it came out plain. He's one danger-ous son of a bitch."

Coop's bold dark eyes looked me straight in the face. "But he ain't going to scare my mouth shut. Only . . ." He hesitated, his gaze falling away from me. "Only he's kind of got me worried a little bit about the family, maybe."

"I don't see nothing he could do," I said, doubting my words.

"You know what he did already."

I watched him get up, and followed a little behind him to the house.

Our house that evening, with all the flowers around and Mama locked away in her room and Daddy propped up dumb as a stone on the sofa, seemed like a place I knew so well just only from paying visits. There was talk sometimes and sounds of stirring about the house, but nothing able to do any more than stop and start the silence. It was like the dogs had caught it too, and even the chickens, I thought, because I hadn't noticed our roosters crowing at sundown. Stack finally couldn't stand it anymore and, a while after dark, without a word he got on his motorcycle and left. Dorcas and Mabel would've done the same thing if they'd had any way to. Coop said he wouldn't take them, they were needed here, but that wasn't his only reason for refusing. I'd seen him thinking. When he got his mind made up and got me off in private, I already knew what he wanted.

"Tell me how to get there . . . to the bikers."

"It's hard to find," I said, maybe lying. "I need to go with you."

He saw I wouldn't tell him unless he took me.

Coop's car wasn't really a fine one at all, but it seemed fine to me. Riding along in the dark, going fast, I told him so. He didn't answer for a minute. Finally he said, "If I can get back what I paid on it, that ought to help some."

He really meant it, then. Feeling my rush of gratitude come back, I said, "It won't be enough, though, will it?"

"Naw. Bound to take a lot more. I got to think of something."

All but forgetting the business we were on, maybe with a grin on my face, I sat back easy in my seat. Let him think. I was thinking that there wasn't anybody in the world as smart and good and brave as my brother Coop.

That was a while before we got to the turnoff. By the time we found it, heading into that track through the dark woods, I was thinking that for sure those boys would've told me last evening everything they knew. In fact they had, as it turned out . . . all they knew at the time. It was only today they had found out something else, in a newspaper that one of them had brought back with him from Nashville.

"It was in this county. Your brother kept saying Tipps was in on the thing, getting payoffs from it."

We were all standing around in the car's head lights, Coop and I and more of them than I had seen before. They kept butting in on each other, still excited from thinking at first that Coop and I were the law coming to visit. The one face-to-face with Coop had red hair lying clear down on his shoulders. He was saying, "They caught two of them. Right there in the middle of all those chopped-up cars. It was an old barn near. . . ."

"They say they got some others spotted, though. One of them might be you-know-who. Turdy Tipps."

"A celebration. Gather the tribes." It was the boy that had come on the motorcycle.

Coop, with the newspaper, was reading it in front of one of his head-lights. The voices were still going on, cutting across each other, when it came to me that we hadn't told them about Dud yet. I waited a little while for quiet enough. Then I mumbled, "Our brother died."

That stopped it cold. After a few seconds somebody cussed. All the lighted faces were looking at me. I said, "He was dead when I got home with him."

"Goddamn," a voice murmured.

Coop handed the paper back to the red-haired boy. With all the faces turned on him now Coop said, "It sure wasn't your fault. We're mighty grateful to you."

There were some answers, mumbling ones. Till the red-haired boy said, "We were going to come tell you about this. We find out anything else, you'll hear from us."

"Thank you."

We got back in the truck and left them standing there in the dark.

Eighteen

They brought Dud back the next day, in the afternoon, in a big black hearse instead of that van. The two men who helped bring his box in the house stayed around afterwards just long enough for some words with Coop outside. I couldn't hear what they were talking about but it wasn't long till I reckoned I knew. That came just in the seconds after we opened up the box. It might have been Dud made out of wax, with his cheeks and mouth all ugly pink like they never had been in life. Nobody said a word, not till Eve finally did. She was crying, wanting to know what they'd done to him. The rest of us knew, all right. It was just that for a good while yet, nobody could come up with any words to comfort her.

The grave across by the edge of the woods had been ready since yesterday, but it took a long while to find and fetch Mr. Beasley. By the time we had Dud in the ground and the dirt all rounded smooth on top of him, the old man's voice was sounding off in the last faint wash of daylight. Coop finally had to stop him and lead him, ahead of the rest of us, on back into the now dark house.

Not that changing places was anything more than an interruption for Mr. Beasley. Sitting with the lighted lamp beside him, trying with boney fingers that wouldn't stay still to keep the cup of coffee from spilling over his knee, he was on again with his flow of Bible verses. It was like his quavering voice was just about all there was left of him. Even seeing him there in the full lamplight, you got the notion that bones and shadow was all you'd find if you could see under his clothes. His old melted eyes searched about him in the room, but did they see anything? . . . See even the still lamplit faces listening to his promises of everlasting life? I'm certain he didn't notice a thing when Coop got up and left, or when Daddy's nodding head sank down for good on his chest. Stack finally took him home and I went to my room where Coop had gone.

He was sitting like I expected, propped back against the bedstead. His glance touched me but didn't seem to really take me in. Without saying anything I sat down in the chair to wait, watching and watching him. That was the first in a whole lot of times yet to come, with Coop off all by himself thinking and me just waiting and hoping he'd finally tell me what he thought. Sometimes he would and again he wouldn't, but tonight was a time when he did. It was two different things but it was like they went together. He turned his face my way and said, "I'm going to go down to Nashville, to the law. Tell them about Tipps. I been thinking. It could just as well be like that biker boy was saying. If that paper's right, they got their eye on a couple of more people. What if Tipps is one of them?"

Coop was smart, he'd know what to say. I said, "Tell them how he talked to you. Trying to scare you."

"I'll tell them that and everything else. I'm going to make them believe me."

When his eyes drifted away from me, my mind settled on Tipps . . . how he looked, the way he talked to us, even to Mama. "He hates the lot of us," I said.

"Let him. We can hate hard as he can." He drifted off again and when he finally spoke it was about the other thing.

"I'm going to try something else down there, too. They got what you call 'loan sharks.' Might be one of them would lend us some money. Put up the farm against it. This place is worth a lot more than what we owe on it, for sure. I'm going to try it."

I felt my mouth spreading into a grim. Like all of a sudden everything was going to be all right. When my mind jumped back to Dud out there in the ground, it was with the thought that in a way we could keep him with us now.

That thought kept me a little comforted all night and stayed with me on through the next couple of days. But it was a comfort that had another side to it, because it added still more to the sweat I was in for Coop to go on to Nashville. What held him back was Mr. Sherman, who wouldn't let him off. Coop said that the way Sherman had talked to him made him feel like quiting his job right there and then. He'd considered it hard for a minute and only held back when he thought how much we needed the money he made. He said it was the first time Sherman hadn't talked to him in a friendly way. He hadn't seen why at first, not till Sherman dropped a couple of plain hints meaning that Coop would be a lot better off to cut every last tie with a family sure to drag him down. By then it was clear he knew about Dud, because he mumbled something about being sorry to hear it. In fact, which Coop found out later, everybody knew. It was all in that morning's paper that Coop brought home and showed to Stack and me but not to anybody else.

I said it was "all" in the paper, but really it was "all" of what Tipps wanted people to believe. It was truth and lies together, starting with Dud's getting put in jail on big dope charges and things, and then escaping and finally sneaking back. It said how they chased him through the woods along the river bank, yelling at him all the time to halt, which he wouldn't ever do. It said they shot at him once and thought they'd missed him, till three days later when one of his brothers found him lying dead. The way they told it made Tipps and Willis both sound mighty sorry for the whole thing, like they never wanted to hurt the boy. It made my blood boil up and set me pestering Coop to get going, no matter what Sherman wanted.

But Coop stayed cool till Wednesday, when all at once he had yet another reason. It was a thing that made him get right white around the mouth at first, and a few minutes later, Sherman like it or not, take off straight to Nashville. We hadn't thought anything much about Stack's not getting home by bedtime Tuesday night and it was morning before we found out what had happened. He'd spent almost the whole night in a jail cell. Just on the other side of town, for no real cause, Willis had stopped him. He made Stack drive on in to the sheriff's office before he even told him what it was for. Then he said the charge was speeding and reckless endangerment.

"I hadn't done a goddamn thing," Stack said in a voice you could hear all over the house. For once he was excited enough to straight-out kick a chair over. "The bastard just made it up out of nothing. I mean nothing. Once when I started to get up, he pushed me back so hard it like to busted my head against the wall."

From the look of her, Mama might have been too tired to come up with even a word. But she did, just in a murmur. "How come him to?"

I said, "I know how come. It's to show us. . . ."

"Shut up, Chester." It was Coop's voice and I shut up. He said, "It's the way they are." Then, "Say they fined you thirty dollars?"

"I ain't even got thirty dollars. But I got to show up there with it today."

"Come on," Coop said, heading back to our room with Stack behind him. What he did was write Stack a check and tell him not to talk about it front of the family anymore. Then Coop snatched his coat off the hook and went right out to his car.

It was a long day for me. I hadn't been to school but a few times since it started, back in September, and this was another day I didn't go. A couple of early frosts had got the corn ready to pull and finally, not even asking Daddy to come help, I hitched up the mules and wagon and went to it. The work was some relief, breaking and snatching the ears from the stalks, arching them up and over into the wagon bed. I'd keep forgetting, though. I'd find myself standing with my arms hanging down to my sides, seeing things in my head. Most of the time it would be Dud lying in his box. But again it would be Tipps, looking at us, looking at Coop the way he had.

After dinner, though, Mama put me to a different chore. It was because of Daddy. The battery to his TV had played out. He was pacing back and forth in the house, showing all the signs of a man getting ready to bolt. "You got to," Mama said. "Ain't nothing else'll keep him steady." She put some dollars in my hand, out of the little stash she kept hid away someplace.

Before this, going to town never had been a chore to me. But chore is not the word for a thing that was only hard because it scathed my feelings. Right off I was struck with the notion that everybody in town was watching me, the same thought running through every head. "He's one of them. One of that one's brothers." It wasn't all my imagination, either.

Some eyes and once a voice followed when I walked by, and the fat man in the TV store, looking close at me, said it plain in my face: "You're one of them Moss boys, ain't you?" On my way back through the square to the truck I had to hold off from running. Would it crank? I never before had hoped so hard it wouldn't take more than a second. But it did, a lot more. Along the courthouse walk old heads had turned to watch it happen, listening to it grind and cough just like they'd known it would do. Up on the bridge, when I finally reached it, the river air swept cool as a blessing across my burning face.

I'd let my hopes get blown up too big, and what Coop had to say when he got home late that night left them lying pretty flat for a while. But the first hard thing was seeing the car he parked in front of the house. The one he'd had sure wasn't new, but the look of it made me proud. This one, especially when he opened the door and made the inside light turn on, was the kind of a car I'd a whole lot rather not take out in the daytime. But it struck me harder another way. It was like a warning not to hope for Coop to be bringing good news.

"It runs pretty good," he said, pushing the door hard shut to make it latch. "I'll clear maybe a hundred dollars on it, too."

But my thoughts jumped right past that. "What'd they say . . . the law people?"

Coop was slow. He rested his arm on top of the car. "They didn't say much. Listened to me, though, finally . . . after I told them everything. Said they'd look into it. It was a tall skinny detective. Watched me like a hawk the whole time. I think he'll do something, though. I felt like he took me serious."

"What'll he do?"

"Nose around, I hope. I don't know. We just got to wait and see."

I looked away from him, looked at the car. The front fender had a big hunk torn out of it. I thought to ask, already knowing the answer, "Would they lend you any money? The loan sharks."

"Laughed at me. I tried three of them. You'd have thought they were the president of something."

We went in the house and to bed without talking anymore except once, in the dark, when Coop asked me, "Did Stack get it settled all right?"

"He took them that check. They told him they were going keep their eye on him, so he better watch hisself."

Coop didn't answer but not because he was falling asleep. I don't know whether he went to sleep at all or not. The last time I looked he was lying with his eyes open, and somewhere along in the night, missing him in the bed, I heard him prowling around the house. That was just the first time. In the nights to come I pretty near got used to finding him gone.

That was when I started really noticing a change, another bigger change, in Coop. It was a sort of drawing-in on himself, the way people do when they're going deaf. It was like you had to do something special, touch his shoulder, to get his attention. Not that those quick dark eyes of his weren't looking out, they just weren't looking out at you . . . unless you took the trouble to get right in front of them. Maybe at first I was the only one to notice it much, but after the things that happened in the next week or so, it got where nobody in the house, not even Daddy, could miss it. I wondered if he behaved that way at work, too. Sherman, he'd told me, was down on him plenty enough already.

That skinny detective in Nashville hadn't wasted any time. Just the next weekend there was already some mixed-up talk about him, which Coop picked up at the crap game where Mama sent him to keep his eye on Daddy. Coop said they had the detective's name wrong — it was Gannon instead of Gant — but it was him for sure. He'd been poking around town, asking questions in a sly kind of a way, and he'd spent some time talking to both Judge Norris and the president of the bank where Tipps did his business. Exactly what he wanted to know was anybody's guess, but it was something about Tipps, who Gannon hadn't talked to. Dope dealing and moonshining were the crap shooters's guesses. Nobody said a word about the car-stealing thing.

Gannon had done his investigating on Friday. The next week, as far as we could tell, he hadn't been seen again. On Tuesday when Coop couldn't stand it any longer, he tried calling Gannon from a pay phone in town. All he got back, from a woman in Gannon's office, was that Mr. Gannon didn't discuss cases. That could have meant something or nothing at all, Coop said. So what else could we do but wait and see?

What came of Gannon's poking around, though, was a far cry from what we'd been hoping for. As smart as Coop was, he hadn't really looked at the thing from another side. He'd figured Tipps would hear about Gannon, all right, but he sure misjudged how Tipps would take the news. If it gave him a scare, it was anything but the kind of scare to make him hunker down. It was plain he already hated our guts. Now, all of sudden, he showed us right out how far he was ready to go.

On Saturday morning Mabel walked all the way from town to tell us. She finally got it out through all her sobbing, telling it again to make it clear. I don't think Coop said one word. I looked just in time to see him heading out the door, and ran after him and and got in the car before he could get it started. His face was white all over and he still didn't say a thing, just drove . . . too fast in that old car down the winding highway slope.

"You better go easy," I said. "Look what they did to Stack."

But he didn't slow down, not till we got across the bridge and started into town.

"What we going to do?" I said, and when he didn't answer I said, "Don't go running in there looking mad."

"I won't."

In fact, after we stopped outside the municipal building, Coop didn't even get out for a minute. Some color had come back in his face, too, and I sat a little easier there beside him.

"Let's go."

I followed just a step behind him and kept the office door from slamming shut when we went in. It was Willis at the desk, looking down, paying no mind to the two of us standing in front of him. Till Coop spoke, I was afraid to look at his face, for fear of seeing it gone all white again.

"I come about my sister, Dorcas Moss."

Willis wasn't in any hurry about looking up. When he did, taking us both in, you'd have thought he never had laid eyes on us before. He had a heavy-lidded blink. He said, "All right. Charged with prostitution." Then, "Street-walking, that is."

I waited, not looking at Coop's face, still afraid to. That was when I noticed something else. From behind the counter to my left the two women were watching us . . . watching close, thinking. . . .

I heard Coop's voice, almost natural sounding. "How was that?"

Willis leaned easy back in his chair. "'That' was soliciting on the public street. Last night. Which is a Class B misdemeanor. Her bail's sixty-five dollars. You get it back when she comes to trial."

"Trial." Coop just said the word, like saying a word he hadn't heard before. Right after that was when the office door in back of Willis came open.

Tipps was standing there, those agate-looking eyes of his already trained on Coop. They shifted just enough to take me in for a second before, quick as a bird's, they darted a glance at the women behind the counter. For once he lacked a hat to hide how his knotty forehead beetled out. He said, "Mosses just keep on coming, don't they? 'Fore long we'll have them all."

I saw Willis's mouth do something that made a kind of a grin. Coop's didn't do anything.

His eyes on Coop again, Tipps said, "Come in here, boy," and turning, left the doorway empty.

I don't know whether the slow way Coop moved was on purpose or because he felt like somebody headed into a dangerous place. In fact, he didn't go far inside . . . a step across the threshold. That was where he took his stand, with his head quartered so I could see just his cheek and the side of his forehead. At first, if anything at all was being said in there I couldn't tell it. All I could see of Tipps was in my head, him behind a desk, just standing, his hard eyes fastened on Coop that way. Then I heard a voice but not any words. It wasn't Coop's, I could see his mouth never moved. I heard the low voice speaking again, and then, because of a typewriter starting up, not even that much anymore. When Coop finally turned around, his face was the same fish-belly white I'd seen on the way from home.

It had to be cash money, Willis told him, so we had to walk down to the bank and get it. Coop wouldn't tell me what Tipps had said to him. "I'll tell you later." By the time we got back it was just his mouth that had that white look still.

I waited outside the office this time. Willis came out and went through a door at the end of the hall where the jail was. Before I saw it open again, Coop was at my side, looking where I was looking. Willis came out, not even holding the door open for Dorcas to come through behind him, and passed us by like he didn't see us there. Dorcas saw us. It made her stop. It made her mouth come open but not say anything and her eyes drift away from us, and down. Her yellow hair. I never had seen it falling this drab and stringy onto her shoulders.

"Come on, Sis." Coop had a different voice. He took her arm and walked her past two men who turned their heads to look, outside and on to where the car was parked. With her head bowed, hunkered down on the seat between us, she seemed to me like a little girl just half the size of herself. Her small voice said, "I want to go back to my room."

"Naw." Coop put his hand on hers. "You come on back home with us. Everybody's waiting for you."

"I didn't do nothing. I went for a hamburger. I just talked to a fellow a minute or two. They made up lies.

"We already knew that. Let's go home. Mabel's up there, too."

We took her home but she went right straight and shut herself in her room. Mabel went in for a minute, and Mama a little later with milk and a plate of food. It was dinnertime but nobody came till the food on the table was near too cold to eat.

Outside where his old car was parked, leaning against a fender, Coop finally told me.

"Said of course he knew I was the one got that detective up here. Said he called up the State Bureau to make sure. He claimed they told him it was just the kind of routine check they did when they got a complaint. Told him they hadn't found anything, so he could forget about it . . . except he ain't going to forget about it. He couldn't have made that any plainer to me. What the bastard really wanted to do was pull out that pistol and shoot me."

Coop turned his face toward the woods, thinking.

"Didn't he say anything else?"

"Yeah. He said even if we did know anything on him, which we don't, nobody'd believe it . . . from a low-down family like ours. Said we'd just got started paying for the damage we'd done him. He kind of gave himself away right there, saying that." Coop paused, looked down at his clenched fingers. "No way it could hurt him, though . . . just me to hear

176

him say it. It's nothing but plain old revenge now. It don't even make sense, the way he hates us. And he ain't going to stop till he runs us clear out of the county . . . or something worse."

I watched Coop's slow hand clenching and unclenching. "What else can he do?" I murmured.

"I don't know. I don't know what we can do, either. I got to think."

I watched him thinking. The sun went behind a cloud and then came out again, casting a gauzy light on things that made them look not quite real.

Nineteen

In those months when Coop was working for Mr. Sherman, he'd come to seem like a different person to me. Looking back on it, though, I can see how little the real difference was . . . like a skin he was able to sluff clean off when the season for it came. Then he was back to being my brother again, a Coop only changed by knowing a lot he hadn't used to know.

But now, along in the fall, especially after they did Dorcas that way, what I could see taking a stronger and stronger hold on Coop was something else again. There were times it would show up plain in his eyes, like the sun had struck and put a glaze as hard as rhinestone on them. He never had been somebody to talk a whole lot, wasting words, but now, except for spells once in a while, he might have had to strain words out of his throat. It got where I couldn't tell when he slept, if he did sleep. I'd feel him turning and turning in the bed beside me, and wake up later and find him gone. I know about feeling nervous. I worry and fidgit and pace the floor, but that's the whole thing with me. With Coop, maybe right in the middle of pacing around, it was like his nerves would all of a sudden lock up and bind him tight and hold him standing still as a post for minutes at a time.

He'd lost his job at the factory . . . or quit, would be as true to say. It happened less than a week after Dorcas got arrested and by that time, as seemed to me, he was already about as bitter as a man could get. From what he told me, his last talk with Mr. Sherman, which was a lot more than just a talk, had a build-up to it from a couple of days before.

That time, when Sherman started in on him about our family and how Coop was just going have to break off with us for good and all, Coop held on to his temper. Instead of blowing up at Sherman, he set in telling him about Tipps, the whole story, and that Tipps was the one responsible for just about all the things that made our family look so bad. He said Sherman listened him out, though the look on his face didn't make it easy for Coop to keep his voice down. Afterwards, though, Sherman did say he'd talk to some people and see what he could find out about Tipps. So that was it for two or three days.

Maybe Sherman did talk to some people, but from the kind of details he brought back to Coop at their last meeting it sounded like he'd talked to just one person, Tipps. What he said on every single point was just exactly what Tipps would say, right down to the business of Dorcas's getting caught flat-out trying to pick up a man on the street. And almost as bad was his way of telling it back to Coop, not leaving Coop a decent chance to even get a word in. It was like Coop was the one had done wrong, making charges without any evidence and bringing that detective in here to damage an honest public man's reputation. Another thing got to Coop. It was his first time to notice the cold, steady, measuring look that Sherman held on him through those gold-rimmed glasses. That look was new to Coop but not to me. My one meeting with Sherman months ago had left it set clear as a picture in my mind.

But the last straw, the thing that finally broke Coop's temper loose, was Sherman saying he guessed he could understand it. What he understood was how a young man rightly ashamed of his family could talk himself into really believing the blame was somebody else's. So maybe that was some excuse . . . he'd let it pass, this time.

But Coop wasn't about to let it pass. It was right there he lit straight into Sherman, the way I'd seem him do sometimes, not sparing anything, just the same as asking to get fired. So Sherman obliged him . . . with, I'll bet, a face about as drained of blood as Coop's face probably was. It was even whiter than that if Coop talked to him the same way he talked to me about him. It wasn't just that he used cuss words. He said the only difference between

Sherman and Tipps was that Sherman had money instead of a badge, that if he was to get in Tipps's shoes he wouldn't do a bit different. Both the same, just different calls to use the power they had. Give him a reason and Sherman would be as ready as Tipps was to stomp our family out. It wouldn't surprise him a bit, Coop said, if Sherman knew the real story.

In those spells when he felt like talking, Coop would say these things over again . . . to me but nobody else. And it didn't happen many times before Uncle Clarence started getting into it. Coop wanted to know did I remember the things Uncle Clarence said, about the law and how it wasn't anything but a way of hiding the real truth. To paint a thing like the people in charge wanted it to look. I remembered, and I thought I kind of understood now what he meant. That got my mind back on Uncle Clarence and it got to where, trying to start Coop talking, I'd bring up other things about him. How nice he'd been to Eve, giving her that gold pen, was one. And how he warmed up to us, telling us all those things he knew like we might have been his own children. And in the prison hospital, how he thanked us for helping him out. This, him dying there, brought me back to a question I'd thought a lot about at first. I said to Coop, "Where you reckon they buried Uncle Clarence? Looks like they could have sent him back here, to his own people."

"Likely as not, they dumped him in a garbage pit someplace," Coop said and fell quiet all over again.

Coop had to do something with himself, and soon after he helped me finish pulling the corn he got another job. It wasn't much of a job, at Mr. Cutchins's sawmill where Daddy used to work, off and on. In a week, because he was so sharp, he was made the head sawyer, but even that pay wasn't more than we needed to keep us in food and such. Especially with the girls back home — to stay, it looked like — you could add up what he and Stack both made in a month and still not have enough left over to put a good dent in the sum we owed on the place. If there was any hope at all left, I didn't know where it was. Unless it could somehow come from whatever Coop was thinking about.

At least I knew his mind was working on something, and I reckoned money was it. Did he have some plan he was figuring on? He wouldn't give me a start of an answer to even one of my questions, so I quit asking, just went on waiting. Some nights he went out and stayed for hours, but the next morning early he'd go off to the saw mill . . . every day just like the one before.

As long as Dorcas and Mabel stayed on, every day around the house was just about the same, too. I'd plain stopped going to school, and so had Eve, finally, because she could tell that nobody really wanted her to. Mornings just after sun-up Coop would go out, and Stack on his motorcycle would leave a little while later. That motorcycle would make me think about Dud's old car still down there behind the municipal building, but like everybody else I was afraid to go claim it. It was like none of us wanted to go anywhere we didn't have to go. I did our bit of grocery buying at Simmon's little store, down the highway, and always came straight back. My one real outing was when I loaded up the corn, what we didn't have to keep for feed and meal, and drove over to Chatham to sell it . . . for $21. Except for Coop and Stack, I don't remember anybody else in those weeks going as far as a mile away from the house.

So finally it got to be almost like our family was living under some kind of a spell. There was a late, long Indian summer up in November that kept everything quiet outdoors, with nothing but chickens clucking and dry flies from out in the woods making a low hum you couldn't hear till you listened. And no wind, not even a breath to stir the rusty-red and yellow leaves hanging bright on the trees. In the house you could hear Daddy's TV running, but Mama made him keep it low. Except sometimes when he'd disappear for a hour or two — which would be for a whiskey run across the ridge to Sodic Hollow — Daddy would be there humped in his rocker, his eyes locked in on those flickering pictures. Even Dorcas didn't make much noise, just brooding, drifting around. But helping Mama, too, for a change, in the same kind of muffled way. Along in the afternoon when Mama was ready, Dorcas and the other girls would go with her to hunt for the wildflowers she liked to put on Dud's grave. They never missed a day. Sometimes you couldn't see the mound for all the fresh flowers piled on top of it. Looking at them I couldn't help but think how, soon, there wouldn't be anybody at all left to put them there.

I reckoned now there wasn't any more use in hoping Coop would save us. Not that he hadn't kept right on in the same silent, restless way. But nothing seemed to come of all his mulling, and when he started bringing little presents home — candy sticks for Eve, a wooden bowl he'd shaped at the mill for Mama — I took it to be his way of trying to make up for his failing. That was why, on the evening he brought me a hunting knife he'd ground out of an old saw blade, I couldn't seem to make a show of being rightly grateful. He looked at me straight with his quick dark eyes. He'd read what I was feeling. It did give me a little boost when he finally said, "Don't give up on me yet, Chester," but it wasn't enough to last long. That night was the same as the ones before, and so was the next morning when he went out on his way to the mill again.

There was a change that day, though. It was only a change of weather, bringing in heavy clouds and bitter wind by nightfall, making an end to the long Indian summer. But looking back from now on that day, I've got in my memory that it struck me like a sign of something coming, something that wasn't just winter. I remember doing nervous work around the place, tarring up cracks between the wall logs and knocking soot out of the stove chimneys. Lately it had got to where Mama, looking straight out ahead of her so much of the time, wasn't the noticing woman she used to be. But she noticed my doings that day, followed me with her eyes. When she finally said, "What's eating at you, Chester?" I just said, "Winter's coming down," and went on with my business. But I think maybe she was feeling some of what I felt, too.

But Coop came home for supper and his not eating much didn't mark any difference in him we hadn't got used to by now. If he was getting leaner all the time and his hair longer, it happened so slow that nobody but maybe Mama and I noticed. He got up from the table along with the rest of us and, just like he did most nights, sat a while in the front room with his eyes fastened on something that wasn't the TV. It wasn't unusual either when he went off without saying anything, because he'd been doing just that a couple of times a week. So I didn't know why I kept on feeling the way I did.

I couldn't sleep and it sure wasn't because of the cold wind blowing gusts of rain against my window. I got up three or four times to go for a look at the kitchen clock by the light of a match. The last time it was way past midnight and after that my heart started beating heavier than ever. I knew something was coming. I couldn't even lie down again and I was sitting on the side of the bed facing the window when all of a sudden I saw car lights. The lights went out but I could hear how the car kept on coming and finally stopped on the other side of the house where the truck was. I moved just enough to face my open door, and waited.

To move as quiet as he did, Coop must have had his shoes off. After the faint, faint tap of the front door shutting, all I could hear, getting closer and closer to me, was the muffled creak of floorboards under his feet. Soon there wasn't even that to hear, and the bulk of him at my doorway just made the darkness darker. There was another sound, I could hear him breathing. A minute more and it didn't seem to me like natural breathing. It stopped, I reckon he could see I was sitting up in the bed. He stepped as quiet as feathers into the room and, just as quiet, reached and shut the door. My first try at whispering to him failed, and I tried again. "What's the matter?"

He moved, a shadowy step or two across to the bed. "Find me a rag," he whispered. "An old shirt or something."

"What for?"

"Just do it."

Trying not to make a sound, I eased across to the corner closet. Reaching behind the curtain I found a shirt, any shirt, and held it out to where his hand could take it. "Here."

"Tie it around my arm. Up under my shoulder. Tight." He took the shirt and put it in place, ready for me to tie it. "Come on."

The second I lifted my hands to his arm I knew what it was my fingers touched. I didn't say it. I wrapped the shirt around and around and got it finally knotted tight with the sleeves.

"That's good." He turned around and sat down easy on the bed.

I waited but he didn't speak, and I couldn't seem to gather up boldness enough to ask him. So I stood there, on and on, using that for a way to press my question. And finally, so low I had to cock my ear, he said, "I made a mess, Chester."

That gave me my voice back, or enough of it to say, "How?"

"I thought it'd be easy. I never thought to do her any harm. Just to take her money, was all."

"Who?" I breathed.

He was a long time answering, so long I started getting afraid he wasn't going to.

"A fortune-teller woman. A dope seller mainly, though." He paused again, like he was going to stop right there. Then, "In a trailer down there outside of Cold Springs. Calls herself Madame Shula or something."

I'd seen that trailer, passed it by.

"I just thought to scare her into showing me where her money was. I finally managed that, all right, but then I turned my fool back on her. That was when she got me with her kitchen knife. Fighting her off was when I threw her up against that iron cookstove. She's a little woman. Kind of old."

I waited. I could see how he was sitting with his head bent down, his good arm held across his chest so his hand could rest on the bandage. I whispered, "Then what?"

"She didn't get up."

In the stillness after, drops of rain tick-ticked on the window glass. What came to me first like a jolt inside my head was a voice speaking out-loud. Not Coop's voice, nothing from Coop, who hadn't stirred a hair. It came from beyond the wall, one of the girls, Dorcas complaining in her sleep. I stopped hearing it. To Coop's dark bent-down head I whispered, "She wasn't dead, was she?"

"Naw. She was breathing. I picked her up and put her on her bed. After that I saw her hand move a time or two . . . kind of jerking." He hushed for a minute. "I ought not to left there like I did."

"What else could you do?"

"I ought to've waited." Coop lifted his head but he didn't say anything more for a little while. When he spoke, his voice was louder than a whisper, making me start again. "I got to go back."

"You can't do that."

But he got to his feet, almost touching me.

"What good would it do?" I whispered. "You can't."

"I got to."

He moved and stepped past me but I reached out and caught him by the arm. I said, "I'm going with you."

"Naw you ain't." He went on out. But seconds later I came behind him carrying my clothes.

Because I was already feeling maybe just what he felt, I figured I knew why he decided to let me come along. It was a feeling of being not just by himself, but by himself in a far, far place where he couldn't see any way at all of ever getting back. All ways the same, and no way back to home. That was why he let me come and why, driving on through the rain, he spent the whole time explaining how he'd got to where he was.

He told me what he was doing those nights when he went off after supper. He figured, since there wasn't any right way he could get the money, he'd have to learn from the kind of people who knew how to get it the wrong way. It wasn't too hard to find them. He said he went to about all the likely joints in the county and buddied up to the people he thought were the kind he was looking for. He had to buy a lot of beers for people to get them talking to him. Till he finally got around to a place the other side of Silver Hill. That was where he heard about Madame Shula. He heard it said that for all the looks of her, she'd made a pile at dealing and such. And more than that, among other rumors about her, he heard she kept it all hid somewhere in or around her trailer. That was when Coop's mind got busy working up his plan.

Her trailer was a little way out of town where there weren't any houses real close by. Coop said he spent a good many night hours parked so he could watch the place, seeing if she went in and out by night and when people were likely to sneak up and knock on her door. Sometimes he sneaked up close to watch and just by luck overheard something he couldn't have done without knowing. It was a pass word. She wouldn't open her door at night unless you gave it to her.

So he picked this rainy, windy night, late, an hour after he'd seen that last shadowy customer sneak away. He left his car parked on a dirt track off the road and walked through a little thicket to the trailer. By then the trailer was all dark. He didn't have any real weapon, just a pocket knife, and he hoped he wouldn't need even that to scare her with. He meant to do that just with his voice and shining a flashlight in her face, keeping her blinded. He climbed the steps and knocked. It was about the third time of knocking, standing there in the wind and rain, before he heard her footsteps. Then her voice inside the door wanting to know who was out there. He said the password, "Jack-of-diamonds." A latch and then another one clicked and the door opened a crack.

He was all set to do the way he'd planned, and the second he saw that crack he hit the door shoulder-first. It knocked her backwards but not down, and right off he had his flashlight shining in her eyes. He remembered thinking they were like a cat's eyes, with barely even any fear in them. He couldn't remember what he said to her, only that it was threatening words, in a voice he made up to show how much he meant them. Of course, she said she didn't have any money, and finally, to let her know he meant business, he had to pull his knife and hold the blade up shining in the light. That did it, put a little flash of fear in her eyes. Right after that was when she said the one thing that, along with the way her face twisted around those broken teeth, stayed on like something wedged in the back of his mind. "Boy, you going to be goddamn sorry you done this."

She led him to a refrigerator. It was under there, she said, in through the back of it, but the thing was too big for her to move by herself. That was when he should have figured she meant to trick him, but he didn't. He just told her to stand back and, still holding the flashlight, put his shoulder against the thing and started pushing. All that saved him was a little clicking noise she made before she came at him with the knife. He turned sideways enough to take it there on his arm instead of in the middle of his back. In the stab of pain and the blind rage that hit him, he just grabbed hold and threw her away like throwing a sack of grain. He heard a hollow-sounding thump, another duller thump, and nothing after that. His flashlight lay still-burning on the floor. When he put the beam on her, she was lying flat with her mouth open and eyes that looked all white under her half-shut lids. For a minute or two he couldn't do a thing but stand there looking down at her.

She wasn't dead, though. She was breathing and, in spite of his own pulse thumping even in his fingertips, he could feel the life still in her stick of an arm. Knocked out, was all, he told himself. Then he saw he couldn't just leave her there on the floor and he started to pick her up. That was when he found out how much his left arm hurt him. He managed it with his right one and got her to and on the bed and even pulled the blanket up over her naked legs. But her small wrinkled face, especially the stark slips of white showing under the eyelids, looked scary when he trained his flashlight on it. Then one of her hands, her fingers, moved . . . jerky movements lasting a second or two. Knocked out was all she was.

Turning slow away from her, he shifted his light back to the refrigerator. He'd moved the thing enough so he could see the backside of it and into the space where the coils and motor were. There was nothing else to see, though he leaned for a closer look. Nothing there . . . the way she'd used to trick him. At the same time, like the gust of wind that all of a sudden blew in through the open door, it came to him that he didn't care any longer and that he'd better get out of there as fast as he could go. The only thing that slowed him down was making sure he'd left the door so the wind wouldn't blow it back open.

That was what Coop had told me on the way . . . that and one more thing. He said he'd got in too big a hurry to think. Instead of heading into the thicket, he went straight on to the road. There was a car coming, pretty close. "He had me in his headlights a second before I even thought to turn my fool face away." Coop fell quiet, thinking. "It wasn't but just a second, though, and he wasn't up real close to me then. And I had on my hat and this big old coat. I could've been just about anybody . . . I hope."

Watching the glistening rain come at us through the headlights, I finally said, "Anyhow, it was likely just a stranger passing through."

Where we slowed down was just beyond an unlighted house, with thicket on our side of the road. We passed the trailer, hard to see, back off in the rainy dark. A little farther on, Coop turned the car around and, passing the trailer again, pulled off into the thicket. He didn't move to get out, not for a minute or two, just sat there waiting, listening. The sizzling rain was all there was to hear. "You stay here," he said and opened his door. I stayed, but not for long. Before he got out of sight through the trees, I was coming on behind him.

I wasn't but a few steps back when he got to the trailer and I stopped because he did. I could see his hand was lifted, held there shy of the door. He stayed like that for a while, before his hand moved and touched the door with what I could barely hear was a knocking sound. Then waiting again. His hand moved down to the knob and pushed and the door fell slowly back. One quick step, up and over the threshold, and his flashlight beamed in the room.

He was standing by the bed when I came in, holding his flashlight straight on a face that startled me like a shout. I'd seen dead people before and I knew a dead face when I saw one. No use, it was foolishness, for Coop to reach out like he did and lay his hand in a testing way on her chest and then her neck. Just those eyes, white-staring at nothing from under the lids, were plenty to tell him so. He took his hand off. He let it fall away and hang there straight down at his side.

It seemed like neither one of us was ever again going to move or say anything or even think about anything but what we were looking at. I can't even guess how long we went on staring at her that way. But long or not, the time came and my mind went back to working. It was working at something my eye had struck on the floor not far from my feet. I made out it was a knife lying there, the size of a butcher knife. My mind shut hard on a notion. "Coop," I said.

He turned his face to me.

"Let's fix it so they can't tell. They'll think she just up and died."

"They can tell."

"How can they? Shine your light around."

After a second he did, the bright beam slowly sweeping the room. I said, "It's nothing but that ice box out of place. And that knife lying there. We can fix it easy."

"They'll find out anyhow."

But I was already moving. Humping with my shoulder I pushed the refrigerator back in place against the wall. I stepped across and picked up the knife. "Let's go. 'Fore somebody comes," I said and headed straight to the door.

But when I looked back, Coop hadn't moved. He was shining his light on that stark face again.

"Come on! We need to hurry."

He switched off his light and turned and came on, but not like hurrying.

At the foot of the steps another thought hit me. It was what I'd seen on the TV, and I dodged past Coop and from on the steps set to wiping the doorknobs clean with my shirttail. "For fingerprints," I whispered, closing the door. But Coop wasn't even watching.

"Let's go!" I whispered.

This time he followed me, through the thicket back to car, where we had to sit and wait a minute till a car on the road got past.

Still whispering I said, "I'll throw this knife in the creek or something. They won't know. They'll think she. . . ."

"They'll know. They always look to see what killed a person." He cranked the car and backed out onto the road like there wasn't any reason for us to hurry.

Twenty

Coop was sick the next day and the day after that, and it wasn't mainly because his arm hurt him. Where he was really sick was in his heart. He didn't come out and say that, but I was sure. In fact, in those two days he didn't say much of anything, just a few words to Mama and me once in while when he had to, and once, to me, when he didn't have to. Of course, Mama saw right off he was hurt, the blood showed her that. Coop told her a lie, that he'd got in a fight, but I could tell she didn't believe him. I think she probably had heard him come in and go out again that night, but even if she hadn't she'd have seen from the way he just lay there on the bed not moving, with his eyes shut or else open staring at the ceiling, that it was a thing bigger than a fight. The time he talked to me when he didn't have to was just to say, "If it wasn't for that goddamn Tipps being sheriff, I'd turn myself in.'"

I mumbled something about it not being his fault, he hadn't meant to do it. Coop didn't answer. The other thing he said was, "Want you to go to town and see what you can hear. Look in the newspaper."

I did, though by then it was noon of the second day, because all of a sudden I had a job. When I first went to tell Mr. Cutchins that Coop was sick, he offered me a job stacking lumber, which I took because of the money. I went to work the next day and it was noon break before I got a chance to walk uptown for a few minutes. There wasn't any mention in the newspaper yet and in the time I had I couldn't see a chance to find out anything. So we had to wait till the next day.

Then it was in the paper. Coop was back at work now and at noon we both went up there to look. It wasn't at the top but it was on the front page. Coop's face reading it didn't change a bit, even when he got through and handed it to me like it was any old paper. It told about them finding her on her bed and how the coroner said her neck was broken. They hadn't got any suspects yet, but they'd found some marijuana and also money hid in a place in the wall. So they figured it was likely one or more of her customers come to rob her, who'd tried to force her to tell them where it was. That was all except for some bragging words from Tipps about how he was going to track her killer down.

When I looked up Coop's face was just the same, like there might not be a thought in his head except what came from watching people pass along the sidewalk, the way they do on a winter day, humped a little in their coats, walking some faster than in the summertime. I knew they weren't especially noticing us. It was just my feeling that they were, in secret, pretending not to know. But if Coop felt even a little that way it sure didn't mark his face.

In fact, it struck me now that just those two days lying in bed had cured the last of his heartsickness. That was my notion at the time, and in his car driving back to the mill he made it a whole lot stronger. Not as much to me as to the road out ahead of him he said, "I might as well have had that money. I ought to kept on looking for it."

I wasn't sure I liked hearing him say that, so I didn't answer. Later on, though, even if they did sound kind of hard-hearted, I could see the good sense behind his words. What was the use to keep crying over something you couldn't help, when you had plenty of serious stuff on hand to worry about? Like Tipps, first of all, bragging that he'd track the killer down. That was how I stayed of one mind with Coop in the days to come.

But it seemed to me I worried more than Coop did. I kept thinking of things like fingerprints and tire tracks in the mud and about the man in the car that night who had got Coop in his headlights. When I said these things to Coop he'd always make me feel better for a while. He'd point out how, if they did find any fingerprints, they had no way of knowing the prints were his, and that all the rain that night for sure would've melted down the tire tracks. And the person in that car? All he'd got was a glimpse of a man dressed in a coat and hat. Then, even if it was foolishness, I'd say, "They know how bad we're needing money, though." And Coop would answer, "Yeah. And they'd have them about a thousand suspects just here in Clayton County."

Talking to Coop was always a help but this time it never really cleared my head. I hurried every day to get hold of that newspaper and I spent all the time I could easing up close whenever I saw people talking to each other on the streets. But days and days went by and I never learned one new thing. Sometimes at the sawmill stacking lumber I'd feel the whine of that big bandsaw dragging and dragging like a file across a nerve between my ears.

I don't mean Coop didn't worry; there were times when I could see it. Once he said to me, "It's not the things you think of, it's the things you don't think of that get you caught." He didn't stew like I did, but the real difference between us wasn't just a matter of how much. I came to notice it more and more. It was almost like getting caught wasn't what worried him, it was getting caught by Tipps. That was part of it for me, too, but not the big part. I'd think about Coop in the electric chair or locked in the pen the rest of his life. Tipps was what Coop thought about, and those other things, life in the pen or worse, might have been nothing but just bad dreams that slipped up on him sometimes. It was like Tipps got so big in his mind that Coop couldn't see any further.

And that was even before what happened just when Christmas was coming. Not that it turned out bad. For once in all those months a thing that had our family expecting the worst ended in a surprise like a gift unwrapped. But it's Coop I'm talking about, and the whole thing, no matter for our good luck this time, was just more fuel to feed his hate for Tipps.

We'd known all along it was finally going to happen. But because it was a thing nobody wanted to even think about and, so, kept pushed back out of sight, that summons caught us way off guard. Worse than that, though, I'd never known Dorcas to get so quiet, looking like maybe her heart had stopped on her. And after he took the thing out of her hand and put his eyes on it, Coop didn't look much different for a space. Then he said something I couldn't hear, just with his lips, making his teeth flash.

By that time Mama knew, and even Daddy, I think, sitting there in his rocker in front of the TV. I don't know why I remember what was coming out of that screen at the time, something about a cream that made your skin get smooth. Then Coop's voice saying, "It's for Friday. Two o'clock." He wadded the paper in his hand. If ever I saw Coop having thoughts to make your hair stand up, it was in that minute. Dorcas went back to her room, and Mabel behind her. A little later dinner was ready but neither one of them came. And Daddy, for once, didn't finish the food he'd put on his plate.

They had a lawyer for Dorcas and she had to be down there the next day and talk to him in his office. She said he was a little pinch-faced man named Sanders, new in town, she thought, who didn't say much but seemed to listen hard while she told him everything. On Friday afternoon Coop and I were there in the courtroom where we could see him sitting with her up front and maybe reading something he had in his lap. He was little, all right, but he didn't look as little as Dorcas did. She sat in kind of a drawn-up way like she was trying to hide in her chair, not ever lifting her head and just her yellow hair to make us sure which one she was. It was a long wait, with different people, mostly two at once, going up in front of the judge's big table and talking so you could hear them just about half the time.

Because of Coop, we were sitting farther back in the room than I would have chosen, back behind the loafers who'd come for nothing except to watch. Pretty soon, though, I understood Coop's reason. I never had seen him look so close to letting go of himself. I'd see his knuckles go bare-bone white and stay that way for a whole minute or two, and more than once I heard his teeth working. For maybe a half hour it didn't get any better with him and then, all of a sudden, it was different. If he'd been a snake drawn up to strike he couldn't have got any stiller. I saw why. Tipps was up there, off in a corner where a flag stood, talking quiet to a man with a badge on his shirt. That cocked elbow was because Tipps's hand lay resting on the pistol butt at his side. He turned and went out through a door in the back wall, but it was a while yet before I saw Coop blink away the hot stare in his eyes.

We'd missed something. Out of nowhere, in a spruced-up uniform too tight across his back, Willis was standing in front of the judge's table. He was already talking, a few words getting to us, telling his lies straight into the judge's face. That went on for a couple of minutes and then, in a voice that made me think of a jaybird, the little lawyer, who was on his feet now, cut in on Willis. Most of what they said didn't come clear to me. There was something, repeated two or three times, about an exchange of money and what the law said on that. Willis was already mad. He'd turned clear around to face the lawyer, and because he'd lifted his voice I could hear him saying how he'd been watching Dorcas for a long time.

"Lying son of a bitch!" But that was Coop beside me, his whispered words finishing off with a gust of breath through his teeth.

In those next minutes I lost all track of the argument passing between them. But a notion in my head was getting clearer. The little lawyer was the one winning the argument. I could hear that much in Willis's voice, getting louder, and then still more when all of a sudden the judge's voice shut him up. It was a plain put-down. Then the judge, so his bald head caught the light, was sitting up straight behind his table. In a voice I could hear plainer than any one before, he said, "It won't stand up, Deputy Willis. Case dismissed." He brought that little hammer down.

Even so, it was only the sight of Coop's grinning face that made me finally sure of what had happened. With the grin not even faded much, he stepped out into the aisle and walked to where Dorcas was standing . . . just standing, posed there like a person caught out in a heavy shower of rain. Then Coop was saying something, thanking the lawyer. I might have gone up to thank him, myself, if it hadn't been for Willis close by with his eyes fastened on them.

Later on I told Coop what had come into my head about the lawyer. It was my notion that being new in town, like Dorcas mentioned, he hadn't found out yet what his right place was. Coop thought a minute and then said, "Give him a little time. They'll teach him."

Dorcas getting off that way wasn't really a big enough thing to make us all feel hopeful. But it did, and for longer than you might have thought. It was just that we'd about lost the habit of looking for anything good, and this made it easy for us to think maybe our luck had changed. Besides, it was almost Christmas, a time for change of luck. Later that same afternoon all of us, all us children, went down in the woods where I knew a perfect cedar was and brought it back and set it up in the front room in the corner by the TV. It couldn't have been any better for size, and dense till you couldn't see your hand in among the branches. All fresh that way in the heat of the stove, it set a winey taste in the air I couldn't breathe enough of.

But the next day, Christmas Eve, when we got the tree all fixed, is even better in my memory. The girls made a long snow-white chain of the popcorn Mama popped, and threaded it round and round the tree to the point where the ceiling touched. They cut out shapes, stars and little animals and angel wings in colored paper and tinfoil, and pasted shards of colored glass on ribbons to hold them up. Then feathers, the little pin-feathers from a white hen Mama had killed, set floating like on air in the cedar rush. The candles came last, cut to thimble-size, perched, it seemed, on branches growing a little apart from the rest.

We waited till after dark to light the candles. Then we did, all standing around, watching each one start to life by the match in Mama's hand. Then the whole tree like a vision blooming right there in front of our eyes. I heard Bucky suck in his breath and Eve give a little cry. But Daddy, as I remember it, came up with the only words. "Lordy Lord-a-mighty. Ain't that a sight to see." We all just went on standing there goggling at the tree.

It might be partly true that that Christmas is set so deep and warm in my memory just because it was our last one. But I think it really was, at least in some ways, the best one of them all. Coop had got back the bail money he'd put down on Dorcas and he didn't stint to spread it out among us. So there were presents like never before and a Christmas dinner I thought was a dinner fit for any king. There wasn't a turkey but there were three of the fattest hens we had and a guinea and a bunch of partridges Stack had gone out and shot on Christmas Eve. There were two red candles burning, too, and I recollect exactly how that light put a glow on the oilcloth table and the plates and smoking dishes and the gold-brown breasts of the chickens and all waiting for us to eat them.

But what most made that Christmas different was the thought we were secretly thinking. A month, or two or three for sure, and where would we be then? Trying to hold it out of mind never was much use. I thought about it when I saw Mama kill those best hens of ours, how we wouldn't be needing them for eggs much longer. And those fine candles Coop put on the table, like even money didn't matter in this house anymore. Where would we be? I'd shut my eyes and try, but every picture I could shape was this place over again. In town somewhere, a house I'd seen? I couldn't call up a single one and see our family in it.

I'm sure Coop was thinking about it too, because once, late on Christmas day, he let it slip out. He said, "We got to figure something pretty soon," and hushed as quick as he said it. I could tell he was sorry, he hadn't wanted to trouble Christmas for me. By now, I reckoned, he had enough room in his head for thinking about such matters. For the best part of a month, except for one thing he took as comforting, there hadn't been another scrap of news. He thought the reward we'd read about in the paper a week ago was a sign they hadn't made any way toward finding out who did it. That was what Coop decided and I thought that made sense. We still had the week after Christmas to go, before the next news came.

Twenty One

I need to pause right here in my story and tell a couple of things we had no way of knowing at the time, things I found out piece by piece after it was all over with. Coop, and I along with him, couldn't be sure, of course, but when the first couple of weeks after it happened hadn't brought any sign of bad news, he settled for thinking he'd got clean away with it. Part of his mistake, I guess, was underestimating Tipps. Hating him the way he did, he couldn't give him credit even for being smart. But it turned out Tipps hadn't been sheriff sixteen years for nothing. Coop and I had gone over and over all the likely ways that Tipps might use to track him, but the one that Tipps did mostly use was one that hadn't seemed likely. Coop had dismissed it almost at a glance, saying he'd been careful not to come out in the open with the questions he asked in those honky-tonks. He hadn't been careful enough, though.

It had taken Tipps a while but he finally came up with somebody that remembered a young man asking questions about Madame Shula. Of course, Tipps still had the problem of getting a clear description. It was at night with the place just halfway lighted, and Tipps's witness had only overheard Coop talking to somebody else in one of the booths. So the guy doubted he'd know either one of them if he saw them again. The best he could do was say it was a young man, slight of build, with dark hair. That could have been a lot of people, but because Coop was on his mind,

Tipps had him right off for a suspect. The trouble was, his suspicion didn't lead him anywhere. So because it wouldn't have been smart to let Coop get wind of it, for several more weeks Tipps just went around with the notion in his head and nothing else.

When he arrested the biker a week after Christmas, I don't believe he even thought, then or later, that he had the right man. In fact, there was more clear reason to suspect the biker than there was Coop. He was one of that gang that hung around scoffing at the law and everything else, and where they lived wasn't too far from Cold Springs and Madame Shula's trailer. There was plenty of evidence they had been buying from her and the one Tipps picked on, named Baxter, had been seen, Tipps said, going in there. What especially singled Baxter out, though, was the man in the car that night who had got Coop in his headlights. Right before he got in touch with Tipps for the second time, he'd seen Baxter in Cold Springs wearing what looked to him like the same big coat and pulled-down hat the person he'd seen that night had on. That wasn't evidence enough, but the boy tried to get away when Tipps went to question him. Then, according to Tipps, the boy's answers just made him look worse and worse. The first we learned was in the newspaper, saying Baxter was in jail on suspicion of murder and that Tipps was downright sure he had his man.

"That's all he needs," Coop said. He'd brought the newspaper home with him, keeping it under his coat till he came in our room. In the bad winter-evening light he had a look like the skin had somehow got stretched tight across his mouth and jaws. "Anybody'll do. Just so he gets somebody."

When I got through reading I looked up at him and said, "He can't prove it, can he, with just those things? He'll have to let him go, won't he, if he can't prove it?"

"He'll come up with whatever he needs."

"How can he? With that judge. Like with Dorcas."

"He won't get careless another time. Not on a thing like this."

Coop was sitting on the bed now, propped up the way he liked to sit, staring at the wall in front of him. His tight face kept me from saying anything else for the time. It was more than just for the time, though.

The whole evening till I finally went to sleep he wouldn't let me bring it up again. And all that while I couldn't stop myself from thinking about what he might be thinking.

He didn't stop being that way, not for several days. Even at the dinner table the look of him, like a man too far away in his head for even a shout to reach, kept the whole family quiet. Every day when noon break came at the mill he'd leave and go uptown and wouldn't let me come with him. I could tell, because he never said anything or brought a paper back, that nothing new had happened. I started wondering how he could keep on like this. And since he'd stopped ever really talking to me, I started doing some thinking of my own.

From what I came to find out in afterdays, I believe my thinking at the time had brought me pretty close to the real truth. It gave a lot of credit to Tipps's brains, a lot more than Coop would allow, but I think it was right. I think he'd read Coop pretty close and figured on him being the kind that couldn't sit still and watch somebody else take the blame for his doings. So really Baxter was nothing but just bait. When finally, after about three days, I put that notion to Coop, he said it couldn't be. "A bastard like Tipps?" he said. "That never had a decent feeling in his life? His kind figures everybody's just the same as them. Shit on that."

Even so, I could tell I'd made him think about it, and I believe maybe that was the reason he didn't go ahead at the time and do what he finally was forced to do. But that, because of what happened next, already had just a few more days to wait.

I think what happened then was nothing but some more of Tipps's slyness. It was in the paper again, Tipps saying he had the evidence he needed now, including a new witness, and that he already had the case scheduled for the grand jury. Which was something he never did, he said, till he had his ducks in a row. Just that and some more bragging was all, but I could see how it had struck Coop. He brought the paper back to the mill with him and didn't say a word when he handed it to me or after I got through reading it, either. Till I said, "He could be making that up, too."

"He's taking it to the grand jury."

"What's that?" I said.

"It's where they make sure he's got a good case. He wouldn't go there if he didn't."

"It could still be to trick you."

"How could he know about me?"

I tried saying more but he wasn't listening. He was due back at the shed where the big saw was but even when they called to him he didn't stir out of his tracks. It was his own thoughts he was listening to, blinking his eyes like to stop and start a thought all over again. About the third time they called him he turned and went and put the saw to running. Stacking lumber, I watched him under the shed, setting the logs and lining them, guiding them slow along the track into that screaming blade. After a while, when the scream got in my head, I'd look and think I was watching him move in a daylight dream I was having.

That night was when he decided. He didn't tell me but I could see it, and after we went to bed, lying there in the dark, I whispered to him, "Don't do nothing yet. He might be just waiting."

"Waiting for what?"

"You. To do something."

"It won't be something he can catch me by."

He did it the next night. An hour after supper he went outside, and the second I heard his car start up I knew he was on his way. I looked at Mama. She'd lifted her head from her sewing, and after the sound of his motor died out she turned her eyes on me. "I wonder where Coop's going," she said, watching me for an answer. I said I didn't know, and setting myself to wait, I watched TV pictures flicker like ghosts across the screen. Daddy's head was nodding, and Stack, spread out on the sofa beside me, was starting in to snore. My eyes fell once on that bank notice, the one that had come today. But it was like I couldn't even remember what it said.

Coop didn't come back till on in the night. From the bed, hoping and hoping that now at last he'd open up to me, I watched the shadow-shape of him getting out of his clothes. He noticed, read my mind. "Everything's all right, Chester. You'll know in a day or two."

But I didn't know in one day and the day after that I only knew because he told me. From the looks of him I'd already guessed things hadn't gone like he wanted. I thought it when he came back to the mill after noon break and even more that night when he couldn't seem to keep his hands still or his eyes from jumping around. Finally, once we were both back in our room, I didn't have to ask him again. He told me about the letter he'd written and not signed his name to, saying he was the one that had done it and not Baxter. He'd taken the letter and, after waiting till everything was clear on the street dropped it in the slot by the door of the newspaper office. "They couldn't have missed it. I thought sure they'd snap it right up and print it, like they do. Two days, now. I couldn't stand sending it to that bastard. He'd probably have just sat on it anyhow."

After I got my breath I said, "I bet that's what they did with it. Gave it to him. Anyhow, showed it to him."

Coop got still for a minute, looking down at his hands gripping each other. "It doesn't matter. The newspaper people saw it, so he can't sit on it."

In a blank sort of way I was starting to feel relieved, when a cold thought came slipping into my head. I'd learned a few things from the TV. Out of a tight throat I said, "They can tell about writing. Whose writing it is."

"It's in typewriting. I did it on that old typewriter in the office down at the mill." In a voice that sounded maybe kind of proud he added, "I wore gloves, too."

Even if there was something blurry about it, my feeling of relief stayed with me this time. "It don't matter," I said, repeating his words, bracing my easy feeling.

Those were words I kept saying to myself later on in the night when thoughts started sawing at my nerves again. Finally, though, they didn't help anymore. I couldn't go to sleep and I saw Coop couldn't either. It wasn't that my thinking —— and Coop's, too, I figured —— had any solid thing to fasten on. It was mainly just a notion, or a feeling, that Coop, when he didn't have to, had stuck his neck out too far. A hunch, I guess, that stayed with me all the rest of the night and still wouldn't go away when morning came. That I didn't have it all to myself was clear from what Coop said to me on our way to the mill. "I'm to blame for that old woman. But there ain't a way in the goddamn world I'd let the likes of Tipps put it on me."

Something about the way he said it raised a tingling chill at the back of my neck. I didn't answer. I just made another try to wipe that hunch clear out of my thoughts.

But all that day it never left me alone and there were times when it took hold like something fit to stop my breath. One of those times was when Coop came back from town with nothing to say. But the worst time came when Mr. Cutchins did something that stopped me in my tracks, frozen under the heavy board balanced across my shoulder. He was standing there a few feet away from the shed, just standing, but I could see where his eyes were looking. It was Coop he was looking at, watching and watching the back of him while Coop was lining a log. That was all, but afterwards it wouldn't go out of my head. It needn't have meant anything, of course, but that evening I told Coop about it. He listened to me, just listened. In fact, on till we put out the lamp that night he never really answered anything I said to him. Then, in the dark when I wasn't expecting his voice, he said, "Might as well go on and sell the mules. They ought to bring a hundred dollars. And those two calves maybe forty. And the hogs. Wait on selling the cow, though."

That was all, though I lay waiting a long while with my heart beating heavy. I didn't know whether he finally went to sleep or not. In the times I was awake, which seemed like all night long, I never heard him breathing like he was asleep. He didn't wallow like I did, either, or even draw up the covers against the cold. Thinking and thinking, I guessed he was . . . maybe trying to figure where he might have made a mistake by writing that letter. But maybe not. Somehow I decided that what he was thinking had nothing to do with the letter.

He'd made a mistake, though. I didn't find out till afterwards what the mistake was, but the first cold smear of daylight that morning showed me for certain he'd made one. I already had half a notion I'd heard something out of the way, but till I heard the dogs and then looked out the window and saw the dim shape of a man stealing along outside the yardfence, I hadn't recognized the sound. It was the sound of a car drifting without the motor running, coasting easy down the sloping road from the highway. They hadn't shut a door or made any kind of a noise and it was only seeing the man out there that brought it to me like a thing blowing up in my face. I'd twisted my head clear around before I remembered Coop was already out, gone to the barn instead of me to milk. I hit the floor in a staggering run and saw as I got to the kitchen Daddy in his longjohns staring through the window over the sink. "Somebody out there," he said.

No, there were three of them. But just in the second I looked, they noticed what I noticed too. It was light in the barn, from the lantern Coop was using. They moved, moving fast, one of them veering off from the others. I saw what he was doing, heading around to the back side of the barn . . . for a trap. I think I had my mouth open to yell, before I thought and went for the back door, through and onto the freezing ground with my naked feet. Then I was running. I yelled, "Coop! Look out!" and saw him, a glimpse in the lighted door, and then the light went out. A man, the one from the other side of the house, was coming behind me.

"Get back, boy!" But this was Tipps, turning his head to snarl at me. "Get back in the house."

But I didn't. I stood looking where Tipps was looking, into the barn where the cow's white face was all I could see in the gloom there. Then Tipps's voice, loud, "He didn't get out over there, did he, Willis?" And Willis's muffled voice from outside the far hall door, "Naw. He's in there."

I saw Tipps draw his pistol. Holding it out ahead of him he stepped right up to the barn door. In a voice all of a sudden loud he said, "Boy, you might as well come on out."

A pigeon started cooing . . . nothing else. Tipps's voice again, "If I have to come in there, I'll kill you."

There wasn't any answer. This time it was our big red rooster crowing.

"All right," Tipps's loud voice said. Then quietly, to the man standing just ahead of me, "Give me your flashlight."

The man —— Billings, I think —— stepped forward and handed it to him.

"Look out, Coop!" This, a scream really, came busting out of my throat. I think I was about to jump right on Tipps's back when Billings grabbed me and threw me spinning so I landed on the ground. Then Tipps was inside with his light, and Billings was in the doorway.

I watched that searching beam of light, watched him move from one stall door to another, drawing each one open, probing inside with his beam. Then his beam climbed the ladder and passed up into the loft. "He's up there." In his loud voice again, he said, "This is your last chance, boy."

It brought silence without even a pigeon or a rooster to mark it.

Managing that pistol and the flashlight both, Tipps started climbing. A rung at a time, as slow as slow, the slowest thing to me I'd ever watched. "Coop," I yelled, but nothing else would come. Tipps's head went out of sight through the square door into the hay loft.

What I have in my memory following that is exactly as if my eyes had seen it happen. The thumps I heard were Coop's feet on the floor, coming at Tipps, and the pistol flash was a fiery stroke of light. I can see Coop's face, all twisted in it, and see the tines of that hay fork plunge clear out of sight in Tipps's chest. And Tipps's body on the floor, writhing and screaming, screaming, spewing blood out of his mouth. What I see in the last few seconds of that memory is not as clear to me and maybe it didn't really happen. It's a vision of Coop, his face still twisted that way, still holding the handle of that fork so Tipps couldn't pull it out.

But everything after that is a memory I really did see with my eyes. There were Billings and Willis at the ladder struggling, trying both at the same time to climb up into the loft. And there was Coop, like something out of the sky, hurtling down from that loft door so close he barely missed me. A thump, too hard, that left him lying a second or two on the ground. But his head came up and then his body. He was on his feet, staggering, pausing there just long enough to look at me and say, "Chester."

Then he was moving, faster and faster, running before he got up there to his car. There was just time enough for a thought that made my heart sink down: that old wreck wouldn't start. But he wheeled away from it. Tipps's car was there close by and I saw him glance inside it. Then he was in with the motor racing and gone too quick to count.

Twenty Two

That early morning when Coop went streaking out of there in Tipps's car, gone for good to God knows where, the story of our family was the same as over with. The rest was nothing but falling away in pieces, first one and then another going his own path in the world. Even at the time, standing there in first daylight, cold, shivering in my longjohns, that thought came plain as a picture in my mind. And after that, in the house, even in among their bodies huddled in front of the window, I couldn't seem to draw heat enough to stop shivering.

Tipps was dead. I think he was dead even before I turned and ran back up to the house. Willis had finally got Coop's old car started and gone for the ambulance. He came back with three or four other cars following behind him, and after that people were milling around out there like the place wasn't ours anymore . . . which I guess it really wasn't. Just one person came to the house, though, a man from the newspaper, but Mama wouldn't tell him anything. Till everybody was gone, which was several hours, not one of us put a foot outside the door.

I didn't go up in the loft that day but I did see where some of Tipps's blood had dripped between the floorboards and made streaks on one of the stall doors. I don't remember feeling anything about it or anything at all except a kind of dull satisfaction in the thought that he was dead. With all the things he'd done to us, there wasn't any reason I shouldn't have felt that way. Besides, what came to light a few weeks later showed everybody what a rascal he was. His death loosened some tongues and Dud's notion about him being mixed up in that car-chopping business was exactly right. Along with Willis, he'd been protecting them for years and making all kind of money out of it. If our family had been "anybody," or maybe if we'd just been smarter than we were, we might have been able to make them give us something back for all the wickedness he did to us. But maybe not. What Coop did to the old woman, and even to Tipps, made our family look to be just that much worse than before.

I found out how Tipps had tracked Coop down. It was that old typewriter in the office at the sawmill. Suspicious like he was and knowing where Coop worked, he checked it out against the letter. I don't know if that would've been proof enough, but it was enough for him to go on. If he didn't have more, he'd have come up with whatever else he needed. Tipps was one smart bastard, I can say that much for him. Though he wasn't smart enough not to climb up in that dark loft with Coop.

Pretty soon they told us our home belonged to the bank. Less than two months later our family, what was left of it, moved into a trailer on a bare lot with three other trailers on the north side of town. There were just four of us, Eve and I besides Mama and Daddy. By that time Dorcas was long gone. She went to Nashville and for a couple of years had jobs as a waitress in several different restaurants. She said that was all she was doing. I hoped it was. Then without even telling us, she left town and went up to Kentucky . . . to Louisville, she finally wrote us. After that it was Chicago where, after a while, we lost track of her completely. By now she could be dead and we wouldn't know. I think about her long gold hair, what a pretty girl she was.

Stack and Mabel —— and Bucky, of course —— didn't move in with us. But Mabel stayed around town for a while and Stack stayed for good. Stack got to be a pretty fair mechanic and always could get jobs. He's still living in the same grubby little house he rents, and never has got married. He drinks some but not too awful much and, till she died, he was good about coming around to see Mama now and again.

Mabel, except in the time while she was divorced, never was good about that. She first married a man, a little plumber from over at

Chatham, that Mama didn't like or trust, but after three years she left him and came to live in our trailer with two yelling babies. Her luck the second time around was some better. He was a real fat man and dull-witted and hardly ever had a word to say to anybody when we saw him. He kept to his job as a tool salesman, though, and made enough so Mabel would stick with him. After they moved away to Haydonville we hardly ever saw Mabel at all.

Bucky, like in the past, would turn up once in a while. I still go visit him down on the river. Except for his thinned-out hair and all the web of wrinkles in his face, he's the same as he used to be.

Eve and I went on living at the trailer till we'd finished high school. I left first, of course. After about six months of working around Riverton, I headed for Nashville to seek my fortune. But I did it partly to make more money and as soon as I found a good job I started sending, or else bringing, a piece of my salary home to Mama every week. Of the girls, though I can't be really sure about Dorcas, Eve was finally the one to have luck with a husband. I wasn't surprised. She was pretty and smart, a good girl every way. She married a young man Mama liked, a lawyer from a farm family come to practice in Riverton. The sad thing was that inside of a few months they moved away, far away, clear out to El Paso, Texas. Eve wrote letters back and once just a month before Mama died came all that way to visit. That was at least some late comfort for Mama.

Living there in that trailer wasn't much of a life for Mama. Or Daddy either, though the way he'd got to be before we ever left home might have kept this life from seeming too much worse to him. He still had his TV, and half the time he was drunk enough not to notice much anyhow. For a while he'd get little jobs like cutting people's grass or cleaning up at stores. Finally, though, nobody would hire him anymore. Except for the help I sent them, it was all on Mama.

A while after we moved in there, Mama got a job at a little grocery out from town, walking to it every morning and home at night. Once the owner saw what she was like, he left about all the work to her. She bought the stock and handled the money and pumped gas at the one pump out in front of the store. Even at that, what she got paid wasn't quite enough for the rent and food and such. She kept that one job for years, till she got sick with the heart trouble that killed her pretty soon. That left it for me to look after Daddy. But by that time he'd got so bad off I was able to fix it for him to go live free at the state home. I still go to see him once in a while, but he barely knows who I am.

And Coop that I loved better than I ever loved anybody except Mama? They found Tipps's patrol car a couple of hundred miles away on a side-street in Memphis. But no Coop. He hadn't left even a toe-track. They had a big bulletin out for him, and his face and name and all on a "wanted" poster, but it never did them any good. It was like Coop had plain vanished off the face of the earth. I'd think about him, wondering how he'd managed, how he'd got money for food and maybe a ticket out of there on a bus. Stole it, maybe? Or maybe he found a gun in the car and used that to get him where he wanted to go. I wondered where that would be.

All these years I've been wondering. I'd bet he's not dead. I know he wasn't dead two years ago, because I found something from him in my mailbox in Nashville. It was a mystery how it got there without any address but just my name on the brown envelope. There were ten fifty-dollar bills inside and there was a slip of paper that had nothing but the words "For Mama" written on it with a pencil. I walked up and down my street for an hour thinking he might be someplace nearby. I kept on that way for a week or two, watching for him, hoping he might step out from behind something and show himself to me. Finally, because Mama was dead by then, I divided up the money four ways and saw my brothers and sisters all got their share. I wished it could have been five ways, with a share for Dorcas, too.

It wasn't long after that when an old notion got itself really fixed in my mind. Now I keep picturing Coop in a desert place with burnt-red rocks behind him, or else in one of those windless dead-end canyons where the straight-down heat of the sun, shining bright, shrivels the tongue in your mouth. And I keep remembering something little Eve said once. It was after Dud escaped from jail and Tipps and Willis came to our house looking, or pretending to look for him. "It's like with Uncle Clarence," she said, after they were gone. She could as well have said it again that morning when Coop lit out. Because it was true. In all the important ways, it was.

Jones, Madison
To The winds

J. 22-46

DATE DUE			
AUG 7 1996			
AUG 23 1996			
SEP 23 1996			
OCT 16 1996			